'Don't look round,' he murmured. 'Keep looking at me.'

'What is it?'

'Machart is watching us from the doorway yonder.'

'Why would he?'

'Perhaps he was hoping to get you alone.' Falconbridge smiled. 'I think we should show him how futile his hope is.'

'How?'

He released his hold on her hand, but only to slide an arm round her waist and draw her against him. His lips brushed hers, tentatively at first, then more assertively. Liquid warmth flooded her body's core and she swayed against him, her mouth opening beneath his. The kiss grew deeper, more intimate, inflaming her senses, demanding her response. She had no need to pretend now, nor cared any longer who was watching. All that mattered was the two of them and the moonlight and the moment.

AUTHOR NOTE

The Napoleonic Wars provide the backdrop for this novel, which is set in Spain in 1812 in the Peninsular Campaign. The story takes place in the months between the Siege of Badajoz and the Battle of Salamanca.

I was once lucky enough to live in the Spanish capital for a while. Madrid is a beautiful and vibrant city, and also provided a perfect base for exploring the rest of Iberia. The impressions and experiences from that time have stayed with me ever since, and from them I have drawn much of the local material for this book. Other sources of inspiration came from Sunday morning visits to the Prado Museum. Goya's paintings—in particular *Dos de Mayo* and *Tres de Mayo*—give a real flavour of the Napoleonic period and the brutal struggle against foreign oppression. The Spanish waged a highly effective guerrilla campaign against the French, and this forms a strand of the subplot in my novel.

However, El Cuchillo is entirely my own invention. Like so many Spanish towns, Ciudad Rodrigo is a wonderful place to visit—rather like taking a journey back in time. It isn't hard to imagine Wellington and his staff walking through the halls of the Palacio de los Castro, or red-coat soldiers manning the walls of the town. These still bear the marks of the bombardment. The *castillo* no longer has a military function; these days it is a parador, one of the many historic state-owned hotels.

HIS
COUNTERFEIT
CONDESA

Joanna Fulford

First published in Great Britain 2011
by Mills & Boon, an imprint of Harlequin (UK) Limited,
Large Print edition 2011
Eton House, 18-24 Paradise Road, Richmond, Surrey TW9 1SR

© Joanna Fulford 2011

ISBN: 978 0 263 21868 8

Harlequin (UK) policy is to use papers that are natural,
renewable and recyclable products and made from wood grown in
sustainable forests. The logging and manufacturing process conform
to the legal environmental regulations of the country of origin.

Printed and bound in Great Britain
by CPI Antony Rowe, Chippenham, Wiltshire

Joanna Fulford is a compulsive scribbler, with a passion for literature and history, both of which she has studied to postgraduate level. Other countries and cultures have always exerted a fascination, and she has travelled widely, living and working abroad for many years. However, her roots are in England, and are now firmly established in the Peak District, where she lives with her husband Brian. When not pressing a hot keyboard she likes to be out on the hills, either walking or on horseback. However, these days equestrian activity is confined to sedate hacking rather than riding at high speed towards solid obstacles.

Recent novels by the same author:

THE VIKING'S DEFIANT BRIDE
 (part of the *Mills & Boon Presents...*
 anthology, featuring talented new authors)
THE WAYWARD GOVERNESS
THE LAIRD'S CAPTIVE WIFE

**Visit www.joannafulford.co.uk
for more information**

For Catherine Pons, whose friendship
has made life so much richer.

Chapter One

Spain 1812

Sabrina surveyed the laden wagon and the damaged wheel and mentally cursed both. Her gaze travelled down the dusty road that snaked through rock and scrub towards the distant sierra. The sun was already past the zenith and they still had many miles to cover before they reached their destination. Now it looked as though they were going to be much later than planned. The wagon driver, a short, wiry individual of indeterminate age, kicked the wheel rim and flung his hat to the ground, muttering an imprecation under his breath. Then he turned towards her, his swarthy face registering an expression that was both doleful and apologetic.

'*Lo siento mucho, Doña* Sabrina.'

'It's not your fault, Luis. This wagon wasn't up

to much in the first place,' she replied in Castilian Spanish as fluent as his own.

'It is no better than firewood on wheels,' he replied. 'Or rather, not on wheels any more. Next time I see that donkey, Vasquez, I shall kill him.'

She shook her head. 'He is an ally, even if he does supply poor transport.'

'*Dios mio!* With allies such as this, who needs to worry about the French?'

'Even so.'

Luis sighed. 'Very well. I shall let him off with just a beating.'

'No, Luis, tempting as it is.' She turned back to the wagon. 'All that matters now is to get this thing fixed so that we can make the rendezvous with Colonel Albermarle.'

Another voice interjected calmly, 'There's a wheelwright in the next town. It's no more than five miles from here.'

She turned towards the speaker, a man of middle years whose black hair showed strands of grey. His tanned face was deeply lined but the eyes were shrewd and alert. Though he was not tall, his stocky frame suggested compact strength.

Sabrina nodded. 'All right, Ramon. You and I will ride into town and fetch help. Luis and the others can stay here and guard the wagon.'

With that she swung back astride the bay gelding

and waited while Ramon remounted his own horse. She nodded to Luis and the three men with him and then turned the horse's head towards Casa Verde.

Town was an overstatement she decided when they reached it about an hour later. It was no more than a large sleepy village. Many of the buildings were ramshackle affairs with cracked walls and sagging pantile roofs. Chickens scratched in the dirt and a hog sunned itself beside an adobe wall. Ragged children played knucklebones before the open door of a house. The narrow street led into a small dusty plaza and Sabrina glanced at her companion.

'Where can we find the wheelwright?' she asked.

'Garcia's premises are located behind the church.' Ramon nodded in the direction of the imposing whitewashed building on the far side of the square. 'Not far now.'

They found the place with no difficulty but discovered the proprietor and two others engaged in removing a wheel from a large supply wagon. Another similar vehicle stood nearby, laden with barrels and sacks. A group of red-coated soldiers stood beside it, laughing and talking among themselves. Sabrina and her companion exchanged glances.

'I'll go and speak with Garcia,' he said.

She took his horse's reins and watched him cross

the intervening space. The wright glanced up from his work. There followed an interchange lasting perhaps two minutes. Then Ramon returned, his expression sombre.

'The man has just begun a new job,' he said. 'He will not be able to help us until tomorrow.'

'What!'

Ramon gestured to the two supply wagons. 'He says he must fix those first.'

'But we're supposed to rendezvous with Albermarle in Ciudad Rodrigo this evening.'

'I think that won't be possible. He says the English soldiers are before us and their commanding officer needs these wagons in a hurry.'

'Yes, and we need ours in a hurry,' she replied. 'I'll speak to the officer. Perhaps he may relent.'

Ramon grimaced. 'I doubt it.'

'We'll see.'

Sabrina swung down off her horse and thrust both sets of reins into his hands. Then, taking a deep breath, she walked across to the group of soldiers by the waiting wagon. As she drew nearer the two facing her looked up, becoming aware of her presence. Their expressions registered surprise and curiosity. Seeing it their companions glanced round and then the conversation stopped. Sabrina fixed her attention on the man immediately in front of her.

'I need to speak to your commanding officer.'

'That would be Major Falconbridge, ma'am.'

'Can you tell me where he is?'

'Over there, ma'am,' the soldier replied, nodding towards a dark-haired figure crouching beside one of the draught horses tethered nearby.

Sabrina thanked him and went across. Though the Major must have heard her approach he didn't look up, his attention focused on the horse's near foreleg. Strong lean fingers ran gently down the cannon bone and paused on the fetlock joint.

'Major Falconbridge?'

'That's right.' The voice was pleasant, the accent unmistakably that of a gentleman.

'I am Sabrina Huntley. May I have a word with you, sir?'

He did look up then and she found herself staring into a tanned and clean-shaven face. Its rugged lines had nothing of classical beauty about them but it made her catch her breath all the same. Moreover, it was dominated by a pair of cool, grey eyes, whose piercing gaze now swept her critically, moving from the tumbled gold curls confined at her neck by a ribbon, and travelling on by way of jacket and shirt to breeches and boots, pausing only to linger a moment on the sword at her side and the pistol thrust into her belt. As it did so a gleam of amusement appeared in the grey depths. Then he straightened slowly.

'I am all attention, Miss Huntley.'

Sabrina's startled gaze met the top buttons of his uniform jacket and then moved on, giving her a swift impression of a lithe and powerful frame. Her heart skipped a beat and just for a moment her mind went blank to everything, save the man in front of her. With an effort she recollected herself and, adopting a more businesslike manner, explained briefly what had befallen the wagon.

'I must get to Ciudad Rodrigo tonight. I need the services of the wheelwright at once.'

'I regret that I cannot help you,' he replied, 'for as you see his services are already engaged.'

'My business is most urgent, Major.'

'So is mine, ma'am. Were it not so I would have been delighted to oblige you.'

'Can you not delay your repairs a little?'

'Indeed I cannot. I must deliver these supplies today or my men won't eat.'

The tone was even and courteous enough but it held an inflection of steel. She tried another tack.

'If I do not get help my men and I will be forced to spend the night in the open.'

'That's regrettable, of course, but fortunately the weather is clement at this season,' he replied.

Her jaw tightened. 'There is also the chance of encountering a French patrol.'

'There are no French patrols within twenty miles.'

He paused, eyeing the sword and pistol. 'Even if there were I think they would be foolhardy to risk an attack on you.'

Her green eyes flashed fire. 'You are ungallant, sir.'

'So I'm often told.'

'Would you leave a lady unaided in such circumstances?'

'Certainly not, but on your own admission you have several men to help you.' He paused. 'May I ask what your wagon is carrying?'

There was an infinitesimal pause. Then, 'Fruit.'

One dark brow lifted a little. 'I think your fruit will be safe enough, ma'am.'

Sabrina's hands clenched at her sides. 'I do not think you understand the seriousness of the case, Major Falconbridge.'

'I believe I do.'

'I must have that wheelwright.'

'And so you shall—tomorrow.'

'I have never met with so discourteous and disobliging a man in my life!'

'You need to get out more.'

Hot colour flooded into her face and dyed her cheeks a most becoming shade of pink. He smiled appreciatively, revealing very white, even teeth. Sabrina fought the urge to hit him.

'For the last time, Major, will you help me?'

'For the last time, ma'am, I cannot.'

'*Bruto!*'

The only reply was an unrepentant grin. Incensed, Sabrina turned on her heel and marched back to where Ramon waited with the horses. The Spaniard regarded her quizzically.

'Do I take it that the answer was no?'

'You do.'

Grabbing the reins, she remounted and turned her horse towards the gate, pausing only to throw Falconbridge one last fulminating glance as she rode on by. As the Major's grey gaze followed her he laughed softly.

Some time later the army supply wagons set out. Falconbridge rode alongside, keeping the horse to an easy pace. From time to time he let his gaze range across the hills but saw nothing to cause him any concern. For the rest, his mind was more agreeably occupied with the strange encounter in the wheel-wright's yard. He smiled to himself, albeit rather ruefully. His response to the lady's plight was ungallant as she had rightly said. No doubt his name was mud now. All the same he wouldn't have missed it for worlds. It had been worth it just to see the fire in those glorious green eyes. For a while there he had wondered if she would hit him; the desire had been writ large in her face. The image returned with force. He knew he wouldn't forget it in a hurry.

Her unusual mode of dress had, initially, led him to wonder if she was one of the camp followers, but the cut-glass accent of her spoken English precluded that at once. Her whole manner was indicative of one used to giving orders. He chuckled to himself. Miss Huntley didn't take kindly to being refused. Under other circumstances he would have behaved better, but he had told the truth when he said he needed to deliver the supplies promptly. She had told him her destination was Ciudad Rodrigo. His smile widened. Without a doubt he'd be meeting her again and soon.

These reflections kept him occupied until the town came into view. He saw the supplies safely delivered and then headed straight to the barracks. He arrived at the quarters he shared with Major Brudenell to find the former already there, seated at the table. Though he was of Falconbridge's age the likeness stopped there. Hair the colour of ripe wheat offset a lightly tanned face whose chiselled lines bespoke his noble heritage. He looked up from the paper on which he had been writing, vivid blue eyes warmed by a smile.

'Ah, Robert. Everything go as planned?'

'Yes, pretty much.'

'The men will be pleased. That last barrel of salt

pork was so rancid it could have been used as a weapon of terror. If we'd fired it at the French they'd have been in full retreat by now.'

Falconbridge smiled. 'Maybe we should try it next time.' He nodded towards the paper on the table. 'Letter home, Tony?'

'Yes. I've been meaning to do it for the past fort-night and never got the chance. I must get it finished before I go.'

'Before you go where?'

'The Sierra de Gredos. Ward has me lined up for a further meeting with El Cuchillo.'

The name of the guerrilla leader was well known. For some time he had been passing information to the English in exchange for guns. Since the intel-ligence provided had been reliable, General Ward was keen to maintain the relationship.

'You'll be gone for a couple of weeks then.'

'I expect so.'

Falconbridge glanced towards the partially written letter. 'I sometimes think war is hardest on those left behind.'

'As a single man you haven't got that worry.'

'Nor would I seek it, notwithstanding your most excellent example.'

Brudenell shook his head. 'I am hardly an excel-lent example. Indeed it has been so long since I saw my wife that she has likely forgotten what I look like.'

'That must be hard.'

'Not in the least. Ours was an arranged marriage with no choice offered to either party. I am quite sure that Claudia enjoys an agreeable lifestyle in London without being overly troubled by my absence.'

The tone was cheerful enough but Falconbridge glimpsed something very like bleakness in those startling blue eyes. Then it was gone. Privately he owned to surprise, for while he knew that his friend was married, he had only ever referred to the matter in the most general terms, until now. The subject was not one that Falconbridge would have chosen to discuss anyway. Even after all this time it was an aspect of the past that he preferred to forget.

It seemed he wasn't going to be allowed that luxury as Brudenell continued,

'Have you never been tempted to take the plunge?'

'I almost did once but the lady cried off.'

'I'm sorry to hear it.'

Falconbridge achieved a faint shrug. 'Don't be. It was undoubtedly a lucky escape. Ever since then I've preferred to take my pleasure where I find it.'

'Very wise.'

'You condemn matrimony then?'

'Not so,' said Brudenell, 'though I would certainly caution against arranged matches.'

'Advice I shall heed, I promise you.'

'Of course, you might meet the right woman. Have you considered that?'

'I've yet to meet any woman with whom I would wish to spend the rest of my life,' replied Falconbridge. 'The fair sex is charming but they are capricious and, in my experience, not to be trusted. Brief liaisons with women of a certain class are far more satisfactory.'

'You are a cynic, my friend.'

'No, I am a realist.'

What Brudenell might have said in response was never known because an adjutant appeared at the door. He looked at Falconbridge.

'Beg pardon, Major, but General Ward requires your presence at once.'

'Very well. I'll attend him directly.'

As the adjutant departed, the two men exchanged glances. Falconbridge raised an eyebrow.

'This should be interesting.'

'A euphemism if ever I heard one,' replied his companion.

'Well, I'll find out soon enough I expect.'

With that, Falconbridge ducked out of the room and was gone.

* * *

It was late afternoon of the following day before Sabrina and her companions crossed the Roman bridge over the Agueda River, and reached the rendezvous in the Castillo at Ciudad Rodrigo. After the siege in January that year, the French had been driven out by British troops. Capture of the town and the big artillery batteries on the Great Teson had opened up the eastern corridor for Wellington's advance into Spain. The Castillo was a hive of activity. The guards at the gate of the fortress recognised the party in the wagon and sent word of their approach, so that by the time they drew to a halt in the courtyard Albermarle was waiting. The Colonel was in his mid-fifties and of just above the average height, but for all his grey hairs he was of an upright bearing and the blue eyes were sharp and astute. When he saw Sabrina his craggy face lit with a smile.

'You're late, my dear. I was getting worried.'

'We had a damaged wheel, sir, and it took longer than expected to repair.'

'Unfortunate, but these things happen. Any other trouble on the way?'

For a moment Major Falconbridge's face swam into her memory. She pushed it aside.

'No.'

'Good.' He eyed the oranges on the wagon. 'And the guns?'

Sabrina nodded to Ramon. He pushed aside part of the top layer of fruit and lifted the sacking on which it rested to reveal the stocks of the Baker rifles beneath. Albermarle smiled.

'You've done well, my dear, as always.' He eyed her dusty garments and then went on, 'Lodgings have been arranged for you nearby. You'll find Jacinta there with your things. When you've had a chance to bathe and change we'll have dinner together.'

'That sounds delightful, sir.'

'Good. We'll talk then.'

Sabrina rejoined him some time later, elegantly gowned in a sprigged muslin frock and with her hair neatly dressed. The meal was good and so far removed from the rations of the last few days that she ate with real enjoyment. Her companion kept the conversation to general topics but, knowing him of old, she sensed there was something on his mind. In this she was correct, though the matter was not broached until they had finished eating and were lingering over the remains of the wine. The colonel leaned back in his chair, surveying her keenly.

'Have you thought any more about our last conversation, my dear?'

'Yes, and my answer is the same.'

'I thought it might be.' He smiled gently. 'Does England hold no charms for you then?'

'I barely remember the place, much less my aunt's family. It is kind of her to offer me a home but I would feel like a fish out of water. My life has revolved around the army. Father could have left me behind in England when he went abroad, but he chose not to and I'm glad of it.'

'I have known your father a long time. John Huntley was always an unusual man, some might even say eccentric, but he is brave and honourable and I am proud to count him among my friends. He is also a very fine cartographer.'

'Yes, he is, and it's thanks to him that I have received such an unusual education. How many young women have been where I've been or done what I've done?'

He chuckled. 'Precious few I imagine.'

'I have sometimes thought that it might be pleasant to have a permanent home and to attend parties and balls and the like, but the bohemian life is not without its charms, too. I suppose the habit has become ingrained, even though Father is gone.'

'You miss him, don't you?'

'It has been four months now, but not a day passes when I don't think of him.'

'His capture was a severe blow to the army.'

'I can't bear to think of him languishing somewhere in a French prison. I cling to the hope that one day he will be freed and I shall see him again.'

'When the war is over who knows what may happen?'

She sighed. 'I think that day is far off.'

'I know how lonely you must be without him.' He hesitated. 'Did you never think about settling down?'

'Marriage?' She shook her head. 'I have never been in one place long enough to form that kind of attachment.'

'Just so, my dear, and it worries me.'

'There is no need, sir, truly. Father took pains to ensure I was well provided for.'

'It is a godfather's privilege to be concerned,' he replied.

She returned his smile. 'When I find another man like you I may consider settling down. In the meantime it is my duty to do my part for king and country.'

'Are you sure, my dear?'

'Quite sure.' She paused, her gaze searching his face. 'There's something in the wind, isn't there?'

'Am I so transparent?'

'I've known you a long time, sir.'

'True. And you're right. There is a mission in the offing.'

'May I know what it is?'

'Even I don't have all the details yet. All I can tell you is that it is top level. I have a meeting in the morning with General Ward and Major Forbes.'

'Major Forbes is one of Wellington's leading intelligence officers.'

'Yes, he is.' He paused. 'What is more, he has asked that you should be present at the briefing tomorrow.'

Her astonishment was unfeigned. While she had undertaken several missions in the last year they were all low-key affairs involving relatively small risk. This appeared to be rather different. Curiosity vied with a strange feeling of unease. What kind of mission was it that required her involvement? What part would she be asked to play?

For a long time after she retired that night she lay awake pondering what her godfather had said. It wasn't just the business of the mysterious mission. It was the matter of her future. At some point the war would end and, God willing, her father might be released. However, conditions in French prisons were notoriously bad and she had to face the possibility that he might not survive. What then? Likely she would have no choice but to return to England. However, she had been independent too long ever to live by someone else's rules. Her aunt meant well but the prospect of life in a small town held no charms. Besides, the only career open to a woman was marriage, an indescribably dull fate after a lifetime of adventure. Happily, that was one problem that wouldn't affect her. She had learned early that, when it came to matters of the heart, what men said and what they meant were very different things.

For an instant Captain Jack Denton's image returned, along with its false smile and equally false assurances. Of course, she had been much younger then, barely fifteen. Having no mother or older sisters to advise her, she had been easy prey for a handsome face and polished manner. They had met at her first dance. Ten years older than she, Denton's attentions had been flattering, and had awakened something inside her whose existence had remained unknown till then. He had recognised it at once. And he had been clever, careful not to move too fast yet leaving her in no doubt of his admiration. Smiles and soft looks and compliments developed into brief stolen meetings, always when her father or his friends were not by, and eventually a tender kiss. It had kindled the spark to a flame that lit her whole being. Utterly infatuated, she never questioned his sincerity or the depth of his feelings.

She swallowed hard. No woman in her right mind would risk making that mistake again. Nor would any woman risk her reputation so foolishly. Her relationships with men were almost entirely professional now. On those occasions when she met them socially she was unfailingly courteous but also careful to keep them at arm's length. It was better to be free and independent. The only person she could rely on was herself.

In the meantime she must find out what Ward and Forbes were planning, and the only way to do that was to accompany her godfather tomorrow.

Falconbridge lay on his cot, staring into the darkness, his mind too crowded with thoughts for sleep to take him. The meeting with General Ward was still vivid. Though his skills as an intelligence agent had been used many times on different missions, Falconbridge knew this one was different. If it succeeded it could change the whole course of the war, but the hazards were great for all sorts of reasons. It had been madness to agree to do it. The fact that Ward had given him a choice showed that he knew just how much he was asking. However, the offered inducement was also considerable—for an ambitious officer. Ward was fully aware of it, of course, and calculated accordingly. He knew his man. There was no knowing if this would work, but doing nothing was not an option. Had it involved only himself, Falconbridge would have taken on the challenge without demur, even knowing the risks were great. As it was… He had expressed his reservations in the strongest possible terms, and been ignored, of course. He thumped the pillow hard. The General had made up his mind and would not be deterred. It argued a degree of calculated ruthlessness that was almost enviable.

The meeting was arranged for ten o'clock. Sabrina had dressed with care for the occasion, donning a smart primrose-yellow gown. Her hair was neatly arranged beneath a pretty straw bonnet. Having surveyed her reflection in the glass with a critical eye she decided the outfit would pass muster. She and Colonel Albermarle presented themselves at the appointed time. Knowing the army as she did, Sabrina had expected a lengthy wait, but to her surprise they were shown straight in.

General Ward was seated behind the desk at the far end of a large room, and Major Forbes was standing beside him. Both men were poring over a map. As they entered Ward looked up.

'Ah, Colonel Albermarle.' As the Colonel came to attention, Ward rose from his seat and bowed to Sabrina. 'Miss Huntley.'

Sabrina returned the greeting and accepted the offer of a chair. For a moment there was silence and she saw the General exchange glances with Forbes. Then he drew a deep breath.

'We have requested your presence today in order to put forward a proposition, Miss Huntley.'

'A proposition, sir?'

'Yes. One of the carrier pigeons recently returned bearing a coded message. In essence, the Spanish agent who sent it has obtained vital military documents concerning French troop movements. However, his responsibilities in Madrid make it impossible for him to deliver the information to us. Like everyone else in senior government positions he is watched, and cannot afford to do anything that might appear unusual. That means someone must go and collect the information from him.'

Sabrina's brow wrinkled for a moment. 'But surely it would be equally suspicious, sir, if he were suddenly visited by a total stranger.'

'Ordinarily it would. However, the gentleman's wife is celebrating her birthday next week and he is holding a ball at his mansion near Aranjuez to mark the occasion. It is to be a lavish affair. Everyone who is anyone will be there. It will also provide a perfect opportunity to get hold of the information he has obtained.'

She nodded slowly. 'I can see that, but I confess to being at a loss as to my role in all this.'

'Our agent is to impersonate this gentleman's

cousin, the Conde de Ordoñez y Casal. The real one lives on his estate in Extremadura. Apparently he prefers the pleasures of country life to those of the city and almost never goes there.'

'But isn't there a chance someone will know him and spot the deception?'

'It's an outside chance but one we have to take,' the General replied.

'I still don't understand how all this involves me.'

'The Conde de Ordoñez is a married man. As such, his wife would certainly attend the ball with him. Our agent must therefore be so accompanied.' Ward glanced at Forbes who nodded. 'My informants tell me that Ordoñez's wife is French and blonde. As I am sure you will appreciate, ma'am, there are not many blonde-haired women hereabouts, and even fewer who speak fluent French as well as their native tongue. Your skill in both languages is well known to us.' He paused. 'And you have helped us before.'

'You want me to pose as the Conde's wife?'

'Just so.'

Beside her Colonel Albermarle gave an exclamation of astonishment and disgust.

'The whole thing is highly improper, sir, and I would in no way sanction it,' he said. 'Besides, which, it would be unthinkable to put my goddaughter in such a dangerous situation.'

The General regarded him with a cool and level stare. 'I have not said all.'

'You mean there's more to this confounded business, sir?'

'Yes. We are not expecting Miss Huntley to take such a risk without offering something in return.'

Ward paused and glanced at his companion. Forbes smiled.

'Your father is unfortunately confined in prison in France,' he said. 'Negotiations are underway for the release of certain English military personnel in exchange for high-ranking French officers currently in our hands. If you agree to help us we'll make your father's release part of those negotiations.'

Sabrina swallowed hard as she tried to marshal her thoughts. 'If I were to agree, what guarantee would there be that my father would be released?'

'We would ensure the man we offered in exchange was of sufficient importance that the French would be most unlikely to refuse.'

'How soon would my father be free?'

'In a matter of weeks.'

A matter of weeks! Her heart thumped in her breast. Her father need not die in a foreign prison after all. They would be reunited at last. Surely that was worth any risk, wasn't it? She bit her lip, unable to ignore the ramifications of her decision. If she agreed she might be putting her life on the line; would be reliant on the help and cooperation of a complete stranger. She did not think that Ward and Forbes would have chosen anyone but the best for this task; they couldn't afford to. All the same, this man's first care was to see that those plans got back to Wellington. If it came to a choice between that and her safety it didn't take a savant to work out which would come first. She would be expendable. The intelligence service needed those plans and its agents were prepared to go to considerable lengths to get them. That also included the ruthless exploitation of her emotions. Her father was of no real monument to them. Had it been otherwise they would have negotiated his release already. The knowledge caused the first faint stirrings of anger. It was an emotion she couldn't afford. Forcing it down she met the General's gaze with apparent composure.

'May I have some time to reflect?'

'Time is of the essence. The ball is eleven days hence. The journey will take nine. I need an answer today.'

Her godfather laid a gentle hand on her arm. 'You don't have to do this, my dear. Your father would never ask it of you. I know how much he means to you and I care for him, too, but as your guardian I urge you to think most carefully.'

'I cannot leave him to die in prison, sir.'

'Consider, Sabrina. You know nothing about this man they would have you accompany.'

'I assure you, sir, that the gentleman is of good family,' Ward replied. 'He is the younger son of the Earl of Ellingham and is currently carving out a distinguished career for himself as a member of Wellington's intelligence staff.' He paused. 'His background might be considered among the best in England. Good enough, one would think, to be a fit companion for your goddaughter.'

Seeing Ward's haughty expression, Albermarle reddened. 'My goddaughter is also of good family, General. John Huntley has no reason to be ashamed of his connections.'

'I never meant to imply any such thing, Colonel.'

Recognising the signs of impending wrath on her godfather's face Sabrina interjected quickly. 'I am sure you did not, sir.'

Albermarle threw her a swift glance and held his temper. 'Connections are all very well,' he went on, 'but what is the man's character?'

'I have never heard anything to his detriment. On the contrary, he has shown himself to be capable and resourceful in the undertaking of his duties.'

'I am quite sure of that or you would never have chosen him. What concerns me is his moral character. After all, my goddaughter will be alone in his company for weeks. Her reputation…'

'Will be untarnished,' said Ward. 'The proprieties will be observed, sir. Miss Huntley will take her maid, as befits a lady of rank, and our agent will be accompanied by some of his men, in the guise of servants.' He paused. 'It goes without saying that arrangements for accommodation will be quite separate.'

'My goddaughter will have more than just her maid for protection. If she goes at all I insist upon Ramon and Luis attending her as well.'

Forbes raised a quizzical eyebrow. 'Ramon and Luis?'

'Partisans, I believe,' said Ward.

'Two of my father's most trusted companions, sir,' Sabrina explained. 'They have guided him on numerous expeditions and have accompanied me on every mission I've been on. They are most able men.'

Forbes and Ward exchanged another glance. Then the latter nodded.

'Agreed.'

However, Albermarle wasn't finished. 'Apart from the dubious nature of this proposal, Aranjuez is deep in the heart of enemy territory,' he said. 'If anything were to go wrong there would be no possibility of outside help. The consequences mean death or imprisonment.'

'That's true,' said the General. 'It is a risk, albeit a calculated one.'

'In my view the whole thing is utter madness, but the final decision is not mine.'

Ward turned to Sabrina. 'Then may we know your mind, madam, or do you wish a little more time to consider?'

Sabrina knew that time would make no difference in this case. The choice was made as soon as he had talked of her father's freedom.

'I'll do it.'

There came a muffled exclamation from Albermarle, but he said nothing.

Ward smiled. 'Good. It's a brave decision, Miss Huntley. Believe me, we are most grateful.'

'Does your agent know about all this?' she asked.

'Yes, he was briefed earlier.'

'What did you offer him?'

For a second he seemed taken aback, as much by the dryness of her tone as by the directness of the question, but he recovered quickly. 'Promotion to Lieutenant Colonel.'

'I see.' An ambitious man, she thought. That knowledge wasn't particularly reassuring. 'When do I meet him?'

'At once,' replied Ward. He glanced at Forbes. 'Tell him to come in.'

Sabrina closed her eyes for a moment, willing herself to calm. She must do this thing. There was no other choice. Her father's liberty was all that mattered. She heard the Major's footsteps cross the floor and then the sound of the door opening. He spoke briefly to someone outside. Two sets of footsteps returned. She clasped her hands in her lap to keep them still and forced herself to look up. Then her heart leapt towards her throat and she found herself staring into the grey eyes of Major Falconbridge.

Chapter Two

Suddenly it was harder to breathe and her cheeks, so pink before, went pale. Impossible! It couldn't be he! Of all the men in His Majesty's army... Sabrina came out of her chair and darted a glance at Ward and then at Forbes but saw nothing in their expressions to contradict it. Dear God, what had she agreed to? The idea of walking the length of the street with this man was unappealing, never mind spending weeks in his company. The temptation to renege on her promise and walk away was almost overpowering. Then she thought of her father and took a deep breath.

If Major Falconbridge had noticed aught amiss it wasn't evident. Having observed the necessary social courtesies he got straight to the point.

'I believe that you are to accompany me on this mission, Miss Huntley.'

Somehow she found her voice. 'Yes, sir.'

'I take it that you understand exactly what that entails.'

'I understand.'

'All the same, I should be grateful if you would afford me an opportunity for private speech later.'

With an effort she kept her tone neutral. 'As you will, Major.'

In fact, Falconbridge had seen the fleeting expression of dismay when she realised who he was. Under any other circumstances such a meeting would have been most entertaining, but just now he felt no inclination to laugh. For a moment he had expected her to refuse point-blank to enter into the bargain, but then she had seemed to regain her composure. Forbes had apprised him of her situation and he understood now just how much her father meant to her. After their first meeting Falconbridge knew he must be the last man in the world she would ever have chosen to go anywhere with, let alone Aranjuez. He also knew that his memory hadn't done her justice. From the beginning he had considered her attractive. Seeing her now he realised she was much more than that—spirited, too. However, looks and spirit were only part of it; she had other attributes. Ward had assured him of her linguistic ability in French and Spanish and of her usefulness to them in the past. It still hadn't stifled his doubts. Yet somehow those documents had to be obtained and brought back for Wellington. Promotion and the release of John Huntley, though highly desirable, were secondary considerations.

His thoughts were interrupted by General Ward. 'You will complete your briefing today and leave for Aranjuez in the morning.'

Sabrina's heart lurched. So little time! Then she reflected that it might be better so; if she had more space to consider she might well refuse to go through with it. This man unsettled her too much. Such a mission required clear-headedness and a certain amount of detachment. The knowledge that she was failing in both areas only added to her mortification.

Ward drew the meeting to a close shortly afterwards. Since Falconbridge was to be detained for a while he asked for directions to Sabrina's present accommodation.

'I will call upon you there very soon,' he said.

With that they said their temporary farewells and she and Albermarle left the room. For a while they walked in silence, but when they were away from the headquarters building he paused and drew her round to face him.

'Are you quite sure you know what you're doing, my dear? This mission truly is most dangerous.'

She nodded. 'I know but my mind is made up.'

'Very well. It's your decision, of course, but I cannot pretend that I like it.'

The words stayed with her long after he had gone. Though her reply had sounded confident, she was far from feeling it. However, the die was cast. Unwilling to spend too long thinking about the possibly dire consequences of her actions, she turned her mind to the practicalities. She would need to speak to Jacinta and then the two of them would pack all the necessary items for the trip. Later she would talk to Ramon and Luis. It was all very well for others to commandeer their services for this mission, but it was not the usual low-key affair, nor were they soldiers being paid to risk their lives. They needed to know of the dangers and be given the chance to opt out if they wanted to.

Jacinta listened impassively while Sabrina explained where she would be going. She did not go into details about why, since it was classified information, but only said that it concerned her father's safety, an explanation that she knew the maid would accept without question.

'Aranjuez?' she said then. 'I know of it, of course, but I have never been there. It will be interesting to see.'

'It will also be dangerous, Jacinta. Are you sure you want to come?'

The girl lifted one dark eyebrow. 'Do you think you can prevent it?'

Sabrina smiled ruefully. 'I doubt it, but I wanted you to know what you're agreeing to first.'

'If it were not for your father I would be dead now. He saved me after French dragoons burned and looted my village, and gave me a place in his household. Never shall I forget what I owe to him.' Jacinta's dark eyes burned now with inner fire. Her face, too angular for beauty, was nevertheless arresting and it concealed a sharp brain. In her mid-twenties, she had been with the Huntleys for the last five years. Ordinarily she never spoke of the past and Sabrina did not pry, though she knew the broad outlines of the story. If Jacinta wanted her to know the details she would tell her.

'I miss Father so much.'

'I, also,' Jacinta replied, 'but he is a brave and resourceful man. God will surely help him to win through.'

'I pray he may.'

'Meanwhile, not everything can be left to God. We play our part too, no?'

'As well as we can.'

Jacinta turned towards the clothes press. 'Then perhaps we should begin by relieving the Almighty of the task of packing.'

They were thus engaged when a servant appeared

to say that Major Falconbridge had just arrived. Sabrina drew in a deep breath. This had to be faced and it would be as well to get it over with.

He was waiting in the small salon. Hearing her step he turned, watching her approach. For a moment or two they surveyed each other in silence. Then he made her a neat bow.

'Miss Huntley. Thank you for receiving me. I am sure you must be busy.'

She kept her expression studiedly neutral. 'It is of no consequence, sir.'

'I shall not keep you long, but there are things that must be said.' He gestured to the open French windows that gave out onto the garden. 'Will you oblige me?'

As he stood aside to let her pass, she was keenly aware of the gaze burning into her back. It was one thing to be with this man in the company of others and quite another to meet him alone. It ought not to have bothered her; after all, the army had been a large part of her life. She was quite used to the company of men but none of them discomposed her like this one. But then none of them had his rugged good looks either, or that confoundedly assured manner. He had presence, no doubt about that. It was only enhanced by the scarlet regimentals; the jacket with its gold lacings might have been moulded to those broad shoulders. She had thought she was tall, until now. It gave him an annoying advantage since she was forced to look up all the time.

It was warm in the garden, the sunlight brilliant after the relative gloom indoors. They walked a little way down the path between the flower beds until they came to a wooden bench. There he paused.

'Shall we sit awhile, Miss Huntley?'

She made no demur and watched as he joined her. His gaze met and held hers.

'I'll come straight to the point,' he said. 'I was not…am not…in favour of your coming on this mission. It is difficult and dangerous and certainly no place for a woman.'

'And I am the last woman you would have chosen into the bargain.'

One dark brow lifted a little. 'I did not say so.'

'You didn't have to,' she replied. 'But then you are the last man I would have chosen, so in that way there is balance.'

'I am well aware that our first encounter was not calculated to make us friends, Miss Huntley, but personal feelings do not enter into this. My objections are based solely on the risks involved.'

Sabrina's chin lifted. 'It was my choice to come, Major. The risks were explained to me.'

'Were they?'

'Colonel Ward made it clear that capture would probably mean death.'

'Death is the best you can hope for if you are captured,' he replied. 'Before that there is always interrogation, and the French are not noted for their gentleness in such matters.'

'Are you afraid I would talk?'

'Everyone talks by the third day, Miss Huntley.'

Suddenly the sunshine wasn't quite as warm as it had been. 'Are you trying to frighten me, sir?'

'No, only to make you fully aware of what you are agreeing to.' He paused. 'The fact that you are a woman brings very particular perils.'

It was impossible to mistake his meaning and, under that cool scrutiny, she felt a hot blush rising from her neck to the roots of her hair. Immediately she was furious with herself. He saw the deepening colour and thought it became her. It was a most agreeable foil for her eyes.

'I consider the end to be worth the possible perils,' she replied.

'General Ward told me about your father. I'm truly sorry.'

The tone sounded sincere and it took her by surprise. 'If there is any chance that he might be released I have to take it. Surely you see that?'

'I understand your motives and applaud your courage, but...'

'You cannot dissuade me. I am set on going.'

'Very well, but know this: I shall expect you to

obey my orders to the letter. Both our lives may depend upon it.'

'I understand.'

'I hope you do because I shall not brook disobedience.'

The threat was plain and she had not the least doubt that he meant it. Did he think her so unreliable?

'I assure you, Major, that I will do nothing to jeopardise the success of this mission.'

'Good.' He paused. 'Then we may be able to deal tolerably well together after all.'

It was, she knew, an oblique reference to their first encounter. Unwilling to go there she sought safer ground.

'There must be many things I need to know, about the Condesa de Ordoñez, I mean.'

'I shall brief you on those while we travel. There will be time enough for you to assimilate the details.'

'As you wish.'

He stood. 'Until tomorrow morning then, Miss Huntley.'

Sabrina rose, too, and held out her hand. It was in part a conciliatory gesture. Whatever had happened before, it must not be allowed to get in the way now.

'Until tomorrow, sir.'

She had wondered if he would shake hands with

her or consider a curt bow sufficient. Strong fingers closed around hers and, unexpectedly, lifted her hand to his lips. The touch sent a tremor through her entire being. For a moment the grey eyes held hers, but she could not read the expression there. Then she was free and he turned to go. She watched until he was lost to view.

Early next morning, as the trunks were loaded onto the carriage and the horses put to, Sabrina came down to find her godfather and her large travelling companion already waiting. With a small start of surprise she saw that Major Falconbridge had changed his uniform for civilian dress. He was clad now in fawn breeches, Hessian boots and a coat of dark blue superfine that might have been moulded to his shoulders. Snowy linen showed at wrist and throat and a single fob hung from a cream-coloured waistcoat, completing an outfit that was at once simple and elegant. It also enhanced every line of that powerful frame and rendered it more imposing.

Unwilling to let her mind travel too far down that road, she turned her attention to their escort. Ramon and Luis were reassuring presences. As Jacinta had told her, when asked they had made it quite clear that they took their presence on this journey as read. Nor would they be dissuaded.

'Your concern does you credit, *Doña* Sabrina,' replied Ramon when she had told them her plans, 'but I believe I will make up my own mind.' The words were quietly spoken but carried an undertone that she recognised all too well.

She made a last-ditch attempt. 'Aranjuez is far behind French lines.'

'*Madre de Dios!* Can it be true?' Luis threw up his hands in mock horror. 'In that case, Ramon and I shall remain safely here and tell your father later that we let you go alone into the lion's den. I am sure he will understand.'

'My father would not ask this of you.'

'Your father is not here,' said Ramon, 'which means that we two are *in loco parentis* until his return.'

'Loco is right,' replied Luis, 'but even crazy parents are better than none, eh?'

Unable to think of an immediate answer to this, Sabrina had given in. With Ramon and Luis now were two of Falconbridge's men, Corporal Blakelock and Private Willis. She recognised them from the encounter in Casa Verde. Both men seemed to be in their mid-twenties but there the resemblance ended: Blakelock's thin, rangy frame and shock of fair hair were a complete contrast to Willis's shorter, more compact build and straggling brown locks. They touched their caps and greeted her respectfully, neither one giving any indication that they recalled what had taken place that day in the wheelwright's yard. She wondered whether it was natural tact on their part or whether Falconbridge had spoken to them. They were to travel in the chaise with Jacinta. Ramon and Luis would take it in turns to drive the coach. The entourage certainly looked like that of a wealthy man and, in this instance, appearances were everything.

Sabrina had not expected that the farewell to Albermarle would be easy, and in this she was right. The craggy face surveyed her for a moment in silence and the blue eyes softened.

'God bless you, my dear. I wish you all good fortune.' He hugged her closely. Then he shook hands with Falconbridge. 'Take care of her, Major.'

'You have my word on it, sir.'

Albermarle handed Sabrina into the carriage before turning back to the man beside him and bestowing on him a vulpine smile. Then he leaned closer and lowered his voice so that only the two of them could hear.

'If you let any harm come to her I'll personally cut out your liver.'

The Major met his eye. 'I'll try by every means to keep her safe, sir.'

'You'd better.' Albermarle smiled at Sabrina and watched her companion climb into the coach. Then he stepped back and rapped out a command to Luis on the box. The horses leapt forwards.

Sabrina drew in a deep breath as the coach pulled away; this was it, the beginning of the adventure. Yet she knew nothing about this man with whom she was to spend the next few weeks. This was only the second time they had been alone together. She would have preferred it to have been somewhere other than the close confines of the carriage, for she was only too keenly aware of the virile form opposite. Just then she would have given a great deal to know what he was thinking, but his expression gave nothing away.

What was running through his mind just then was a strange mixture of emotions. Chiefly he wished with all his heart that she had not come. He was also hoping with all his heart that their mission would go without a hitch. The thought of what might happen if she ever fell into enemy hands turned him cold. Any woman would have been in danger, but a woman who looked like Sabrina… It was why he had tried to talk her out of coming along. She really was lovely. The green travelling dress and matching bonnet became her well, enhancing the colour of her eyes. The shade was unusual, reminding him just now of sun-shot sea water. Those same eyes darkened to emerald when she was angry, he remembered. At that moment their expression was unfathomable. He sighed inwardly. Like it or not she was with him now and he knew it would be better if they could at least get along. The fact that they didn't was, he admitted, in great measure due to him.

'It doesn't seem quite real, does it?' he said then.

The words were so exactly what had been going through her own mind that she wondered if he had somehow read her thoughts.

'No, indeed it doesn't.'

She wondered if he would attempt to make polite conversation now. In truth she had no wish for it. However, it seemed that was not his intention.

'Since we are to spend some time together perhaps I should begin by telling you something of the lady you are to impersonate.'

She acknowledged privately that it was an adroit touch. He had her full attention now. 'I would be glad if you did. I know so little, apart from the fact that the Condesa is French—and blonde.'

'Her family's name was De Courcy. They came from Toulouse but left France during the revolution, just before the Terror, and settled in Asturias where, I understand, the family had lands.' He paused. 'Marianne de Courcy married Antonio Ordoñez three years ago.'

'Was it an arranged marriage?'

'Yes, though with the consent of both parties apparently.'

'Children?'

'A son called Miguel.'

'And they live retired.'

'Happily for our purposes, yes. The Conde prefers country life.'

'All the same, there might be someone at this party who knows him or his wife.'

The grey gaze met hers. 'Let us hope not, for both our sakes.' He reached into the inner pocket of his coat and drew out the object that reposed there. 'Incidentally, you will need this.'

'What is it?'

'A small detail, but an important one if our subterfuge is to be believed.' He held up a gold ring.

She stared at it for a moment and then at him. 'I had not thought of that.'

'How should you? It is a husband's concern, is it not?'

He reached across and took her hand, sliding the ring on her finger. It fitted well, almost as though it belonged there. However, she was not so much aware of the gold band as of the hand holding hers, a strong lean hand whose touch set her pulse racing. It lingered a few seconds longer and then relinquished its hold. He smiled faintly.

'The adventure begins, my dear, for better or for worse.'

They settled into silence for a while after this, each occupied in private thought. Sabrina's gaze went to the window but in truth she saw little of the passing countryside. The presence of the wedding band on her finger was a tangible reminder of the role she was expected to play now. It might have been easier if the man opposite had been a less charismatic, less attractive figure. A plainer, duller man might have made it easier to concentrate. She forced her attention back to what she had been told, committing the detail to memory. She couldn't afford to make a slip. Thus far she had not allowed herself to think too far ahead but now the implications of their mission crowded in, and the dangers it posed to them both.

At noon they stopped to rest the horses and to partake of a light luncheon. The inn was humble but clean and boasted a vine-covered terrace to the rear overlooking the hills. It was a far more appealing prospect than sitting indoors, and Sabrina readily agreed when he suggested they repair thither to eat. It was good to be out of the swaying vehicle for a while, and to have the opportunity to stretch her cramped limbs. While the Major bespoke luncheon, she walked to the end of the terrace and stood for a while looking out towards hills now hazy in the heat that shimmered over rock and scrub. Nothing moved in the stillness save a buzzard circling high on the warm air currents.

'It is a fine view, is it not?'

She had not heard him approach but a swift glance revealed the tall figure at her shoulder. His close-ness was disconcerting so she returned her gaze to the hills.

'Very fine.'

'Spain is a beautiful country, at least those parts of it I have seen.'

She nodded. 'Yes, it is. My father always thought so, too.'

The mention of her father brought unwelcome emotions to the fore and she resolutely changed the subject.

'The journey has made me hungry. Shall we eat?'

He could hardly miss the hint and smiled faintly. They moved back under the shade of the vines. The meal was simple and unpretentious: tender, home-cured ham, slices of Manchego cheese, green olives, pieces of spicy chorizo, freshly baked bread and a jug of red wine, but Sabrina had no fault to find with it. On the contrary, she ate with enjoyment. The ham was particularly good, almost melting in the mouth.

Falconbridge owned to some surprise, initially wondering if she would turn up her nose at such plain fare. Perhaps the lengthy travels with her father had accustomed her to such things. It pleased him to find it so. This mission would be difficult enough without being saddled with a captious female.

For the most part they ate in silence. When at last they had finished he leaned back in his chair, surveying her keenly.

'Would you care to walk a little? It may be some time before we get another chance.'

She nodded acquiescence and rose with him. By tacit consent they strolled together towards the arroyo some hundred yards off.

'I find that I know nothing about you, or almost nothing,' he said then.

She glanced up at him. 'What do you want to know?'

'Now that's a leading question.'

'I have nothing to hide.' That wasn't completely true but she had no intention of mentioning Jack Denton. Anyway it had no bearing on their mission.

'Then tell me a little about your background, the things that General Ward did not say.'

'There is not a great deal to tell. My mother was a Frenchwoman whose family fled Paris when the revolution came. She died when I was twelve. Father refused to leave me with relatives and brought me with him to Iberia.'

'An unusual upbringing for a young woman.'

'I suppose it must seem that way to other people, though I have never considered it so.'

'You clearly have a gift for languages.'

'We spoke both French and English at home so the facility came early. I learned Portuguese and Spanish after my father's posting to the Peninsula.'

'I see. Did you never have any formal schooling?'

'I had a governess when I was little. My father also taught me many things; more perhaps than most young ladies learn.'

'Such as?'

'Such as learning how to defend myself.'

Recalling their first meeting, Falconbridge smiled. 'So the sword and pistol weren't just for show, then?'

'Hardly.'

'Have you ever been called upon to use them?'

'Yes. Father's work took us to some remote places and once we were attacked by robbers. Fortunately Ramon and Luis were with us and we were able to drive our attackers off, but it's not an experience I would choose to have again.'

'I can well believe it,' he replied. His curiosity mounted. 'Did you never settle in one place?'

'No, though there were some fairly lengthy spells in different locations.'

'Did it not bother you to be always on the move?'

'Home was wherever we happened to be. So long as Father and I were together I didn't mind.'

'His capture must have come as a severe blow.'

'Yes, it did.'

'I take it you were not there on that occasion.'

She shook her head. 'My horse was lame and Father was only going to be away for two or three days. That was four months ago. I have not seen him since.'

'I'm so sorry.'

Sabrina was struck again by the apparent sincerity in his tone. It was much at variance with the man she had met before.

'I should have been with him,' she said. 'Perhaps then I could have done something to help.'

'If you had been with him, my dear, you would have been killed or captured yourself.'

'Perhaps.'

'Soldiers are not known for their chivalrous behaviour.'

She smiled innocently. 'So I've noticed, sir.'

'Touché!'

Her riposte had been justified, he admitted. All the same he hadn't missed the mischievous glance that had accompanied it. There had been no malice in the look. On the contrary, it had been quite unwittingly seductive. The fact that it had been unintended made it all the more effective. He smiled in self-mockery. Any overture to Miss Huntley would likely result in him getting shot, or run through with a sword. She was more than capable of holding her own. It didn't displease him. Whatever else, it meant that the journey wasn't going to be dull.

Their stroll had brought them to the arroyo, but the stream in its stony bed was reduced to a mere trickle now. A few stunted trees clung to the margins. Heat struck upwards from the baked earth and carried with it the scent of wild thyme and dry grass.

'Despite the shortcomings of some members of the military,' he continued, 'you are fortunate to have a friend in Colonel Albermarle.'

'He has been kindness itself. He and my father go back many years.'

'When this mission is over you will see your father again.'

'I pray that I may. I cannot bear to think of him in a foreign prison.'

Her expression grew wistful and he was unexpectedly touched. Her affection for her parent was clearly genuine, as was her desire for his freedom. Her youth made her seem more vulnerable. Once again he felt the weight of his responsibility.

'How old are you, Sabrina?'

'I'm nineteen.' Her eyes met and held his. 'How old are you?'

His lips twitched. 'Eight and twenty.'

'Now you know about me will you not tell me something of yourself?'

'You will find it dull. Unlike you I had a most conventional upbringing: Eton, Cambridge and the army. As the younger son I was expected to carve out a career for myself. My father bought me a commission and then let me get on with it.'

'Do you have any sisters?'

'One. Her name is Harriet. She is four years younger than I and married now with children of her own.'

'And your brother?'

There was an infinitesimal pause. 'Hugh, who is two years older.'

'Are you close?'

'Not especially.' It was, he thought, a massive understatement. The antipathy he had come to feel for his brother had, at one point, come perilously close to hatred.

'Is he married?'

The grey eyes glinted. 'Yes. His wife is called Clarissa and they have two children.'

It had been easier to say than he had imagined. It was said that time salved all wounds; it must have made more of a difference than he had ever envisaged.

Sabrina smiled. 'I find it hard to see you as an uncle.'

He regarded her steadily. 'Do you?'

'Yes, the soldier in you seems to preclude it.'

'In truth I have seen little of my nieces and nephews,' he admitted, 'but that is due to the demands of the army and not to any shortcomings of theirs. I happen to like children.'

The statement was surprising and oddly pleasing. It was a side to him that she would never have suspected. They turned and began to walk back towards the inn.

'How came you to be involved in army work?' he continued. 'It is an unusual occupation for a young woman.'

'It was at my own request,' she replied. 'I wanted to do something towards the war effort.'

'A noble aspiration, but not entirely without risk.'

'The risk has been minimal, until now.'

He regarded her steadily. 'You've taken a dangerous gamble, my dear.'

'So have you.'

'True, though I think the odds are stacked more in my favour.'

Sabrina was unable to decipher what lay behind

that for the tone was compounded of several things.

'The odds are always stacked in a man's favour,' she replied.

'Doesn't that worry you?'

'Of course, but then much depends on the man, does it not?'

'And I have done little to impress you thus far.' He paused. 'I admit that on the occasion of our first meeting my behaviour was abysmal. I suppose there's no chance of my being forgiven?'

'Not the least chance, sir.'

He sighed. 'No, I imagine not.' There followed another brief pause. Then, 'Did you deliver your fruit safely, by the way?'

For a moment she stared at him, unable to believe her ears. Then she saw the gleam in his eyes and, unable to help herself, gave a gurgle of laughter.

'Yes, I did deliver it, no thanks to you, you odious man.'

His enjoyment grew. 'I knew you wouldn't disappoint me.'

It was hard to know what to make of that either, but she had a strong suspicion he was quizzing her.

'Anyway,' she continued, 'it wasn't just fruit.'

'What then?'

'Guns for the army.'

'Good lord! Did your godfather know?'

'He sent me.' Seeing his expression she lifted one finely arched brow. 'Why should he not? The risk was small. Besides, I can take care of myself.'

'No doubt,' he replied, 'but now that responsibility falls to me.'

'A worrying thought, sir.'

'Do you doubt my ability to protect you?'

The green eyes gleamed in their turn. 'Well, yes. Did you not abandon me to spend a night in the open with five men and a broken wagon?'

'Wretch! You're not going to let me forget it, are you?'

'Certainly not,' she replied.

At this point all his preconceived ideas had vanished; she was unlike anyone he had ever met. In his experience young women did not usually meet his eye in just that way, and certainly didn't engage in verbal sparring. Beauty and wit were an attractive combination. She wasn't afraid of him either. He wasn't even sure if she liked him. On balance, he suspected not.

They returned to the inn and paid their shot before resuming the journey in a more companionable silence. Sabrina's gaze went to the window but in truth she saw little of the passing countryside. Her mind was focused on the man sitting opposite. Thus far she had not allowed herself to think too far ahead, but now the implications of their relationship crowded in. For the first time in her life she was thrown together with a man whom she knew hardly at all and in circumstances that required a certain amount of intimacy. Falconbridge was unlikely to do anything that might jeopardise the success of their mission, and he didn't seem the type to force unwanted attentions on any woman. However, she had learned early not to put her trust in appearances. Faith was a loaded pistol and she had a brace of them, should the need arise.

As for the rest, the villages they passed were few and mean, little more than clusters of hovels whose inhabitants eked a subsistence living from a grudging soil. It didn't shock her for she had seen it many times on her travels, but it did occur to her to wonder where they would spend the night. In the past she had slept in many places and knew that she would infinitely prefer a well-kept barn to a dirty inn. Even sleeping in the open was better than that. She decided to ask. The answer was immediately forthcoming.

'We shall stay at La Posada del Rey.'

'The King's Inn. It sounds quite grand.'

'I doubt if the king would be seen dead there,' he replied, 'but at least it's clean and well run. I've used it before on occasions.'

'I'm sure it will be satisfactory.'

'Don't expect luxury or I fear you'll be disappointed.'

Sabrina laughed. 'I became accustomed to rough living very early on. A clean inn is a luxury compared to a bed on open ground.'

He regarded her in surprise, not so much on account of her reply as the way in which laughter lit her face. It occurred to him again that she was rather more than just a pretty girl.

'I hope never to subject you to such rude accommodation,' he replied. 'Rather I promise you a comfortable chamber all to yourself.'

Though the words were blandly spoken they were also meant as reassurance and she knew it. The matter of their sleeping arrangements had been on her mind since they had set out. She suspected he had guessed as much, and also that she would rather have died before mentioning the subject.

'I shall hold you to that, sir.' Her tone was equally bland.

The grey eyes gleamed. 'I was certain you would, my dear.'

Unsure what to make of that she searched his expression for clues, but the rugged features gave nothing away.

Chapter Three

The journey resumed uneventfully next morning and, over the next few days, they made good progress, whiling away the time in conversation and sometimes with cards. Sabrina also took the opportunity to learn as much as possible about the woman she was impersonating. Her companion supplied as much detail as he could. All the same, she could already see potential pitfalls, such as the fact that she had never been to the Languedoc. Falconbridge did not seem unduly unconcerned.

'The Condesa must have been very young when the family left Toulouse,' he said. 'It's entirely possible she wouldn't recall very much anyway.'

'That's fortunate. There may be French officers present at this party.'

'I imagine there will. Try to steer the conversation away from potentially dangerous topics.'

She smiled faintly. 'If things look dangerous I'll ask the officer to talk about himself. Then I won't have to do more than nod and smile for the next hour or so.'

'You think any man could speak for so long about himself?'

'In my experience it's usually a favourite topic of conversation; present company excepted, of course.'

The dulcet tone elicited a faint smile. 'I'm relieved to hear it. I should hate to think that I was such a bore.'

'Hardly that.' Sabrina thought that *bore* was the last word she would use to describe him.

'Another load off my mind,' he replied. 'Is your knowledge of men so extensive?'

With those words Jack Denton's image resurfaced and with it a recollection of hurt and humiliation. She pushed it aside, forcing herself to remain collected. 'How am I to take that?'

'Given your unusual upbringing, you must have met many of my sex. Were they all such confoundedly dull dogs as your remark suggests?'

'No, not all. Some were good company.' She was minded to add a rider to that but refrained.

'Indeed? And did your father allow you to keep such company?'

An indignant retort leapt to mind immediately. Just in time she caught the sardonic glint in his eye and realised he had been quizzing her again.

'That was an outrageous suggestion.'

'Yes, I suppose it was.' He didn't look or sound repentant. 'I find myself curious, you see.'

'About what?'

'Given your bohemian lifestyle it cannot have been easy to meet eligible young men.'

'I never thought of them in such a way,' she replied. 'Some were my father's friends, others were officers whom I met in the course of events.'

'But none for whom you felt a particular partiality?'

'No,' she lied.

'You're never going to tell me that they looked upon you with similar indifference.'

'I really have no idea. You'd have to ask them.' Another lie, she thought. Somehow it went against the grain to tell a falsehood to this man, but the truth was a nest of hornets and best left alone.

He continued to regard her steadily. 'And yet you have been of marriageable age for some time.'

'You make it sound as though I were quite on the shelf.' The words were spoken without rancour.

'I beg your pardon. It's just that most young ladies I've ever met are on the lookout for a husband from the time of their coming out.'

'I never had a coming out,' she replied, 'so perhaps that has coloured my view of the matter. In any case I was enjoying my life too much to want to relinquish it for marriage.'

'You think that all enjoyment ends with marriage then?'

'I don't know. I didn't mean to imply that all marriages are dull, especially not where the couple marries for love. That must be agreeable, surely.'

'I'm sure it is.'

She eyed him curiously. 'Did you never wish to wed?'

There followed a brief hesitation. 'I once fancied myself in love but, as it turned out, I was mistaken.'

'Oh. I'm sorry.'

'No need,' he replied. 'Besides, I am now happily married to my career. Romantic entanglements are for other men.'

They lapsed into silence after this, each seeking refuge in private thought. Unable to tell what lay behind that impassive expression, Sabrina could only ponder his words. He had spoken lightly enough but she sensed that more lay beneath. Clearly he considered marriage an unnecessary encumbrance and perhaps in his line of work it really was. The thought caused an unexpected pang. Even in the short time she had known him he had made an impression, more so than any man of her acquaintance—apart from one. While she didn't equate the two, the first had taught her a valuable lesson. Since then she had kept her male acquaintances at a courteous and professional distance. She intended to do the same now. Her father was the reason she had become embroiled in this affair. His freedom was what really mattered. She must not forget it.

As usual they stopped that evening at an inn and Falconbridge requested rooms and a private parlour in which to dine. The *patrón* was delighted to welcome such exalted guests and assured them that he could offer a most excellent parlour. However, he regretted that he only had one bedchamber available. Falconbridge cursed inwardly. He had always realised this was a possibility but had hoped that it wouldn't arise. He glanced at Sabrina who was just then engaged in conversation with Jacinta. Mistaking that look entirely, the *patrón* hastened to reassure him that it was a large room.

'A truly commodious chamber, *señor*. The lady will be most pleased.'

Falconbridge seriously doubted that. Unfortunately, with dusk coming on, further travel was out of the question. The road was dangerous after dark. He had no desire to run into any of the brigands who frequented the hills, or a French patrol if it came to that.

'We'll take it.'

'*Si, señor.* You won't be disappointed, I guarantee it.'

Just then disappointment was the last thing on Falconbridge's mind, which was turning instead on Sabrina's probable reaction. In spite of the extraordinary circumstances in which they found themselves, a shared bedchamber was a step too far and, hitherto, separate accommodation had been obtained as a matter of course. Thus the proprieties had been observed. He could well understand the importance of that to any woman. Now though, matters were about to become deucedly awkward. Taking Sabrina aside he explained the situation briefly, watching her face, bracing himself for the explosion of wrath, which must surely follow.

'I'm truly sorry about this,' he said, 'but it cannot be avoided. There isn't another decent inn for twenty miles.'

Contrary to his expectation she didn't fly into a passion or refuse to stay a moment longer, though she could not quite conceal the expression of alarm fast enough to escape his notice. He could not know how hard her heart was thumping.

'We'll have to manage as best we may,' she replied.

Once again he owned to surprise and, privately, to relief. She was proving to be a much easier travelling companion than he had ever envisaged.

When inspected, the room was indeed quite spacious and, she noted with relief, it was clean. It was dominated by a large bed. A dresser and washstand occupied much of one wall. A low divan stood opposite. It was the first time she had been in a bedchamber with any man, other than her father. Major Falconbridge's presence was different in every way from the gentle reassuring figure of her parent. Somehow he seemed to fill the space.

'You take the bed,' he said. Then, glancing at the divan, 'I'll sleep over there.'

She nodded, forcing herself to a calm she was far from feeling, reminding herself that she had elected to come on this mission. What had happened was a temporary but unavoidable inconvenience. When their luggage had been carried up, Falconbridge took himself off for a mug of beer, leaving the room free for Sabrina. She was grateful for the courtesy. With Jacinta's help she washed and dressed for dinner, donning a green muslin gown. A matching ribbon was threaded through her curls. Sabrina surveyed her reflection critically. It was hardly sensational but at least she looked neat and presentable.

'It will serve,' she said.

Jacinta smiled. 'It looks very well.'

'Good enough for present circumstances.'

Sabrina did not add, 'and for present company'. In all likelihood Falconbridge would not notice what frock she had on. Not that there was any reason why he should. Theirs was a purely business arrangement. He had never given the least sign that he was attracted to her at all, and that, of course, was a great relief.

A short time later she heard a tap on the door. On being bidden to enter Falconbridge stepped into the room. For a moment they faced each other in silence; his practised eye took in every detail of her costume. He had no fault to find. The cut of the gown was fashionable and elegant. That shade of green really suited her, too, enhancing the colour of her eyes. For the rest she looked as neat as wax.

'I need to change,' he said. 'I beg you will forgive the intrusion.'

'Of course.'

He spoke to Willis, who had been waiting outside the door. The acting valet touched his forelock to Sabrina and then busied himself with a chest of clothes. Jacinta eyed both men with cold disapproval and then, with determined slowness, began collecting up her mistress's discarded garments.

Sabrina bit back a smile and, taking a book from her own travelling case, retired with it to the divan on the far side of the room. Aware of Falconbridge's presence to her very fingertips she kept her attention sedulously on the pages in front of her. Out of the corner of her eye she saw him peel off coat, waist-coat and linen, affording a view of a hard-muscled torso. Water splashed into the basin on the wash-stand. He bathed his face and hands and sluiced his neck. Willis handed him a towel and he dried himself vigorously. Once, he threw a glance her way but Sabrina's attention was apparently fixed on the book. Jacinta glared. He smiled faintly.

Then he turned and took the clean shirt offered him. Sabrina glanced up from beneath her lashes, caught a glimpse of a lean waist and narrow hips and very long legs, and looked away again. Spots of colour leapt into her face. Years spent in the wake of the army meant that she was no stranger to the sight of semi-dressed men, but this one possessed an almost sculptural beauty. Its effect was to make the room seem a lot warmer.

Unaware of the sensations he was creating, Falconbridge finished dressing. Sabrina surveyed him closely now, making no more pretence at read-ing. The dark coat might have been moulded to his shoulders. Waistcoat and linen were faultless. The cream-coloured breeches fitted like a second skin. She drew in a deep breath. Becoming aware of her regard he smiled faintly.

'I'm sorry to have kept you waiting.'

'Oh, no, I beg you will not regard it,' she replied. 'I have been quite entertained.'

Across the room Willis made a strange choking sound and received an icy stare from Jacinta. Falconbridge raised an eyebrow. Sabrina's cheeks went scarlet.

'With my book, I mean.'

'But of course,' he replied. 'What else?'

The innocent tone didn't deceive her for a moment. He was outrageous. Moreover, he was enjoying himself. She heard him dismiss the two servants. When they had gone, he took the volume from her hand and examined the cover.

'Lazarillo de Tormes. Does your father know?'

'Of course he knows. He lent—' She broke off, seeing the slow grin spread across his face. The gleam in the grey eyes was deeply disconcerting.

'Did he? Well, he really has attended to every part of his daughter's education.'

She wondered if he were shocked. It was, she admitted, a real possibility, for, while the concept of the picaresque novel was hardly new, this one could be read on different levels—particularly its numerous sexual metaphors.

'Do you disapprove?'

'Not at all.' He paused. 'Do you care?'

'No.' The word was out before she could stop it. She hurried on, 'I beg your pardon. I didn't mean to be rude.'

'You weren't—just beautifully frank.'

'Father always encouraged me to read widely.'

'So I gather.' He glanced again at the cover. 'And it is a wickedly good book, isn't it?'

'Oh, yes, very.'

'Wicked or good?'

His expression drew a reluctant laugh. 'Both, since you ask.'

'Good girl.'

Unsure how to take this, she eyed him quizzically. He laid the book aside and then gestured to the door.

'Shall we?'

Dinner that evening comprised local fare but it was well cooked. Sabrina was hungry, too, after their day on the road. The conversation was kept to general topics but she found her companion informed on a wide variety of subjects. It came as no surprise now. She was forced to acknowledge that none of the officers she had met in recent times had interested her half so much. He had told her something of his background but only the essentials. All in all, she thought, he volunteered very little about himself. It roused her curiosity.

'Tell me some more about your family,' she said. 'Your brother, for instance.'

The genial expression became more guarded. 'What about him?'

'You said you weren't close. May I ask why?'

His fingers tightened on the stem of his wine glass, but when he spoke his voice was perfectly level. 'We had a disagreement. It was some years ago.'

'And you've never been reconciled?'

'No.'

'How sad. What did you argue about?' The question had been innocent enough but the grey eyes hardened. Sabrina was mortified. 'Forgive me. I had no right to ask that.'

'It doesn't matter.' He paused as though inwardly debating something. Then he said, 'It was over a woman, as it happened.'

'Ah, you both liked the same one.'

The accuracy of the observation startled him. In spite of himself he experienced a certain wry amusement. 'Yes. My brother won.'

'Was she very beautiful?'

'Very.'

'What happened?'

He swirled the remaining wine in his glass. 'She married Hugh.'

'Oh.' For a moment she was silent, uncomfortably aware of having strayed into dangerous territory. Yet having gone there, she found herself wanting to know more, to understand. 'That could not have been easy.'

He bit back a savage laugh. The understatement was huge, though she could not have known it. Did one ever truly recover from a blow like that? 'It was some years ago,' he replied, 'and one gets over disappointment. The incident belongs to the past and I am content to leave it there.'

It was a clear hint. They changed the subject after that, but the conversation had given Sabrina much to think about. For all his quiet assertion to the contrary it was evident that the lady had hurt him. Perhaps she hadn't meant to. She had clearly loved his brother more and one couldn't dictate to the human heart. Her gaze rested on the man opposite. Had his earlier experience made him wary? Was that why he had never married? It seemed increasingly likely. It was also a reaction she found quite understandable.

Falconbridge tossed back the rest of his wine and then got to his feet. 'We have another long day on the road tomorrow and it would be as well to get some rest.'

Sabrina rose, too, though rather more reluctantly, for the sleeping arrangements were etched on her consciousness. He stood back to let her precede him out of the door, and then accompanied her to the stairs. Then he paused.

'You go on ahead. I need to speak to Willis and Blakelock about arrangements for the morning.'

It was tactful and once again she was grateful. On returning to the room she found Jacinta waiting. With her help Sabrina undressed and donned her nightgown. Then she sat at the dresser while the maid unpinned her hair and brushed it out. In the looking glass Jacinta's dark eyes locked with hers.

'Do you wish me to remain here tonight?' she asked. 'As a chaperone?'

Sabrina smiled wryly. 'I assure you I am quite safe from Major Falconbridge.'

'Are you sure?'

'Why should you doubt it?'

'Because he is a man.'

'He did not create this situation. It was always possible that it would happen at some point.'

'Maybe so, but I have seen the way he looks at you when he thinks himself unobserved.'

Sabrina shook her head. 'You are mistaken. He has never shown the least regard for me, other than as a…a colleague.'

'He does not look at his other colleagues in that way.'

'I am sure there is not the least occasion for concern.'

'Best make certain. Put a pistol beneath your pillow.'

'I cannot afford to shoot the Major, Jacinta.'

'Very well, your knife then. The wound need not be mortal.'

Sabrina laughed. 'I have no intention of stabbing him either.'

'Please yourself.' The maid sniffed. 'But don't say I didn't warn you.'

She finished brushing Sabrina's hair and then, having watched her climb into bed, pulled the covers up to her chin and tucked them in tightly.

'Colonel Albermarle would not approve of this arrangement,' she told her charge severely.

'Colonel Albermarle isn't here,' replied Sabrina. 'Anyway, it's only for this one night.'

'That's what you think. I'll wager that in future there will be many inns with only one bedchamber.'

Sabrina gave an involuntary gurgle of laughter. 'And I suppose you also think that Major Falconbridge arranged it in advance, in order to have his wicked way with me.'

'Man is tinder, woman is flame and the devil is the wind. What man can resist temptation put in his way?'

'He will not be so tempted. There is too much at stake.'

'I hope you are right.'

With that sobering comment the maid departed. Retrieving Lazarillo de Tormes, Sabrina tried to occupy herself with the book but somehow it was difficult to concentrate. Jacinta's words lingered in her mind bringing with it an image of Falconbridge's lithe and powerful form. For all the maid's assertions to the contrary, Sabrina was fairly certain he wouldn't do anything foolish. Then, unaccountably, the memory of Jack Denton returned. She had trusted him, too. Involuntarily her gaze went to the trunk across the room where her pistols currently resided. Frowning, she laid aside the book and climbed out of bed.

Ten minutes later footsteps sounded outside and the door opened to admit her new room-mate. Her heart leapt. Now more than ever she was conscious of his sheer physical presence. It seemed to fill the room. He surveyed her in silence for a moment and then closed the door and locked it. She drew a deep breath.

'Everything is arranged for the morning,' he said then.

'Good.'

He crossed the room and peeled off his coat, tossing it over a chair. Sabrina feigned to study her book, comforted by the bulky mass of the pistol beneath her pillow. Under her covert gaze Falconbridge began to unfasten his neckcloth. Having done so, he pulled his shirt over his head. The sight of the powerful naked torso beneath did nothing to calm her racing heartbeat. Could she trust him? Irrationally she wondered how it would feel to be held in those strong arms. The idea was as shocking as it was unexpected. She had not considered him in that way before. She certainly could not afford to think of him in that way now. With a start she saw him cross the room and approach the bed. Her throat dried. She must have been mad to send Jacinta away, to get herself into this situation. Her free hand crept towards the pistol butt.

'May I trouble you for a spare pillow and a blanket?' he asked.

'Er, yes, of course.'

Having gathered the requisite items he retired to the divan and then glanced across at her.

'Do you want to read awhile longer or shall I blow out the candle?'

'Oh, no. I'm done.' She laid the book aside and snuggled down beneath the covers.

'Goodnight then, Sabrina.'

'Goodnight.'

He extinguished the candle and the room was plunged into gloom. She heard the divan creak beneath his weight and then the softer sound of the blanket settling around him. Her hand stole beneath the pillow and closed round the pistol butt. Its reassuring presence drew a faint smile. Then she closed her eyes, trying not to think about the man lying just feet away. It proved much harder than anticipated. She realised then that for the first time he had used her name. The familiarity should have annoyed her. It didn't. On the contrary, it had sounded a natural thing for him to do so.

For some time Falconbridge lay awake in the darkness, listening. Once or twice he heard her stir a little but then the room grew quiet. In the silence, thoughts came crowding fast. Chief among them was the semi-dressed figure in the big bed just across the room. Just for a moment he let his imagination go down that route. The response was a wave of heat in his loins as sudden as it was unexpected. He glanced across at the recumbent form and, biting back a mocking groan, turned over, mentally rejecting the temptation. For all manner of reasons she was forbidden fruit, and for both their sakes he must remember it.

When Sabrina woke the next morning it was with a sense of well-being. She stretched luxuriously, opening her eyes to the new day. The details of the room returned but a glance at the divan revealed it to be empty save for the blanket and pillow. A swift glance around the room revealed no sign of Major Falconbridge. She frowned and sat up, wondering what o'clock it might be. As yet the inn was quiet, which argued that it couldn't be too late. Throwing the covers aside she climbed out of bed and went to the window, opening it wide. The sun was just over the tops of the hills, streaking the heavens with gold and pink. All around the silent land stretched away until the rim of the hills met the sky. The quiet air smelled of wood smoke and baking bread from the kitchen.

She was so absorbed that she failed to hear the door open. Seeing the figure by the window Falconbridge paused, his breath catching in his throat. The rays of the sun turned her unbound hair to fiery gold. They also rendered her nightgown semi-transparent, outlining the curves beneath. He stood there awhile longer, unashamedly making the most of it. Then he smiled.

'Good morning.'

Sabrina spun round, heart missing a beat. Recovering herself she returned the greeting. 'You must have been up early.'

'About an hour ago.'

'You should have wakened me.'

'You looked so peaceful lying there that I didn't like to.'

The thought that he had watched her sleeping aroused a mixture of emotions, all of them disquieting. Quickly she changed the subject.

'Did you sleep well?'

'Well enough, I thank you.'

His gaze never left her, drinking in every detail from the tumbled curls to the small bare feet beneath the hem of her gown. Aided by the sunlight his imagination stripped it away and dwelt agreeably on what it found. The thoughts it engendered led to others, delightful and disturbing in equal measure. He tried to rein them in; for all sorts of reasons he couldn't afford to think of her in that way. On the other hand, it was damnably difficult not to just then.

Under that steady scrutiny Sabrina glanced down, suddenly conscious of her present state of undress and then, belatedly, the direction and power of the light. The implications hit her a second later. She darted a look at her companion but nothing could have been more innocent than the expression on that handsome face. It was enough to confirm every suspicion. The knowledge should have been mortifying but somehow it wasn't. The feeling it awoke was quite different. Striving for an appearance of casual ease she moved away from the window.

'I must dress.'

'Do you need any help?' he asked. Meeting a startled gaze he hid a smile and added, 'Would you like me to send for Jacinta?'

'Oh. Oh, yes, thank you.'

This time he did smile. 'She'll be along directly.'

Then he strolled to the door. 'Breakfast will be ready when you are.'

When he had gone Sabrina let out the breath she had unconsciously been holding.

Chapter Four

During their journey that day they beguiled the time with cards. On this occasion it was piquet, a game which Sabrina enjoyed and at which she was particularly adept, as Falconbridge soon discovered.

'Is this the sign of a misspent youth?' he asked, having lost three times in succession.

'Misspent?' She smiled faintly. 'On the contrary, I had a very good teacher.'

'So I infer. Your father?'

'No, Captain Harcourt of the Light Dragoons.' Seeing his expression she hurried on, 'It was all quite respectable. He knew my father, you see, for they had had occasion to work together in Portugal and they became good friends.'

'A trusty mentor then.'

'Yes, he was.' It was quite true, as far as it went. Yet she knew she could never tell him exactly how much she owed Captain Harcourt. 'He said that knowledge of gaming was an essential aspect of any young woman's education.'

'Did he indeed?'

'Oh, yes, and he was right. His instruction has proved useful on several occasions.'

'Such as?'

'Such as the time in Lisbon, when Father and I were invited to supper and cards with the officers. One of them was a lieutenant whose honesty was highly suspect.'

'Ah, he was cheating.'

'Yes, marking cards. It took me a while to work out how he was doing it.'

'And then?'

'I played him at his own game. He lost fifty guineas that evening.' Her eyes sparkled with amusement. 'He wasn't best pleased.'

Falconbridge's lips twitched. 'I imagine he was not.'

'It served him right though.'

'Absolutely.'

Sabrina tilted her head a little and surveyed him keenly. 'Are you shocked?'

'By the revelation of a card sharp in the army? Hardly.'

'I mean by my telling you these things.'

'No, only a little surprised.'

'You think it not quite respectable?'

He smiled. 'On the contrary, I am fast coming to have the greatest respect for your skills.'

What she might have said in reply was never known, for suddenly the vehicle slowed and then men's voices were raised in challenge. The words were French. Falconbridge lowered the window and looked out.

'What is it?' she asked.

'A French patrol.'

She drew in a sharp breath. 'How many?'

'Ten—that I can see. There may be more.'

'Regulars?'

'We're about to find out.'

The carriage stopped and Sabrina heard approaching hooves and the jingle of harness. Moments later burnished cuirasses, blue jackets and high cavalry boots appeared in her line of vision. Their officer drew rein opposite the carriage window.

Falconbridge muttered an expletive under his breath. 'I think I know this man. Not his name, his face.'

Sabrina paled. 'Will he know you?'

'Let's hope not.' He glanced at his companion and murmured, 'Say as little as possible, Sabrina.'

Almost imperceptibly, she nodded. Then the French officer spoke.

'You will kindly step out of the carriage and identify yourself, Monsieur.'

With every appearance of ease Falconbridge opened the door and stepped down onto the roadway. The officer dismounted. Sabrina's hands clenched in her lap. She heard Falconbridge address the man in excellent French. On hearing his own language the officer's expression lightened visibly. For a moment or two his gaze met and held that of Falconbridge in a look that was distinctly quizzical. Then it was gone. He examined the papers that were passed to him and, apparently satisfied, handed them back.

'These are in order. You will forgive the intrusion, Monsieur le Comte.' He bowed. Then his glance went to the other passenger in the coach and lingered appreciatively. He bowed again. 'Madame.'

For the space of several heartbeats she felt the weight of that lupine stare. It stripped her and seemed to enjoy what it discovered for its owner bared his teeth in a smile. Annoyed and repelled together she lifted her chin and forced herself to meet his gaze. The rugged and moustachioed face suggested a man in his early forties, an impression reinforced by the grizzled brown hair that hung below the rim of his helmet.

'Colonel Claude Machart at your service,' he said then.

She inclined her head in token acknowledgement of the greeting while her mind dwelled regretfully on the pistols locked in her trunk.

'May I enquire whither you are bound, madame?' he continued.

'Aranjuez,' she replied.

'Aranjuez? That is some way off. May I ask your business there?'

Before she could reply Falconbridge cut in. 'A social gathering.' His tone conveyed ennui. 'One would rather not travel in these uncertain times, but on this occasion it cannot be avoided. Noblesse oblige, you understand.'

'Of course.' Machart smiled, an expression that did not reach his eyes. 'And you will be staying where?'

'At the house of Don Pedro de la Torre.'

'Then you must be attending the ball.'

Falconbridge evinced faint surprise. 'You are well informed, Colonel.'

'It is my business to be well informed, monsieur.'

'I'm sure it is.'

Machart threw him another penetrating look. 'Well, let me not detain you further. Madame, monsieur, I bid you good day and a pleasant journey.'

Falconbridge climbed back into the coach and regained his seat. As he did so the Colonel remounted and, having favoured the travellers with a nod, barked an order to his men and the patrol thundered away. Sabrina made herself relax.

'He didn't recognise you.'

'No, or we would be under arrest now.'

'Do you recall where you saw him before?'

'Yes, on the battlefield at Arroyo de Molinos last October. He was leading a detachment of cavalry.' He paused. 'My men engaged with them at close quarters. But it was many months ago and the scene chaotic. It is unlikely he would remember every face he saw that day.'

She knew the battle had resulted in a heavy defeat for the French. That would certainly have been held against them if Machart had remembered Falconbridge.

'He struck me as being an unpleasant character,' she said.

Her comment drew a faint smile. 'What makes you think so?'

'I've met enough military men to recognise the type. Let's hope we've seen the last of him.'

Falconbridge mentally echoed the sentiment. He had a good memory for faces and the ability to read those he met. For that reason he could only agree with her assessment.

Sabrina felt more than a little shaken by the incident, and suddenly Aranjuez did indeed begin to assume the quality of a lion's den. One false step would put them at the mercy of the French, of men like Machart. She shuddered inwardly, recalling what Falconbridge had told her earlier about the risks of capture and interrogation: Everyone talks by the third day. He had warned her but she had elected to come. There was no choice now but to see this through. Her father's freedom depended on it.

She was distracted from these thoughts by a strong hand closing on hers. Its clasp was reassuring, like its owner's smile. The effect was to create a sense of melting warmth deep inside her.

'Don't worry,' he said. 'Our stay in Aranjuez will be brief. Once the ball is over I shall have urgent business requiring my return.'

'That's good to hear.'

He gave her hand another gentle squeeze and then released his hold again, leaning back in his seat, surveying her quietly. The sensation of inner warmth intensified. She resisted it. He had meant only to be kind. It would be foolish to refine on something so trivial.

'I should not like to spend much more time in Colonel Machart's company.'

'No, though I believe he would not say the same of yours.'

'It means nothing. He's French so he can't help it.'

Falconbridge bit back the urge to laugh. 'How so?'

'All Frenchmen are demonstrative in that regard.'

'Are they?'

Sabrina saw the bait and refused to rise. 'So it is said.'

'And Englishmen are not demonstrative?'

'Not in the same way.'

His expression was wounded. 'What a body blow.'

'I never meant it to apply to you. I was speaking in general terms.'

'Based on your considerable experience, of course.'

'Certainly not. I never meant to suggest...' Too late she saw the expression in his eyes and knew he had been teasing her again. 'You knew that, you horror.'

'I beg your pardon.' The apology was belied by a smile. 'It was irresistible.'

Her chin came up at once. His smile widened. For a short space neither one spoke, though every fibre of her being was aware of the gaze fixed on her face. Even worse was the creeping blush she could feel rising from her neck to her cheeks.

'I wish you wouldn't look at me like that.'

'Forgive me. I was trying to be more… demonstrative.'

For a second or two she could only stare back but his smile was infectious and, unable to help it, she began to laugh.

'No you weren't. You were roasting me and enjoying it.'

The accusation left him unabashed. 'I can't deny it.'

'You are quite shameless.'

'So I've been told. I fear the habit is deeply ingrained now.'

'I am sure of it,' she retorted. 'However, I shall try not to be so easy a prey in future.'

His enjoyment increased. Better still, the apprehension he had glimpsed in her face after the encounter with Machart was gone, just as he had hoped.

'Good. I like a challenge.'

She shook her head. 'It's no use, sir. I shall not succumb. I'm wise to you now.'

'What a pity.' He sighed, eyeing her speculatively for a moment. Then, 'Now that you mention it, I think we should both be more demonstrative, don't you?' He watched the green eyes darken to emerald, their expression most attractively indignant, and waited in anticipation.

'Do you?' The tone was icy. 'And what put that thought in your mind?'

'Aranjuez. People must believe we are man and wife.'

Sabrina bit her lip. 'Oh, yes. I see.'

His expression registered concern. 'You did not think I meant anything else by it?'

'No, of course not.' Scarlet cheeks belied the words. Her heart was beating uncomfortably fast. 'I will do whatever is necessary to convince people.' She paused, eyeing him with less than perfect trust. 'What did you have in mind?'

'Oh, I don't know. The usual sort of thing: tender looks, melting smiles—a kiss or two.'

Her heart turned over. This was beyond all bounds. 'I will not kiss you, sir!'

Then she saw the familiar glint in his eye and knew he'd done it again. Furious with him and with herself she glared at him, only to see that he appeared to be choking. Her immediate response was alarm. Then she realised it was nothing of the sort; he was suppressing laughter. In reply she hurled the folded travelling rug at him.

They saw no more evidence of French troops that day, a fact for which Sabrina was devoutly thankful. However, the road became increasingly bumpy. The mud of winter had long since dried but it had left some deep ruts and although Luis did his best to avoid them, the vehicle lurched and swayed. It was well sprung but Sabrina knew she wouldn't be sorry to reach their destination that evening. It seemed that her companion's thoughts were moving along the same lines.

'Not far now,' he said.

'I'm glad to hear it. This is one of the worst stretches of road I've experienced in a long time.'

'One day someone is going to lay a good permanent surface,' he replied. 'I suspect that the last people to try were the Romans.'

She smiled. 'I'd guess no one has touched this road since then.'

'Maybe not even then.'

Before she could answer him the vehicle gave another violent lurch. Sabrina was thrown sideways, unable to save herself. She gasped as her head hit the side of the carriage. The blow was cushioned by upholstery but the impact jarred nevertheless. Then she realised they were no longer moving and that the coach was leaning at a drunken angle. Outside she could hear voices swearing in Spanish. Then a strong arm drew her upright and she was pressed against her companion. Her cheek brushed his coat. The cloth smelled faintly of spice—cedar or sandalwood perhaps. Underneath it was the scent of the man, sensual and disturbing.

'Are you all right, Sabrina?'

'Yes, I think so.'

Subjected to close scrutiny she felt the familiar warmth rising into her face. He was so close that if he bent his head their lips would touch. Almost immediately she recalled their earlier conversation and his teasing, and felt ashamed. Of course he wouldn't kiss her. The husband-and-wife act was precisely that, and anyway there was no one nearby who needed convincing. Just then the door opened and Ramon's face appeared.

'Are you hurt, *Doña* Sabrina? *Señor?*'

On hearing them answer in the negative he looked relieved.

Falconbridge straightened. 'What the devil happened?'

'A deep rut, *señor.*'

'Confound it.'

Sabrina watched him reach for the edge of the door and climb out of the vehicle. Then he turned and leaned in, holding out a hand to her. She felt the strong clasp tighten. Then it swung her up and out of the interior with what appeared to be a minimum of effort. A hard-muscled arm lifted her down beside him. It remained casually round her waist while he surveyed the damage to the coach. The offside rear wheel was sunk deep in the road surface. Behind them the chaise had also come to a halt and, leaving

Jacinta in charge of the horses, his men hastened forwards to help.

'Is anyone hurt, sir?' asked Blakelock.

'Fortunately not,' Falconbridge replied. 'It's just a delay we could have done without.'

'The next town is not far off, sir.'

'Just as well. It's going to take some time to right the coach.' He glanced round. 'Luis, take charge of the horses. Ramon, give the rest of us a hand here.'

Ramon nodded. '*Si, señor.*'

Falconbridge peeled off his coat and handed it to Sabrina with a wry smile. 'Would you oblige me, ma'am?'

'Of course.' As she took the garment his hand brushed hers. The casual touch sent a shock along her skin. She tried not to stare at the lithe form revealed to such advantage by the shirt and close-fitting breeches.

Unaware of the sensations he was creating, he rolled up his sleeves. Then he turned to the others.

'All right, lads, let's get this vehicle out of here.'

Sabrina looked on, feeling unusually helpless but knowing there was nothing she could do to assist in this instance. Only sheer physical strength was going to solve the problem. Falconbridge clearly had no qualms about involving himself in the work either; she guessed that was in part why he had the respect of his men. On their first meeting he had been delivering food supplies for their benefit. She had been angry with him at the time but, seeing the situation more objectively now, decided he probably couldn't have done anything else. Of course he would put the welfare of hungry men first. The decision had inconvenienced her but it hadn't left her at risk and he knew that when he made it. She had thought him ruthless then, but now was less certain. She would have liked to learn more about his military career. It was a side to him that she knew little about and suddenly she was curious.

In the event, it took the combined efforts of all the men and the sweating horses to free the coach. Had the road been wet and muddy they might not have succeeded. As it was they were all perspiring freely by the time they had done. However, relief was short-lived. Ramon, examining the righted vehicle, shook his head.

'The accident has damaged the axle, *señor.*'

Falconbridge frowned. 'Badly?'

'See for yourself.'

He pointed to the crack in the shaft. Falconbridge saw it and gritted his teeth.

'It'll get us into town, but no farther.'

'At least the final stretch of road looks a little better,' said Ramon. 'Relatively speaking that is.'

Falconbridge nodded. 'Once we reach town I'll seek out the wheelwright.'

Sabrina heard him with a wry smile. It seemed that history was repeating itself.

Progress was slow, but they reached town with no further problems and while Falconbridge organised the necessary repairs, Sabrina obtained rooms and a bath at the inn. Jacinta laid out fresh clothes and then took herself off to brush out the dusty travelling dress. Sabrina shed her hot garments and slid into the tub with a little sigh of pleasure. It had been days since she'd had the luxury of bathing properly. Making do was all very well, up to a point. Years of travel had made her quite resilient but the woman in her still enjoyed a certain amount of pampering. Of late it had been hard to come by. It was a delight to soap herself all over and wash away all the perspiration and grime of the journey. It was a delight to wear pretty dresses more often, too, or rather to have a reason to wear them. That reason wasn't just confined to present circumstances, as she now admitted. She bit her lip. It would take more than a pretty frock to attract Robert Falconbridge. Sometimes she thought he didn't object to her company, once or twice that he found her person pleasing, but never more than that. His heart was his own. They might have been thrown together for the duration of this mission, but his interest in her went no further. Not that she wanted it to, of course. Once bitten… It occurred to her that he, too, had known disappointment. That was painful enough without the added humiliation of seeing the woman he loved marry his brother.

A door opened and she glanced across the room, assuming Jacinta had returned. However, the outer one remained firmly closed. Instinctively she darted a swift look at the connecting door that led to the adjoining bedchamber. It was open and Falconbridge stood on the threshold. Then, taking in the scene before him, he stopped in his tracks. Sabrina's cheeks flamed scarlet and instinctively she crossed her arms over her breasts, aware that her heart was thumping uncomfortably hard. Her startled thoughts went off in a dozen directions at once, the ramifications of which sent an unexpected flood of heat through her which had nothing to do with the temperature of the bath water.

'What are you doing here? How dare you burst in like this?'

For the first time since she had met him he seemed at a loss. 'I…er…forgive me. I didn't mean to startle you. I didn't realise you would be bathing.'

'But I am, sir.'

'Yes.' He knew it sounded inane but his tongue seemed temporarily to have lost contact with his brain. His legs had, too, rooting him to the spot.

'Well?' She held the lid down on indignation. 'Was there something you wanted to say?'

He cleared his throat. 'Only to let you know that repairs are underway on the coach.'

'That's good to hear.'

'With any luck we should be able to leave tomorrow morning, albeit a little later than usual.'

She nodded, supremely conscious of having the undivided attention of that steady gaze. It was both contemplative and appraising, taking in every detail. As it did so its habitual coolness was replaced by keen appreciation and a warmer light kindled in those grey depths. Her heart thumped harder. She needed to bring this interview to a close and soon.

'Thank you for letting me know.'

It should have signalled dismissal but still he made no move to go. Did he intend to stand there all day? Along with indignation her inner demon awoke.

'I take it there were no problems then?'

He seemed to recollect himself. 'None at all. Why, did you think there would be?'

'I couldn't help wondering if someone else might have had a prior claim on the wheelwright's services.'

'Such as?'

'An army officer perhaps?'

Amusement filled his grey eyes. 'I suppose I deserved that.'

'Well, yes.'

'On that note, ma'am, I had better leave you to finish your bath in peace.'

'I'd be grateful, sir.'

The sweet smile didn't deceive him for a moment. It was also unwittingly provocative. For a moment more he indulged the fantasy of showing her just how provocative, before self-control reasserted itself. He sighed and, with a last backwards look, took himself off.

As the door shut behind him she leaned back and breathed a sigh of relief. It wasn't that she suspected him of anything untoward—his surprise on finding her thus had been genuine enough—but rather that his presence aroused untoward feelings in her. Feelings she could not afford to indulge. She had never met anyone quite like him; he was somehow larger than life. It was difficult enough being thrown together with a total stranger but when the stranger was Robert Falconbridge it lent an added dimension to the whole situation.

The sound of another door opening caused her to start, but this time it was Jacinta. For the second time Sabrina let out a sigh of relief. The water in the tub was growing cool now so she climbed out and wrapped herself in a linen towel. If the maid noticed her preoccupied air she made no comment on the matter and busied herself with hanging up the newly brushed travelling dress. Sabrina bit back a smile, thinking it was as well her companion had not returned earlier. Goodness only knew what construction she would have put on Falconbridge's presence. Possibly she might have shot him herself.

The subject of her thoughts had bespoken a bath for himself and lost no time in stripping off and sinking into the tub. He scrubbed himself vigorously, mentally rebuking himself for what had just passed. Not that he had had any idea of what he would find when he opened the door to her room. He knew he should have left right away but at the time his wits had deserted him. His behaviour had been reprehensible and he knew it, but for the life of him he couldn't regret it. The memory would remain with him for a long time. He had discovered early that Sabrina's image was not easy to banish at any time but particularly not when seen unclothed. One look at her bare shoulders and the swelling breasts partially revealed by the soapy water and all his good intentions had gone up in smoke. The knowledge was disturbing, as was the depth of his desire. Every part of him had wanted her, wanted to lift her from the bath and carry her to the bed and possess her completely.

Once again he reined in his imagination hard. They had a task ahead of them and that should be the focus of his attention. A lapse of concentration might spell disaster for them both. The consequences of being caught meant death, and he had no wish to see Sabrina led before a firing squad or delivered up to the hangman. She was his responsibility in every way. He had promised Albermarle that he would protect her; a promise he intended to keep. He sighed. She would be a test of any man's self-control but he must resist the temptation she represented. The trouble was he hadn't expected to feel like this again. After Clarissa he had believed himself immune. It was a shock to discover he had been wrong. Even so, only a fool would allow himself to fall again, and especially for a woman he hardly knew.

The following morning Sabrina rose early and went out, wanting a little time and space on her own. After what had passed between them the previous day she didn't feel equal to being shut up in a carriage with Falconbridge again until she had cleared her head. Perhaps some sketching might help to restore a degree of perspective in every sense of the word. Accordingly, she took her pad and, having informed Jacinta of her intention to visit the local shrine, the two of them set out.

A little later Falconbridge went down to the break-fast room. As Sabrina had not made an appearance yet he assumed she was still in her room. In the meantime he sent Luis round to the wheelwright's yard to check on the repair work. Within a quarter of an hour he was back. Hearing his footstep Falconbridge turned away from the window.

'Well? How are things progressing? I want to be gone from here before noon.'

'I regret that may not be possible.'

'What?'

'I went to speak with the man but he was not there.'

'Not there? Then where the hell is he?'

'It seems he was called away to a neighbouring village some five miles distant in order to mend a cartwheel for the cousin of his brother-in-law's aunt. However, he will be back this afternoon, according to his wife.'

'Back by noon!' Falconbridge's expression grew thunderous. 'The rogue promised that he would have the wheel fixed by then.'

'That is so, *señor*. However, I fear it will not be possible now.'

'Confound it, I cannot afford the delay.'

'I think it cannot be avoided.'

'We'll see about that. He cannot have taken the entire workforce with him. There must be a competent apprentice who can complete the job.'

'It is possible, I suppose.'

'Go and find out.' Then as Luis turned to leave, 'No wait. I'll come with you. Two voices may be more persuasive than one.'

He had reached the outer door before he realised that Sabrina had not yet come down. Being keen to sort out the immediate problem he left a message for her with the *patrón*. Then he and Luis set off.

The outcome of their excursion did nothing to improve his mood. Having gone to the wheelwright's premises and spoken to the man's wife, it transpired that there was only one apprentice, the son, who had gone off with his father. She assured him they would be back by noon. Having a sound understanding of the local concept of time, Falconbridge had not the least expectation of seeing the man or his son before the late afternoon. Frustration mounted, and with it, annoyance.

This was not helped when he got back to the inn and found that Sabrina was not there. He checked her room and then all the other rooms where she might conceivably be, only to draw a blank. Then he sent for the *patrón*.

'The Condesa has gone out, *señor.*'

'Gone out where?' he demanded.

'I do not know, *señor.* The lady did not honour me with her confidence.'

'Did she take her maid with her?'

The *patrón* nodded. 'She did indeed, *señor.*'

When this elicited an expression of unmistakable ire, the man added quickly, 'I will send a boy to seek for them at once. The village is not large. I am sure they will be found very soon.'

Falconbridge bit back the savage comment that would otherwise have escaped his lips. 'Never mind. I will look for the Condesa myself. If she returns in the meantime, ask her to wait for me here.'

'Certainly, *señor.*'

Gritting his teeth Falconbridge went out into the street again, looking left and right in the hope that he might see Sabrina before she had gone too far. Not that there was far to go; as the *patrón* had said, it wasn't a big place.

The end of the street brought him to a small plaza where some of the local women were fetching water from the pump. He could see no sign of Sabrina or her maid. A swift look into the few small shops proved no help either. Then at last he spied Jacinta emerging from a building across the street. He lost no time in accosting her.

'What are you doing here? Where is your mistress?'

'I came to buy fruit, *señor*.' If she had noticed his expression, her own gave no sign of it. '*Doña* Sabrina said that she wished to take the air and do some sketching.'

'Oh, did she? And you let her go off alone?'

'*Doña* Sabrina goes where she wills.'

His jaw tightened. 'Not on this trip she doesn't. Where is she?'

She nodded towards the street leading out of the plaza. 'Visiting the shrine of San Ignacio. It is not far.'

'She had no business leaving the inn and nor do you. Go back there at once.'

The tone was peremptory. Jacinta's dark eyes flashed but they swiftly veiled. 'As you wish, *señor*.'

He watched her walk away and then set off in the direction she had indicated. People glanced up as he passed but, on seeing his expression, hurried out of his way. He barely noticed their presence. All his thoughts were turned inward, focused first on finding Sabrina and then what he was going to say when he did.

In fact Jacinta had spoken the truth. The shrine was not far, and set by the edge of the road. It was little more than a stone niche containing a picture of the saint and some fresh flowers. However, Sabrina wasn't there. Falconbridge swore softly and looked swiftly about, casting in every direction. Then at last he saw her, sitting on a stone in the shade of a tree not fifty yards away. Since her attention was on the sketch pad on her lap she did not notice his arrival until his shadow fell across it.

He heard the sharp intake of breath as she looked up and saw him, and then saw her relax as she recognised him.

'Good morning. It's a fine day, is it not?' Then, as she became aware of his expression, 'Is something wrong, Major?'

'Yes, there's something wrong. What the devil do you think you're doing?'

'I beg your pardon?'

'You heard me. What are you doing here?'

The tone caused the green eyes to widen a little. 'I am sketching.'

'Don't you know better than to wander off on your own like that without even your maid in attendance?'

'Oh, Jacinta went to buy some fruit. She is not far.'

'She has returned to the inn,' he replied, 'on my instruction. I'd be much obliged if you would do the same.'

'But I do not wish to return just yet.'

'I am not offering a choice as to whether you go or not, merely the means by which you might get there.'

'I don't understand.'

'Plainly then: you may walk back or you may be carried.'

The tone had been perfectly even but it also bore a distinct shade of menace. More than anything at that moment she wanted to call his bluff, but somehow didn't quite dare.

'I will walk back, sir.'

'I thought you might.'

Sabrina gathered her things and rose to face him. 'Why are you so angry?'

'Because I am responsible for your safety. Don't you know how dangerous it is for you to be out here alone, you little fool? These hills are crawling with bandits, to say nothing of the odd French patrol.'

For the first time she felt a small twinge of guilt. 'I did not think there could be any danger so near to the village.'

'There is danger everywhere now and you would do well to remember it.' He took her arm in a firm grip and led her back towards the roadway. 'There are enough problems ahead of us without you adding to them.'

Sabrina bit her lip. 'I'm sorry. I did not mean to cause you any anxiety.'

The tone was contrite, like the accompanying look, and his anger began to cool a little. As it did he acknowledged the first stirrings of remorse. He let go of her arm and sighed.

'I am a brute, am I not?'

She shot him a swift sideways glance. 'How truthful would you like me to be?'

His lips twitched. 'Wretched girl. You deserve that I should carry you back to the inn.'

'You really would have done that, wouldn't you?'

'Yes, and enjoyed it what's more.'

His words had the ring of perfect sincerity. However, the cold anger so conspicuous before was missing now.

'I promise I won't do it again. Go off without telling you, I mean.'

'See that you don't.'

They walked on a little way in silence. Then another thought struck her.

'Were you looking for me to tell me that the carriage is mended?'

'No, I was looking for you to tell you it is not.'

'Not?'

He explained what had happened earlier at the wheelwright's yard. As she listened she heard his unspoken frustration and understood.

'And after you had found out our journey was to

be delayed, I must needs wander off so thoughtlessly.' She put a hand on his sleeve. 'Can you forgive me?'

He looked down at her in surprise but there was no mistaking the real remorse he saw in her face. And seeing it he was ashamed of his bad temper.

'In truth I should not have taken it out on you,' he said.

'You had good reason to be angry.'

He shook his head. 'Not with you. It was just anxiety when I could not find you.'

'It won't happen again.' Then, as the implications dawned, she added, 'What are we going to do now?'

'Wait till that rascally fellow returns. There's not much else we can do.'

For a wonder the wheelwright did return shortly after midday, and repairs commenced on the carriage. Ramon and Luis remained to oversee the work. It was slow and thorough but it became clear that the vehicle would not be ready until the late afternoon. At that point there would be only another four hours of daylight left.

Falconbridge sighed. 'It can't be helped. We'll use what time we have and find somewhere to stop before it goes dark.'

Blakelock nodded. 'Yes, sir.'

'It's a good thing you've got someone standing over that wheelwright, sir,' said Willis. 'He was only going to stop for a siesta.'

'What!'

'True enough, sir,' said Blakelock. 'Only then Ramon had a word and persuaded him not to. Feller didn't like it above half, but money's a powerful inducement.'

Falconbridge glared. 'So is my boot.'

'Ramon said the same, sir. Hurried things along no end.'

It was approaching four when they eventually did set off again. With only a few hours of daylight remaining Falconbridge was keen to try and make up lost ground. Fortunately the road surface was better and they were able to make reasonable speed.

'Will the delay be totally disastrous?' asked Sabrina then.

'I hope not.' Seeing her anxious expression her companion smiled. 'No, my dear, provided there are no more we should reach our destination in time.'

'I am relieved to hear it.'

'I think we must be due for some better luck.'

She nodded, truly aware now of a sense of urgency. Recent events had shaken away any feeling of complacency: so much hung on this journey. Thinking of her behaviour earlier that day she was quietly mortified. She must have seemed like an empty-headed little fool. He had been justifiably angry. No doubt in his place she would have felt the same. She was privately resolved that he should have no further cause to criticise her actions; that she would strive in every way to be the companion he needed. It came to her then that his good opinion mattered where only a few days ago it would not have. Just why that should be or how it had come about she could not have said.

Chapter Five

In fact their journey continued without further mishap or incident and, although they were half a day later than anticipated, they came at length to the house of Don Pedro de la Torre on the outskirts of Aranjuez. Barely a mile from the royal palace and standing in its own extensive grounds, it was an imposing stone building that testified to the wealth and importance of its owner. On their arrival, liveried footmen hastened forwards to open the carriage door and let down the steps. Falconbridge descended first and then extended a hand to Sabrina, a firm, reassuring grip accompanied by a smile that warmed her more thoroughly than the sunshine. Together they walked to the open doorway and into a marbled hall where their hosts awaited them.

Don Pedro was a tall, upright figure whose grey hair and beard lent him a distinguished appearance. Sabrina guessed him to be in his early fifties. His wife, *Doña* Elena, was ten years younger, a handsome woman with dark hair and eyes and an elegant figure. They greeted their guests with great courtesy and, over refreshments, enquired after their journey.

'Did you meet with any French patrols?' asked their host.

'Only one,' replied Falconbridge.

Don Pedro lifted an eyebrow. 'Then you were fortunate.'

'My thought exactly.'

'The French are everywhere. It is almost impossible to travel without encountering a patrol or a road block.'

'Fortunately we didn't encounter any difficulties.'

'Long may it continue,' replied Don Pedro. 'Apart from the French there are many renegades who take advantage of the situation to prey on travellers. I am glad you did not meet any.'

'So am I.' Falconbridge smiled. 'It is good to have arrived.'

'It is good of you to come. We are most happy to welcome you here and, of course, your beautiful wife.' Don Pedro smiled at Sabrina for a moment. She returned it, conscious of the role she was expected to play. Even so it sounded strange to hear herself referred to in that way. Just for a second she indulged the fancy. What if Falconbridge were her husband? It came as a shock to discover that the thought was not totally unwelcome.

Don Pedro threw Falconbridge a meaningful look. 'Later, when you have rested, we shall talk.'

They had been allocated a spacious apartment, beautifully furnished, with an adjoining dressing room and a balcony that overlooked the gardens to the rear. For the space of a few heartbeats they surveyed it in silence. There was, Sabrina saw, only one bed, albeit very large, but mercifully two couches as well. If need be she would appropriate one for her use. The pretence at marriage only went so far: she could not share a bed with her companion. The notion sent a frisson down her spine that had nothing to do with fear. She pulled herself up abruptly. Such a thought should never even have entered her mind yet the memory of the mishap with the coach was vivid, especially the part where Falconbridge had held her in his arms. How would it be to lie in his arms, to lie in his bed? The notion set her pulse racing. All the disgust she had experienced before was absent now, and she knew instinctively that he would treat a woman with gentleness. He was not like Denton. Falconbridge had a wicked sense of humour but he hadn't taken advantage of her. If he made any overtures to her it would only be by invitation. If she were foolish enough to do that she would lose what respect he had for her, a thought she didn't want to entertain. Aware of him now to the last fibre of her being she drew in a deep breath. Then she went to the French windows that led onto the balcony and opened them, looking out with a gasp of genuine delight.

'How beautiful!'

The garden was laid out in terraces connected by sweeping steps and a series of fountained pools that led the eye away towards a high wall where bougainvillea grew in vivid bursts of pink and magenta and purple. On either hand flowering beds lined the pathways and beyond those, to right and left, stern lines of cypress were relieved by fruit trees and blossoming shrubs.

'It's very fine, isn't it?' he said.

He was standing just behind her, his shoulder brushing hers, so close she could detect the faint scent of sandalwood from his clothing. She glanced up for a moment and then returned her attention to the view, hoping no part of her inner turmoil showed.

'A truly romantic place,' she said. 'All it lacks is moonlight.'

He smiled faintly. 'Perhaps nature will oblige while we are here. The moon is near to the full.'

'I hope so.'

'You are fond of gardens?'

'Yes, aren't you?'

'When they're like this one and there is the possibility of a moonlit stroll,' he replied. The tone was ambiguous.

She turned to look at him then, suspecting that he was teasing. However, his expression revealed no such indication. On the contrary, the grey eyes that searched hers were entirely serious. Before she could ponder the matter, he took her shoulders in a gentle clasp.

'Now we step into our new roles in earnest. Are you ready?'

'As ready as I'll ever be,' she replied, trying not to think about his closeness or the warmth of his hands through her clothing.

'Every second of our stay we are the Conde and Condesa de Ordoñez y Casal. Marianne and Antonio. Don't forget it.'

'I won't forget.'

'Good girl.' He paused. 'Joking apart, some show of affection between us will not go amiss.'

Even as he spoke she knew that, on her part at least, it would be no mere show. Just how that change had come about she couldn't have said, but something in her had altered, and on a fundamental level. With a calmness she was far from feeling she met his gaze. 'Tender looks and melting smiles, was it not?' She did not complete the original sentence.

The grey eyes gleamed. 'If you feel equal to it.'

'I shall play my part, sir.'

'I am sure you will.'

For a moment they faced each other in silence. He knew that she had meant the words and they cost him an unexpected pang. Close companionship and cooperation were essential to their mission, but he knew in that instant that he would have liked more than this necessary pretence. It wasn't just about physical attraction either, though he acknowledged it was strong. Combined with wit and intelligence it was a heady combination. Her company was more than congenial to him. With her he experienced emotions that he hadn't expected to feel again. He also knew he couldn't go there. It would be foolish and wrong. Too much was at stake for both of them. He relinquished his hold on her shoulders.

'No doubt you would like to rest awhile,' he said.

She nodded. 'It would also be good to get out of these clothes.'

'In that case I shall repair to the dressing room and leave the field to you.'

A knock at the door announced the arrival of Willis and Blakelock with the trunks. It was a welcome diversion. While they carried Falconbridge's boxes into the dressing room, Jacinta saw to the ordering of hot water and linen towels. When eventually the other servants had gone and the dressing room door was securely closed, she bustled about laying out a change of clothes for her mistress. As she did so she cast a comprehensive and disapproving look around.

'Only one bed,' she observed.

'Yes.'

'Your reputation…'

'Will be quite safe. I'll sleep on the couch over there.'

'All the same, he should marry you after this.'

'Nothing is more unlikely.'

'Would you refuse if he asked you?'

Sabrina drew in a deep breath. 'He's not going to ask me. This is a business arrangement, nothing more.'

'When a man looks at a woman in that way it is because he is thinking of a great deal more, believe me.'

'Enough, Jacinta.' The words came out with more force than she had intended and she was immediately ashamed. It was unlike her to get so rattled. 'I'm sorry. It's just tension speaking. I'll be myself again when we get out of here.'

Her companion lifted an eyebrow. 'Will you?'

'Of course. Why would I not?'

The maid clearly took it for a rhetorical question, because she made no reply. Sabrina busied herself with removing her travelling dress. In truth she was glad of the distraction for Jacinta's words had left their mark. What if Robert Falconbridge were to ask her? She gave herself a mental shaking. It was no use to think that way; theirs was just a business arrangement and she must remember it. Had she learned nothing from the past? She had been thrown together with a man who was handsome and charismatic. Although she didn't think Falconbridge was in any way like that other, if she allowed herself to fall for him it could only result in heartache.

Having removed her outer garments she bathed her hands and face. It was a delight to be rid of the dust of travel. Then she sat while the maid unpinned and brushed her hair before rearranging it into a becoming style, dressing it high so that it fell over Sabrina's shoulders in a profusion of curls. When it was done she donned the yellow gown that had been laid out for her. It suited her colouring and brought out the warm tones of her skin. The low neckline plunged into a tempting décolletage. A gold necklace and earrings completed the outfit. Looking into the mirror she surveyed her reflection in thoughtful silence.

Falconbridge emerged some time later clad in pale breeches, flawless linen and a lovat coat so expertly cut that it might have been moulded to his form. He looked across the room and opened his mouth to speak but the words dried on his lips. For a moment or two he could only stare, but his critical eye found nothing lacking. She looked every inch the golden girl. For a moment he let his gaze strip away the fabric of her gown and dwell on what lay beneath. He was aware, too, of the bed just a few feet away. In his imagination he laid her down there and made passionate love to her and tasted her passion in return. Recalling himself abruptly, he made her an elegant bow.

'If you are ready my dear, we will go down.'

She smiled. 'Quite ready.'

He offered his arm and felt the light pressure of her hand on his sleeve. It felt natural and right, as though it belonged there.

Dinner that night was a lavish meal with a dozen guests at table. The conversation flowed easily on a variety of topics. Sabrina kept up her part, occasionally glancing across the table at Falconbridge. Once, he met her eye and smiled, but otherwise seemed engrossed in what his companion was saying. She noticed that hers were not the only eyes to turn his way. Several of the ladies present evidently found him attractive, too. He stepped easily into his part, she thought, adopting the aristocratic manners that came so naturally to him. No one would question his identity. With his dark good looks, arrogant bearing and impeccable Spanish he might indeed have been the hidalgo he presented.

'Do you stay long in Aranjuez, Condesa?'

Sabrina turned to her companion, an ageing and portly gentleman who had been introduced as Señor Jorge Gonzalez, who had some government role in the capital.

'I regret not,' she replied.

'What a pity.'

'My husband does not like to be long away from home.'

'Well, in these times it is understandable. No doubt he prefers to live quietly and manage his estates.'

'Yes, indeed.'

'And you, Condesa, do you not hanker after the bright lights of the city?'

'The social whirl of Madrid holds few charms for me, *señor*,' she said. It was true as far as it went.

He snorted. 'It holds few charms for anyone since the usurper Joseph took the throne.'

'Can he hold it, do you think?'

'Not if the Spanish people have their way. He'll be sent packing and the sooner the better.'

Don Pedro glanced across the table. 'Our alliance with the English will put paid to Bonaparte's ambitions in our country.'

'The way things are going, his upstart family will soon govern most of Europe,' replied Gonzalez.

Murmurs of agreement greeted this. Sabrina looked across at Falconbridge and met his eye again. His expression was enigmatic. He had not taken a leading role in the discussion that evening, seeming content to listen for the most part. Given his guise as Ordoñez, it was understandable. However, she knew he missed nothing.

'The French will not long hold Spain,' said Don Pedro. 'Already the guerrilla tactics of the partisan forces are telling.'

Gonzalez nodded. 'Men like El Cuchillo, you mean.'

'Exactly,' his host replied. 'Hit the French and then run. It's an effective strategy. All the same, there will be more battles before the enemy is driven from our soil.'

As she listened, Sabrina thought of the plans she and her companion had come to collect and hoped that they would provide the key to allied military success. So far as she knew no private conference had yet taken place between Falconbridge and their host, but it would soon enough. Once he had the plans their real task would begin. In the meantime, there was the ball. Part of her was looking forward to it; in her life such events were rare and thus the more valued, but it carried a strong element of risk. If anyone present actually knew the real Conde de Ordoñez. She shivered inwardly. The penalties for spying were severe. It was a chance one took. She had always known that.

Later, when the ladies withdrew to the drawing room, the conversation took a different direction and Sabrina was content to listen. Once someone asked about her putative son, Miguel, and she made what she hoped was a convincing reply. It occurred to her then for the first time that it might be pleasant to have children of her own one day. Nothing could have been further removed from the life she had been living hitherto, and yet the idea did not displease her. Of course, it would have to be with the right man. Falconbridge's face imposed itself on her memory. In one of their earlier conversations he had told her he liked children. She thought he would make a good father. That was a foolish notion of course, given what she knew of his past. Besides, he had no interest in her beyond the completion of a duty. He had told her he was married to his career. Knowing that, she was unaccountably saddened.

The gathering broke up just after eleven. Everyone knew that the following night would be a late one, for the ball would go on into the early hours, and had decided to be well rested for the event. Sabrina could see the point. In any case, the journey had been tiring and the thought of a good night's sleep was not unwelcome. Then she remembered that to-night she and Falconbridge would be sharing a room again. No one else would think anything of it. After all, were they not supposed to be man and wife? The thought sent a frisson along her skin. She had to trust him.

As she had told Jacinta not to wait up, the room was empty when she returned. Falconbridge had lingered to speak to Don Pedro and she had no idea how long he would remain. Taking advantage of his absence, she undressed and donned her nightgown before sitting down at the dressing table to unpin her hair. She was thus engaged when the door opened to admit him. For a moment he was still, looking on, before closing the door and coming farther into the room. Sabrina forced unsteady hands to continue with their task. In the glass she saw him remove his coat and slowly unfasten his neckcloth. His gaze never left her.

He heard the pins drop into the glass dish on the dressing table and watched her shake her hair loose. It fell over her shoulders in a riot of soft curls. She reached for a brush. Beneath the gentle strokes the wilful gold mass shone in the candlelight. He wanted to reach out and touch it, to run his fingers through it. Conquering the urge he tossed his coat over a chair. The neckcloth followed. He pulled off his shirt and sat down to remove his boots. Having done so, he rose and crossed the intervening space to the bed and retrieved the top cover and a pillow before retiring with them to the nearest couch.

Sabrina's hands paused at their task. 'It's my turn to sleep on the couch.'

He turned, regarding her with a raised eyebrow. 'I think not.'

'Truly, I don't mind.'

'Maybe not, but I do.'

'I should not think the worse of you.'

He smiled faintly. 'No, I believe you would not. Even so, I shall sleep here.'

The tone, though quiet, was implacable. Sabrina had come to recognise it, and also the futility of argument.

'As you will.' She paused. 'Thank you.'

'My pleasure, ma'am.'

'I doubt that somehow, but I appreciate the gesture.'

She laid aside the brush. The mirror showed him the soft swell of her breast beneath the low neckline of her nightdress. The filmy material revealed every line and curve of her body. Almost at once he felt the answering heat in his loins. He wanted her and at the same time knew beyond doubt that to follow his inclination would offend every notion of honour. She was under his protection, and to take advantage of this highly desirable situation would be to violate all trust between them. The only reason she was here was to obtain her father's freedom. She had no interest in anything else.

Drawing a deep breath he watched her cross to the bed and climb in, settling herself beneath the covers. She had shown no fear, he thought, but he guessed at some of the thoughts in her mind. He could not destroy the relationship they had built up over the past days by one ill-judged and lustful act. She deserved better from him.

Sabrina lay still as he blew out the candle and returned to his makeshift bed. Then he finished undressing and climbed in. She closed her eyes, every sense attuned to him, heart thumping in her breast. Once he had spoken about intimacy, of the need to play a part. It had occurred to her then to wonder if he would use that to take advantage and insist she play her part to the full. She knew better now. The thought of sharing Falconbridge's bed should have filled her with horror, but that was not the emotion uppermost in her mind. Horror did not cause the melting warmth at the core of her pelvis, or the sensation of painful longing in her heart. After Jack Denton's betrayal she had thought never to feel desire for a man again. Yet somehow, with no apparent effort, Robert Falconbridge had broken through her guard. It had happened so gradually that she had barely been aware of it. She could no longer deny that she was attracted to him, but it was an attraction that she didn't dare pursue.

Her companion shut his eyes, trying not to dwell on the semi-clad form just feet away from him. With a wry smile he turned his head and quietly bade her goodnight. He heard her reply in kind, and then the faint rustle of bedclothes as she turned onto her side. It was a long time before sleep claimed him.

The following morning Don Pedro solicited a private talk with his guest. For that purpose he had chosen the library. It was quiet and allowed of no possibility that the conversation might be overheard.

'You took a risk coming to Aranjuez, *señor*,' he said, 'but there was no other way of solving the problem.'

'I understand.' Falconbridge paused, eyeing his host keenly. 'But you also took a great risk.'

'In the service of my country.'

'Even so.'

'The alternative is to let the usurper, Joseph, keep the throne he has stolen.' Don Pedro's lip curled in quiet contempt. 'My post brings me into contact with influential people and sensitive information. I put it to good use when I can.'

'Your help has proved most valuable in the past. My superiors are grateful.'

'They will certainly be glad to get these.' Don Pedro turned to the bookcase and drew out a large and weighty tome. He opened it and turned the first few pages. They concealed a hollow section in which lay a flat leather wallet. He withdrew it and replaced the book on the shelf before turning back to his companion. 'This contains the most up-to-date information we have about Napoleon's troop movements, and his future plans for the war in Spain. If they can be exploited it may hasten the end of this campaign.'

Falconbridge nodded. Taking the wallet he opened it and unfolded the papers within, scanning them with a practised eye. As he did so he felt a surge of excitement. 'This is excellent. My government will be most grateful for the information. I take it these are copies?'

'Yes. It would have been too dangerous to remove the originals.'

'I shall do all in my power to ensure that Lord Wellington receives them as soon as possible.'

'Much depends on it.' Don Pedro paused. 'In the event of capture these papers must be destroyed.'

'I understand.' Falconbridge refolded the sheets and returned them to the wallet before tucking it into the inside pocket of his coat.

'If you are captured you must not be made to talk.'

'That eventuality has been considered and the contingency plan is in place.' He hoped that it would never be necessary to have recourse to the small package of pills hidden in a secret compartment of his valise. All the same, one must be prepared for every eventuality.

'Very well. Then it only remains for me to wish you luck, *señor*.' Don Pedro held out his hand. 'You and your charming companion.'

Falconbridge took the hand and clasped it warmly. 'I thank you.'

'She knows the truth, I take it?'

'Of course. It was her choice to come.'

'Then she is a very brave woman.'

'Why so, I think.' Even as he spoke the words Falconbridge knew that they were true.

'You plan to return when?'

'The day after tomorrow.'

'It is well. In the meantime, I hope you will enjoy the ball.'

They parted shortly after this and Falconbridge took himself off to the garden. *Doña* Elena had offered to show Sabrina around it that morning and he had every hope of encountering them there. For a while he wandered among the flower beds but found no sign of them until an enquiry of one of the gardeners elicited the information that the ladies were in the summerhouse.

He found it a little later, a pretty wooden pavilion painted in green and white with elaborate carved scrollwork round the doors and windows and a design of fruit and flowers along the eaves. Hearing female voices he mounted the steps and looked inside. Cushioned seats ran along the inner walls and on one of these he saw Sabrina sitting with their hostess. The latter saw him first and smiled.

'Ah, Conde Antonio. Come and join us, do.'

Sabrina followed her gaze and he saw her smile. He accepted a glass of lemonade and seated himself on a stool opposite. It gave him an ideal vantage point from which to view both ladies. *Doña* Elena was, he acknowledged, a handsome woman. However, his gaze moved on and then lingered on Sabrina, cool and pretty in her figured muslin frock. Sensing his regard she looked across and he raised his glass a little in acknowledgement. She smiled faintly and then returned her attention to what their hostess was saying. However, he found his imagination moving ahead to the ball. He had never danced with Sabrina before. They had never attended such a function together. All the usual social gatherings at which men and women met had been denied them, until now. Courtship had never been a feature of their relationship. He still knew so little about her. Yet there was so much he wanted to know. Perhaps after their mission… He sighed. First things first.

Everything had gone according to plan so far but that didn't mean he could be complacent. This was occupied territory. Anything might happen. He thought of his recent conversation with Don Pedro, and then of the contingency plan he had agreed with Forbes. He hoped that Sabrina would never need to know about that. For all manner of reasons this ball might be the only one they would ever have.

The conversation turned on general topics until a servant arrived to request their hostess's presence in the house. She made her apology and left them. When she was safely out of earshot Sabrina turned to face him.

'Did you have a successful morning?'

'Very successful,' he replied.

'Then the information was all you hoped.'

'It exceeded my expectations in every way.'

'I'm glad.' She smiled. 'Now all we have to do is get it back safely.'

He returned the smile. 'There is no reason why we should not.'

'Your optimism is encouraging.'

'Do you have doubts?'

'No. I can't afford them.'

'I think neither of us can,' he replied.

'Where have you put the documents?'

'In a safe place.'

'You don't trust me.'

'Yes, I trust you, my dear, but it may be safer for you not to know.'

'I see.'

For a moment she was silent, digesting what he had said. It was another reminder of what was at stake. Falconbridge surveyed her keenly but on this occasion found her expression hard to read.

'Have I offended you?' he asked.

'No.'

He finished his lemonade and set down the glass. 'Then will you take a turn around the gardens with me?'

'If you wish.'

They left the summerhouse and strolled together through an avenue of fruit trees, the only sounds their feet on the gravel path and the droning of bees among the flowers. Sweet scents drifted into the warm air. Sabrina breathed deeply, enjoying the moment, every part of her attuned to the man at her side.

'It is pleasant to be in the fresh air again, isn't it?' he said.

'I was just thinking the same thing.' She looked about her and smiled. 'This certainly is a beautiful place. *Doña* Elena is justly proud of it.'

'I collect she has a keen interest in horticulture.'

'Yes. She was telling me earlier about the improvements she and her husband have made to the place since they came to live here.'

'A labour of many years I imagine.'

She nodded. 'And a meeting of minds. I think it must be agreeable to have shared interests like that with one's spouse.'

'I am sure it is, though I suspect it is a rare occurrence in most cases.'

'You may be right. All the same, I should like to have a garden one day.'

'Should you?'

'Yes. I think it would be restful.'

He heard her with some surprise. It was not a subject he would ever have associated with her, but then unpredictability was part of her charm. It also revealed another facet of her mind.

'Perhaps it comes from always travelling so much,' he replied.

'Perhaps it does.'

'Would you not find it dull after all your adventures?'

'Restful is not the same as dull.'

'No, I stand corrected. In truth, it is restful out here, and certainly not dull.' He smiled. 'But then I think one could never be dull in your company.'

The matter-of-fact tone saved it from being outright flattery but it caused her pulse to quicken all the same. In any case he was far from being a flatterer. It seemed most likely that he was teasing her again, but a swift look his way found nothing to substantiate the notion.

'Thank you.'

'I speak as I find.'

She made no reply to that and presently they turned down a path at right angles to their course, and came to a fountained pool where fat carp swam lazily between the lily pads. Sabrina sat down on the stone ledge and trailed her fingers in the water. Falconbridge disposed himself casually beside her.

'Have you ever visited the Moorish palaces of Andalucia?' he asked then.

'No, though I should like to.'

'They, too, have beautiful gardens, albeit on a larger scale.'

'I believe the architecture is very beautiful.'

'Yes, it is, especially in the rooms that once housed the ruler's harem. Beautiful surroundings to house beautiful women.'

'Even so, I pity those women. It must have been an unenviable lot.'

'I imagine that boredom was the biggest enemy.'

'Yes, to have nothing to do all day but think of one's appearance must be dull indeed.'

He grinned. 'And yet there are many women in the first ranks of society who seem to do little else.'

'You speak knowledgeably.'

'I have some small experience of the breed.'

'You sound as though you did not approve.'

'A fair face and fine clothes are no substitutes for an informed mind,' he replied. 'Ideally the three should go together, but rarely do.'

'You have exacting standards.'

'Is that a fault then?'

'By no means, but I think it may be hard to find many ladies who meet the criteria.'

'Precious few, and for that reason their price is above rubies.'

She laughed. 'Then make sure you are not as Othello's base Indian.'

'An injunction I shall heed most carefully, I assure you. A man would be foolish indeed to throw away such a gem.'

The tone was light, almost bantering, but for a moment was belied by the expression in his eyes.

'The same criteria could be used to judge men,' she replied, 'for a handsome face and an elegant coat may conceal a complete fool.'

He grinned. 'True. Do I take it then that intelligence is an important consideration in your evaluation of men?'

'Oh, yes. What woman would want to spend her life with a fool?'

'Many do, my dear, especially where the fool is rich and titled.'

'Then I would guess that they never find true happiness.'

'Happiness takes many forms. It's a question of what the individual is prepared to settle for.'

'That is a mercenary outlook.'

'So it is, and commoner than you might think.'

'But surely it cannot be agreeable to marry where there is no real esteem, no love?' She smiled wryly. 'Does that make me sound very naive?'

'On the contrary, my dear. It makes you sound very wise.'

'Well, that makes a change at least.'

'I have never heard you say anything that was not sensible, except of course when you agreed to come on this trip with me.'

'That was not sensible,' she agreed. 'All the same, I'm glad I did.'

'So am I.'

'You are generous. I know the prospect did not please you at first.'

'It still doesn't—in that way. But the man must be hard to please who did not enjoy your company.'

The words were accompanied by a look that was hard to interpret, but which had the effect of summoning a tinge of warmer colour to her face. It also left her unsure how to respond. She could not tell him that his company was the most agreeable of any man's she had ever met, or that his presence caused her heart to leap. To do so would be disastrous. Such a declaration would be perceived as an invitation to greater intimacy. His regard was not lightly given and it pleased her to think that she had it, albeit in some small measure. She would not do anything to forfeit that.

They walked together back to the house and later rejoined the others for a light luncheon. It was a convivial gathering and, since good manners decreed that they must keep up their part in the general conversation, she had no opportunity for further speech with him then. It was only afterwards when the company went their separate ways for the siesta that they found themselves alone once more.

In the privacy of their chamber he seemed larger than life somehow, as if his presence filled the space.

'We have a late night ahead of us,' he said then, 'and a long journey afterwards. It would be a good idea to get some rest now.'

She nodded. The siesta was a Spanish tradition that she had come to value. 'Yes, you're right, of course.'

'Do you want me to call Jacinta?' he asked.

'No, there is no need.' She took off her shoes and then perched on the edge of the bed while he closed the window shutters and the louvered outer doors to the balcony. Through the dim light she saw him remove his coat and neckcloth and draw off his boots. Knowing she would rest more comfortably if she removed her gown, she reached up, fumbling with the buttons, but they were stiff and resisted her efforts. For a little while he watched in quiet amusement. Then he drew her gently upright.

'Turn around.'

Somewhat hesitantly she obeyed, hoping he wouldn't notice her inner confusion. This closeness had another dimension now; setting her pulse racing, filling her entire being with shameful longing. She felt him lift her hair aside. Steady, competent hands unfastened the gown and gently pushed the fabric over her shoulders. His hands brushed her skin, a touch that sent a tremor the length of her body. She drew in a deep breath, fighting temptation. How easy it would be to let this go further, to let him finish what he had begun and undress her completely, to feel the touch of his hands on her naked flesh. The thought created a sensation of melting warmth in the region of her loins. She darted a glance at the bed. At once the warmth translated to her neck and face. If he knew, if he even suspected…

It seemed he did not for he stepped away then, leaving her to remove the dress, and retired to the couch. Out of the corner of her eyes she saw him stretch out. Those precious seconds gave her time to regain a little more composure. She struggled out of the gown and tossed it over a chair. Then she, too, lay down to rest.

For a little while neither one spoke, but the silence was companionable rather than tense. Then she turned her head and looked across the intervening space.

'What will you do when the war is over?'

'Return to England, I imagine,' he replied. 'And you?'

'The same.' She smiled reflectively. 'Though I think it would seem strange after all this time. Rather like a foreign country.'

He thought it an apt analogy. Going back would be like returning to a past life. Except that one could never go back. The trouble was, while time and people moved on, the reminders lingered.

'Do you have a house in England?' she continued.

'Yes.'

'Will it not seem dull to live there after this?'

He grinned. 'Perhaps.'

'My aunt wanted me to go and live with her in

Reading, but I refused. I know she meant it kindly but it would have been unbearable.'

'I can understand that.'

'She would try to find me a husband, too. I'm sure of it.'

'You dislike the idea?'

'Marriage sounds dull to me, but perhaps it depends upon one's choice of partner.'

'I'm sure it does.'

'Being married to your career you have the ideal partner, do you not?'

'Well, at least my career won't leave me at the altar.'

For a moment she was silent, unsure she had heard him aright. Falconbridge felt his jaw tighten. He hadn't meant to speak of it but somehow the words had come out anyway. Perhaps it didn't matter now.

'Is that what happened?'

'Yes.' He drew in a deep breath. 'Clarissa was very beautiful—the most ravishing débutante of the year. Every man in London was wild about her. I was no exception. I could scarce believe my luck when she accepted my offer of marriage. Our families favoured the match and so a date was set.' He paused. 'The church was packed with our friends and relations; it was one of the most splendid marriages of the season. Or rather, it should have been.

However, when it came to the key question, Clarissa refused to go through with it.'

Sabrina felt intense sympathy for him. While she had heard of brides getting cold feet she had never, until then, known of one who had jilted her fiancé at the ceremony.

'She informed me that she couldn't marry me because she loved another,' he continued. 'With that she fled the church.'

'Good heavens!' His companion stared at him, appalled. 'What did you do?'

'For a little while, nothing. I just wanted the earth to open up and swallow me. Then somehow I got outside; I needed some air, needed to clear my head, try to think…and that's when I saw them. They were standing together by the lych gate, Clarissa in my brother's arms.'

'Your brother?'

'Yes, Hugh, whom I loved; the person I had always looked up to most; the one with whom I had shared so many adventures, the person I had trusted above all others.' He gave a hollow laugh. 'It was Hugh to whom I had first confided my love for Clarissa. Once we were engaged, of course, she and my brother met far more often than they had erewhile. They soon became good friends but, being a gullible fool, it never occurred to me that it was anything other than innocent. At some point she must have realised Hugh's interest was more than brotherly affection and seized her chance.'

Sabrina was genuinely shocked. 'How could she do that? How could any woman?'

'Hugh was the heir to an earldom. I was only the younger son.' He grimaced. 'I realise now that Clarissa never really loved me, but I was too besotted to see it.'

'What did you do…when you discovered the truth?'

'At first I wanted to kill them. They knew it, too; saw it in my face, for both of them were ghastly pale. But…' he let out a long breath '…what would have been the point? When I saw their fear all I felt was contempt, and in the end I just walked away.'

'And then?'

'The scandal was enormous. I had no wish to remain in England to be an object of pity or ridicule so, with my father's help, I purchased a commission in the army. It was a good decision. I discovered that I had an aptitude for the work and enjoyed its challenges. I made some good friends along the way, too.'

'Have you never been back to England since?'

'No, though I corresponded with my father and sister at regular intervals,' he replied. 'When my father died, he left me a handsome competence and one of the smaller country seats. I half-expected that Hugh would challenge the will but he never has.'

'He has that much honour then,' said Sabrina.

'Perhaps his conscience prevented it. Who knows?'

'His conscience must prick him dreadfully. He deserves that it should.'

'Well, it's in the past now.'

'All the same, it must have been very difficult for you.'

His lips twisted in a wry smile at the enormity of the understatement. 'At the time.'

'And now?'

'Not now.'

'You no longer love her?'

'No.' It was true, he thought. Anger and pain had diminished, too. If only memory were so easily vanquished.

'How long ago?'

'Three years.'

'Have you forgiven her?'

He hadn't been expecting that, and the question gave him a sharp mental jolt. The answer, when it came, was no less jarring. His companion was remarkably astute for one so young. No one else had ever dared to probe so far and would have got short shrift if they had tried. This was different, more like speaking to a confidante, even though he had known her for so short a time. Her manner was quite artless and strangely hard to resist. Somehow it invited him to speak of things so long kept hidden; to open up a dark place to the light of day.

'No,' he replied. 'Such duplicity as hers is hard to forgive.'

'Yes, it is.' She hesitated. 'And your brother?'

'Nor him. I never shall.' Now that it was revealed, he thought the dark place looked as ugly as an unhealed wound.

'But if you do not, how can you put it behind you and move on?'

'I have moved on.'

'Have you?'

The answer to that one should have been secure— having thrown himself into his career he had put the past behind him, hadn't he? A sudden and unexpected tension in the region of his solar plexus revealed it wasn't as far behind as he would have liked. The ramifications were disturbing on many different levels.

When he didn't reply, Sabrina didn't press him. The conversation, so innocently begun, had led to places she had never anticipated, and she had no wish to trespass there. Nevertheless, she could not regret that he had told her; it made a lot of things much clearer. For the first time she glimpsed the depth of his hurt and the reason for his anger. After such an experience he would find it difficult to forgive or to trust again. Instead of a loving, supportive marriage it was his career that now provided the stable framework of his life. She didn't care to think of what might happen if he lost that, too.

A swift sideways glance revealed that his eyes were closed. She knew he wasn't asleep but the hint was sufficient. She smiled ruefully. It was none of her business and if he did not speak of it again, she would not.

Chapter Six

When Sabrina woke in the late afternoon her companion was gone. She heard the muted sound of male voices coming from the dressing room and assumed that he was closeted with Willis, no doubt getting ready for the ball. She rose at once and summoned Jacinta. Then she bathed and began the lengthy toilette so necessary for her participation that evening.

When at last it was completed she surveyed her reflection in the glass. Her hair, dressed high on her head, was entwined with a rope of pearls. Another strand decorated her neck and matching pearls hung from her ears. The white satin ball gown, with its daring décolleté, was overlaid with spangled gauze that shimmered with every movement. Satin slippers and long gloves completed the ensemble. The effect was pleasing and she smiled at herself in the mirror. Jacinta smiled, too.

'You look beautiful. Far too good for him.'

Sabrina didn't pretend to misunderstand. 'He will not be paying any attention to me.'

'Oh, is he dead then? I hadn't heard.'

A gurgle of laughter greeted this. 'Of course he isn't dead. I meant he will have other things on his mind.'

'Not when he sees you in that dress, he won't.'

The words caused Sabrina's heart to leap. Falconbridge's opinion should not have mattered one iota but she knew full well that it did. The knowledge added to her feeling of nervous anticipation. It had been many months since last she had attended a ball of any kind, and even then it had not been so splendid a function as this promised to be. Neither had she had so handsome and charismatic an escort. She realised that she was looking forward to dancing with him. It would be the first time. It might very well be the last. The realisation brought with it a sharp pang.

He had long since emerged from the dressing room and taken himself off leaving the field clear for Sabrina. Clearly he had some idea of how long it took a lady to ready herself for such an occasion, and she appreciated the consideration. She could only hope that he would be appreciative of the effort made on his behalf.

* * *

She had not long to wait for the answer. He returned a little later to see if she was ready to accompany him. He took two steps into the room and then stopped in his tracks as his heart performed a sudden and wildly erratic manoeuvre. He had thought that her beauty could not be improved on but he had been wrong. His gaze drank in every detail and found no fault.

'You look gorgeous,' he said, though to his ears it sounded lame. If he knew anything about it, every other man in the room this evening was going to be rampant with envy. The notion was most gratifying. However, if they thought to do any more than look they were going to be disappointed. Tonight at least, she was his.

Sabrina smiled. 'Thank you.'

He crossed the room and took her hand, raising it to his lips. Then he smiled. It warmed the grey eyes and lit his face.

'All set, my dear?'

'All set.'

'Then let us join the fray.'

He retained his hold on her hand and led her to the door. Sabrina drew in a deep breath, partly in trepidation at what might lie ahead and partly because he was near. As always, his slightest touch set her senses alight. It was as well he did not know it.

'Incidentally,' he said as they descended the stairs together, 'don't give anyone else the first dance. I intend to claim a husband's privilege.'

Her heart missed a beat, but she kept the tone light. 'As you wish, sir.'

'It is exactly what I wish. In fact, I feel extraordinarily possessive.'

Her heart skipped another beat. 'Do you?'

His gaze lingered a moment on the décolletage of her gown. 'The sight of you in that dress is enough to heat the blood of a saint.'

'But you are no saint.'

'It hasn't taken you long to realise that.'

'Oh, I realised it the first time we met, sir.'

'Jade.'

She smiled, her expression both unrepentant and irresistible, and he wished very much that they had been alone. For the first time in years he found himself prey to a lot of unexpectedly erotic thoughts. Unfortunately, from his point of view at least, they reached the bottom of the stairs and their hosts were waiting to greet them.

Already the guests were gathering and Sabrina's gaze took in several French uniforms among the elegant crowd. She glanced up at Falconbridge and felt him squeeze her hand. Then they went in

together. Happily, the first people they encountered were other house guests already known to
them: Gonzalez and Don Fernando Muñoz, with
his twin brother, Cristóbal. The latter were in their
early thirties but, although not ill-favoured, showed
signs of over-indulgence at table in their thickening
waistlines. Their short stature did nothing in mitiga-
tion of the fault, but their manners were easy and
pleasant.

Don Fernando made Sabrina an elegant bow, his
gaze taking in every detail of her appearance and
warming as a result. She returned a polite greeting
and, while Falconbridge spoke to Don Cristóbal,
glanced across the room. As she did so her gaze
fell on the small group of French officers she had
noticed before.

'Some of your countrymen, Condesa,' said Don
Fernando.

'Yes,' replied Sabrina. 'I confess I am surprised
to see them here.'

'It does not pay to offend the ruling elite, as our
host is well aware.'

'No, I suppose not.'

'You do not approve of their presence?'

Sabrina contrived a casual shrug. 'It is not for me
to say whom our host should invite to his house.
Besides, I take little interest in politics.'

'Of course not. It isn't a subject that should concern a lady. It is far too tedious.'

Sabrina tried for a vapid expression. 'I confess it is. Antonio tries to explain it to me, but I'm afraid I just can't grasp it at all.'

'A woman shouldn't trouble her pretty little head over such matters.'

'There are so many more interesting things to talk about, are there not?'

'My view exactly,' he replied.

Seeing her chance she seized it. 'What an elegant gown that lady is wearing. I really must try to discover the name of her dressmaker. Of course, she may not wish to divulge it. Perhaps you would introduce us, Don Fernando.'

He professed himself most willing to oblige, and to point out other guests whom she did not know. Sabrina adopted a look of rapt interest. Having diverted him to safer ground she didn't want him to quit it.

In the event, he had no chance because the music started and then Falconbridge was beside her again.

'I believe this dance is mine,' he said.

She breathed a silent sigh of relief and allowed him to lead her away. His expression suggested private amusement.

'What?' she asked.

'Nothing to trouble your pretty little head over, my dear,' he replied.

For answer he received an eloquent look and enjoyed it enormously.

'Eavesdropping is a bad habit,' she said.

'I know but sometimes it's irresistible.'

They walked out onto the floor and waited as the first set formed up around them. Then the music struck up. Moving through the figures, he had leisure to observe that his partner danced well. He could detect no hint of awkwardness in her movements. He was aware, too, that other eyes watched them. It was inevitable, he thought. Men would always watch a woman like Sabrina. While one part of him deplored the attention they were attracting, another part relished their envy.

'Where did you learn to dance like that?' he asked. 'You must have had a good teacher.'

'The best. Captain Harcourt was most insistent on that.'

He frowned, experiencing a stab of something remarkably like jealousy, and determining to know more, but the next manoeuvre divided them briefly. When they came together again he fixed her with a gimlet stare.

'Captain Harcourt again? What had he to do with it, pray?'

The expression in the green eyes was the

epitome of innocence. 'Why, he asked his wife to teach me.'

Falconbridge bit back a laugh, knowing he'd been set up. For the second time that evening he wished they were alone. It would have pleased him very much to exact a fitting retribution. For just a moment he indulged that delicious thought.

'My compliments to the lady,' he replied.

'I'm sure she'd be delighted to know of your approval.'

For a moment her gaze met his again and, involuntarily, they both smiled. The next figure separated them again and he waited for her return.

'Your relationship with the Harcourts seems to have been highly educational.'

'Oh, it was, sir.' She could never tell him why.

'I am sorry not to have made their acquaintance.'

'I think you would have liked them. Father did.'

For a moment he saw a shadow cross her face. Then it was gone. He guessed that the mention of her father brought back the memory of his present predicament. He squeezed her hand gently.

'Don't worry. We shall see your father safe.'

His expression was so patently sincere that it brought a lump to her throat. Once, she would never have thought this man capable of kindness or warmth, and yet she had come to learn that he possessed both.

When the dance ended he led her from the floor where they were joined a moment later by Elena.

'Condesa, there is someone I'd like you to meet.'

Sabrina forced a smile. 'Of course.'

She would have liked to stay with Falconbridge but it was impossible. Good manners decreed that she must go. He smiled at her.

'I'll see you later, my dear.'

Elena led her across the room to another group and performed the necessary introductions. To her intense relief everyone seemed to accept her at face value. The Condesa de Ordoñez y Casal was admitted to their ranks with welcoming smiles. Their conversation turned on general topics to which she listened with apparent interest. Across the room she could see her erstwhile companion engaged in conversation with a small group of grandees. The ladies in the group seemed to hang upon his every word, admiration writ large in their eyes. Admiration and desire. Once, she heard him laugh in response to something that was said. The sound caused an unfamiliar pang. Before she could analyse it a familiar voice jolted her back.

'Condesa, what a pleasure to see you again.'

Sabrina turned round and felt her stomach

somersault as she recognised Colonel Machart, now resplendent in full dress uniform. His lupine gaze swept her in a comprehensive look and glinted appreciatively. Then he bowed.

'May I say that you are looking even lovelier this evening?'

Recovering quickly she made a polite curtsy. 'You are all kindness, sir.'

'I would have the honour of the next dance.'

It was the last thing she would have wished for. Unfortunately there was nothing to be done save consent with as good a grace as possible. He led her out and they joined the other couples on the floor. Machart danced with practised ease but the watchful gaze made her feel apprehensive. It rested often on her bare shoulders and bosom. In it she read admiration and lust and something else that instinctively put her on her guard.

When the dance was over she hoped to slip away, but her partner was not so easy to get rid of.

'Come, don't deprive me of your company so soon. It is not often that I have the pleasure of talking to a Frenchwoman, or one so lovely.'

'You flatter me, Colonel.' She smiled. 'However, my parents left France when I was very young. I regret to say that I have no memory of it.'

'That is a pity.'

'I have always thought so.'

'And they came from?'

'The Languedoc.'

'I also.' He bared his teeth in a smile. 'May I ask your family's name?'

'De Courcy.'

'I know it. An old and respected lineage,' he replied. 'Not that I claim acquaintance, unfortunately.'

His look grew warmer. Sabrina redirected the conversation.

'I have been told that the Languedoc region is very beautiful.'

'Indeed it is. There is nowhere to compare with it.' He glanced across the room towards the group that contained Falconbridge. 'You should persuade your husband to take you there.'

'My husband travels rarely, preferring to live quietly on his estates,' she replied.

'What a shame that you live so retired.'

'Not at all. I have no taste for city life either, Colonel.'

'So lovely a lady should not be buried in the country. It is not generous of your husband to deprive the rest of us of your company.' He paused, casting another look towards Falconbridge. 'Not that I blame him for wishing to keep you to himself.'

'I have no complaint to make.'

'No, that is on my side.' His gaze returned to the front of her gown. Feeling increasingly uncomfortable, Sabrina wanted nothing more than to escape. However, it seemed her companion still wasn't ready to let her go.

'Do you know, when we met on the road I had the strangest feeling that I had met your husband somewhere before.'

Her stomach wallowed. It took every ounce of self-control she possessed to face him. 'Really?'

'Yes. I rarely forget a face.'

'Perhaps it was someone who looked like my husband.'

'Perhaps, but just now the recollection eludes me.' He paused and grinned. 'However, I know that we have met once before, Condesa. Indeed I could never forget it.'

'Nor I,' she replied, with perfect sincerity.

'I should like to know you better,' he went on. 'Do you stay long in Aranjuez?'

Her skin crawled beneath that speculative gaze. 'No, sir. My husband does not like to be away from home too long.'

'Then I must use the available time.' He bowed. 'I shall hope to dance with you again later, Condesa.'

He possessed himself of her hand and raised it to his lips. Feeling the heat of that unwelcome embrace, Sabrina was thankful to be wearing gloves. However, she didn't dare let anything of her inner thought show. This man was a predator if ever she had met one, and he would be quick to sense fear. All the same, she wanted nothing more than to be rid of him.

Across the room Falconbridge watched. Then he turned and murmured something to Elena. Their hostess smiled and left him, making her way casually through the crowd with a smile here and a few words there, until she reached Sabrina's side.

'Forgive me, Condesa, but there is someone who particularly desires to make your acquaintance.'

Sabrina regarded her arrival with real gratitude. 'Of course. Please excuse us, Colonel.'

He bowed again. Sabrina walked away, aware of his gaze burning into her back. Her companion eyed her shrewdly.

'A little of his company goes a long way, does it not?'

'Yes. Your rescue is most timely.'

'Your husband thought it might be.'

Instinctively Sabrina looked over her shoulder towards the far side of the room. Falconbridge was still with the same group, apparently listening with interest to what was being said. However, as though sensing her regard, he looked up briefly and she saw him smile before returning his attention to the speaker. Though it was a fleeting expression it warmed her all the same, like a protective cloak.

'Machart has a certain reputation,' Elena continued.

'I can well believe it.'

'Not just with the ladies either.' Elena lowered her voice. 'There are tales about his military conduct which are not particularly pleasant. Of course, they may have been exaggerated.'

Somehow Sabrina doubted it but kept her own counsel. A few moments later she was admitted to a different group of people. Another casual glance across the room a few minutes later revealed that the French Colonel was engaged in conversation with another gentleman, a short, slight individual of middle years. The lined face with its pointed features and sharp eyes reminded her vaguely of a rodent. Both of them were looking in her direction. Her stomach knotted. Was anything wrong? Had they suspected something? She turned away, telling herself not to be foolish. It probably meant nothing. Machart would know many of those present this evening.

Don Cristóbal was standing nearby so she enquired whether he knew the identity of the man with Machart.

'That is Jean Laroche,' he replied. 'He works for the French intelligence service.'

The knot tightened in her stomach. 'What is he doing here do you suppose?'

'Keeping an ear to the ground, I imagine. He attends all the important social functions.'

She nodded and managed a smile. If that were the case there was no reason to suppose that his presence here had any significance beyond that. All the same, the combination of Laroche and Machart was disquieting.

Her hand was solicited for several dances and that precluded the need for conversation, or kept it to a minimum. After that she went in search of refreshment. The rooms were very warm now despite the fact that the windows along its length were open. A glass of fruit punch would be most welcome.

'A glittering occasion, is it not?'

Her heart leapt and she turned to see Falconbridge at her shoulder. 'Yes, I think that everyone who is anyone is probably here tonight.'

He put a hand under her elbow and drew her gently aside. 'I noticed you speaking to the Colonel earlier.'

She nodded. 'Yes, and I was never more glad to be rescued.'

'I thought you might be.'

'How right you were. I don't care for him at all.'

'No, an unpleasant character all round I gather.'

'He told me that he is sure he knows you.'

'Damn,' he muttered. 'The man's no fool. He'll remember eventually.'

Sabrina paled. 'What do we do now?'

'Act as though nothing were wrong. We have to get through the rest of the evening without attracting attention.' He squeezed her arm gently. 'Tomorrow we'll be on our way.'

'I hope we may.' She paused. 'Has Don Pedro mentioned a man called Jean Laroche?'

'Yes. He pointed the gentleman out earlier.'

'Do you think Laroche's presence here is significant?'

'I think not. I understand he likes to be present at social functions such as this.' As he saw her anxious expression, his face cleared and he smiled. 'As we are here and must remain awhile longer, will you honour me with another dance?'

She returned the smile. 'Of course.'

They returned to the ballroom for the next two measures, and Sabrina forgot about Machart and the other guests thronging the room. Her attention was solely for her present partner, the touch of his hand, his smile, the warmth in his gaze. When he looked at her like that all else became unimportant and she abandoned herself to the music and the moment, content just to be in his company, to be near him.

When at length the second dance ended, she expected that he would return her to Elena or one of the other ladies, but he did not.

'It is hot in here. Would you like some fresh air?'

'Yes, very much.'

'Come then.'

He placed a hand casually under her elbow, steering her towards one of the open doors that led onto the terrace. After the heavy atmosphere of the ballroom the night air was blessedly sweet and cool and scented with jasmine. Overhead the moon rose among a million brilliant stars and silvered the canopies of the trees. Somewhere among the branches a nightingale sang, the pure liquid notes travelling on the still air. Unwilling to break the spell she remained silent. This night might be the only one she would ever spend with him thus. Tomorrow they must leave, must get those secret papers to Wellington. After that… She bit her lip. Would the end of the mission be the end of the relationship?

'A penny for them.'

His voice drew her back. 'I was thinking about the future. Of what might happen.'

'Are you afraid?' he asked.

'Yes, a little.' It was true, she thought, but not for the reasons he supposed.

'Don't be. All will be well.'

'Will it?'

Something in the tone touched him and he smiled

gently. 'Of course. I will do all in my power to ensure it.'

He lifted her hand to his lips. The imprint of his kiss seemed to scorch her skin. She made no attempt to withdraw from his hold for it seemed that her hand belonged there. Heart pounding, she turned towards him, waiting, trying to read his expression. Suddenly he tensed and his fingers tightened on hers.

'Don't look round,' he murmured. 'Keep looking at me.'

'What is it?'

'Machart is watching us from the doorway yonder.'

'Why would he?'

'Perhaps he was hoping to get you alone.' Falconbridge smiled. 'I think we should show him how futile his hope is.'

'How?'

He released his hold on her hand but only to slide an arm round her waist and draw her against him. His lips brushed hers, tentatively at first, then more assertively. Liquid warmth flooded her body's core and she swayed against him, her mouth opening beneath his. The kiss grew deeper, more intimate, inflaming her senses, demanding her response. She had no need to pretend now, nor cared any longer who was watching. All that mattered was the two of them and the moonlight and the moment.

He took the kiss at leisure, every part of him wanting her, in no hurry to end it. This had nothing to do with Machart any more; he kissed her now because he wanted to, because it was what he'd wanted to do from the first. Heart hammering in his breast he drew back a little and looked into her face, trying to read her expression.

'I beg your pardon,' he said. 'I confess I got carried away, but then I had not expected to enjoy it so much.'

Sabrina hid hurt behind a smile. So it had just been an act then. She pulled herself up at that thought. It wasn't as if he hadn't warned her, was it? Tender looks, melting smiles—a kiss or two. How could she have guessed he would be so very accomplished an actor? Her throat tightened, but she swallowed the lump threatening to form there and glanced towards the open doorway. Machart was gone.

'Our companion got the hint,' she said. 'We must have given a convincing performance.'

Falconbridge surveyed her keenly. It hadn't been a performance and they both knew it. What he had felt could not be feigned. Nor had he imagined the spark that had ignited between them. It had been all too real. And that, he acknowledged, was the danger now. A danger she had recognised perhaps, and was seeking to avert? She was right. They could not afford distraction. Resisting the desire to take her in his arms again, he merely nodded.

'As you say, my dear.' He held out a hand. 'I think perhaps we should go back now.'

'Yes.'

She placed her fingers in his and allowed him to lead her back to the ballroom. They did not speak and she was glad of it. Her lips still burned from his kiss, her body remembered the delicious sensation of being held in his arms. She swallowed hard. At all costs she must try and put the incident behind her, forget it had ever happened. She did not deceive herself that it would be easy.

He danced with her again when they returned and then relinquished her to another partner. She performed the steps mechanically now, fixing a smile on her face. Her gaze searched the room but found no sign of Machart. That was a relief at least.

It wasn't until the company sat down to supper that she saw him again, though at the far end of the room. He glanced her way but, much to her relief, made no attempt to approach her.

'May I?'

A tall figure appeared in her line of vision and she looked up to see Falconbridge. She saw him smile and returned it, feeling the answering leap in her heart.

'Of course.'

He took the seat beside her. Now it seemed only natural and right that he should, as though he belonged there. She could not envisage any other man in his place. With an effort she reminded herself that all this was an act performed for the benefit of others, and yet how beautiful the illusion was, and how seductive. No matter what happened later she would remember tonight as long as she lived.

Throughout supper, conversation flowed lightly and easily and she was content to let others do most of the talking. Once again the other ladies present made no secret of their interest in the handsome Conde Antonio, laughing and flirting, seeking his attention. Once or twice she intercepted looks of envy from among their ranks. Outwardly Sabrina ignored them, but she was woman enough to enjoy their response as well, albeit privately. All her senses were attuned to the man beside her, drinking in each detail from the clean lines of the profile at present turned towards her, the easy smile as he responded to the words of a lady opposite, even to the way he held his fork. He seemed perfectly relaxed, quite at home in this company as though he had been there all his life. Of course, she reflected, he had, or its English equivalent anyway. Accustomed to move in the first ranks of the *ton,* he would be at home anywhere.

'May I pour you a little more wine?'

She realised that he was speaking to her. 'Oh, yes, thank you.'

He refilled the glass. 'The chicken is particularly good. Have you tried it?'

'I…er, no.'

'Allow me to fetch you some.'

He retired briefly to the buffet and returned with another plate.

Having tasted a little of the chicken, she nodded. 'You are right. Quite delicious.'

He smiled. 'Much better than some of the fare you have been served of late.'

'It is not the same thing at all.'

'I know it isn't.'

'I meant that you are not comparing like with like and, therefore, the criticism is perhaps a little unfair.'

'Perhaps.' He leaned back in his chair and surveyed her keenly. 'A bit like comparing cheap wine to champagne.'

'Yes, something like that.' Acutely conscious of his scrutiny, she took a sip from her glass with what she hoped looked like casual ease. 'Of course, a true connoisseur would never make that mistake.'

His lips twitched. 'No, indeed, as he could never mistake plainness for beauty.'

'Do you consider yourself a connoisseur of such things?'

'I was not, until recently.' He let his gaze travel from her face to her neck and throat and thence to the décolleté of her gown where it lingered quite unashamedly. 'Now the case is quite altered.'

Her colour fluctuated delightfully. 'Now you are being deliberately provoking.'

He grinned. 'That's right. Is it working?'

She returned him a most eloquent look and then laughed reluctantly. 'You know perfectly well that it is.'

'Excellent. I should have been disappointed else.'

The words brought her back to earth with a jolt. This light flirtation was all part of the act and she would do well to remember it. For all manner of reasons she could not let this man get under her skin. This meant no more to him than a passing amusement. In his world such things were the norm and only a complete gudgeon would read more into it. The knowledge rallied her.

'I should hate to disappoint. Therefore, I shall humour you, sir.'

Hr laughed softly, enjoying her. 'Will you humour me in everything?'

'Certainly not, for then you would grow complacent.'

'Where you are concerned, my dear, I would never be so foolish.'

'I admit that foolishness it not a trait I associate with you.'

'I'm pleased to hear it.' He paused. 'What traits do you associate with me?'

She surveyed him coolly. 'Commitment to duty, attention to detail, thoroughness, a certain degree of ruthlessness and, withal, a touch of arrogance.'

His expression did not change, though for a brief instant the grey eyes were veiled. 'You are honest.'

'I must speak as I find.'

When he thought back to the occasion of their first meeting he could understand why she would consider him ruthless and arrogant. All the same her words stung a little.

'Have I not redeemed myself in any way?' he asked.

'You are quite beyond redemption, sir.' The smile robbed the remark of malice but he was not entirely sure it had been mere banter. It should not have mattered and yet he knew it did. He could not have said exactly how it had come about, but suddenly her opinion of him mattered a great deal.

* * *

When supper was over he rose and, taking her hand, led her out of the room. She had expected that they would part then and go their ways for a while, but he retained his hold on her hand. It was gentle but it would not be resisted. He drew her round to face him.

'Dance with me again.'

'Is that a command?'

The grey eyes glinted. 'Most assuredly it is and, as I am your husband, madam, you are sworn to obey.'

Her chin came up at once and he had the pleasure of seeing a rosy flush mount from her throat to her cheeks. He saw it was on the tip of her tongue to deliver a pithy set down, and waited for it. Instead she smiled sweetly.

'How I could I refuse such a charming invitation?' His enjoyment increased and she saw it. Lowering her voice she added, 'Do you have any idea how odious you can be?'

'Of course, for you told me yourself. Arrogant and ruthless I think you said.'

'Yes, an assessment only too accurately borne out now.'

'But then I did warn you at the outset that I should not brook disobedience.'

'Why, I would never dream of it, sir.'

'Liar. You are contemplating it now, but I promise you it will not be tolerated.'

The tone was disturbingly ambiguous, like the look in his eyes, and suddenly she felt as a swimmer must who inadvertently steps off a shallow ledge into deep water. She should have been afraid but the feeling was more akin to excitement. Unable to think of a reply she tried to focus on the dance but it wasn't easy when every fibre of her being was focused on him.

He kept her with him for another measure and then led her from the floor. After that, they mingled awhile with the other guests. Sabrina cast a surreptitious look around for Machart but did not see him, and for that was devoutly thankful.

As the hour grew later the company began to thin out and as the carriages arrived at the door Falconbridge said their goodnights and steered Sabrina away.

'You look tired, my dear.'

'I confess I am a little.'

'There's time for a few hours' sleep before we leave.'

She glanced at the clock in the hall. The hands indicated half past two. 'Are we leaving today?'

'We are.'

'Is it really necessary?'

'I believe it is.'

He took hold of her elbow and guided her up the stairs and along the passage to their chamber. The room was empty.

'I told Jacinta not to wait up,' she said.

Closing the door behind them, he nodded. 'I can perform the offices of a maid if need be.'

'I can manage.'

'As you will.'

He crossed to the far side of the room and began to undress. Inevitably, he achieved it more quickly and then retired to the couch. Then he lay for a while, watching her complete her own preparations for bed. Conscious of that steady regard, Sabrina did not linger over the matter, shedding her clothing as quickly as possible, save only for the chemise beneath. Then, having removed her jewellery, she seated herself before the glass and unpinned her hair, shaking it loose over her shoulders. She brushed it vigorously, feeling it leap beneath the strokes. When it was done she blew out the candle and bade her companion goodnight before sliding into bed. She heard him reply and then the faint creaking of the couch as he turned onto his side. She smiled in the darkness and then yawned. Snuggling beneath the covers she closed her eyes and in minutes was asleep.

Across the room, her companion lay awake rather

longer, his mind replaying the events of the evening. He had not imagined the spark that had kindled between them, nor was he imagining the attraction he felt now. Given the least encouragement he would have followed his inclination and taken her to bed. Fortunately, she had too much sense to let things get out of hand. She had shown herself to be more than capable of holding him at arm's length, and of doing it with wit and charm. He permitted himself a wry smile. Far from putting him off, it had served only to fuel enjoyment and desire. It was his fault, of course; she had been in no way to blame for what had happened. Yet if he had known the consequences then, would he have avoided that kiss? The answer returned in an instant; he would not have missed it for the world. He knew he was never going to forget it either. As long as he lived he would remember how it felt to hold her in his arms. How could he have imagined that what had begun as a simple ruse would rebound upon him so spectacularly?

Chapter Seven

Sabrina slept soundly and dreamlessly, worn out by the combination of a long journey and the late hour. Ordinarily a ball would have meant a long lie abed the following day to recover. However, it seemed like only minutes, before she was gently shaken awake by a hand on her shoulder. She muttered something and turned over, but the hand was insistent.

'Come, my dear, it's time to move.'

Vaguely recognising the voice, she groaned and opened one eye. 'It can't be.'

'I'm afraid it is.'

'But I've only just gone to bed.'

'Never mind, you can sleep in the coach.'

This time, both eyes opened and focused resentfully on the familiar figure beside her. 'What o'clock is it?'

'Seven, or thereabouts.'

'Seven! We didn't retire till three.'

'I know and I'm sorry, but we cannot afford the luxury of lying abed.'

'Have you no mercy?'

For answer, a ruthless hand drew back the covers. Equally ruthless arms lifted her bodily out and dumped her on her feet. 'Get dressed. We need to be gone. It isn't safe to remain.'

The words penetrated the fog in her brain. 'What is it? Not Machart?'

'Not yet, but there's every chance his memory will return. I want to be long gone before it does.'

Sabrina nodded, coming to at last. 'Yes, of course.' Then she looked more closely at her companion.

Falconbridge was fully dressed and alert and looked as fresh as a man who had had eight hours' sleep, not four. His arm was still around her waist. She could feel the warmth of his hand through the filmy fabric of her nightgown. The memory of what had happened the previous evening returned with force. She couldn't afford any kind of romantic illusions. This man was married to his career. All that could ever happen between them would be a brief affair. The knowledge brought her back to reality.

Disengaging herself gently, she crossed to the washstand and sluiced cold water over her face. The shock woke her completely. She fumbled for a towel. A glance over it revealed the coolly appraising stare that swept her from head to toe. Only then was she fully aware of her own dishevelled appearance and scanty attire. She met his gaze with a level stare.

'If you would excuse me, I need to dress.'

'Of course. I'll see you downstairs.'

'I'll be ready in a quarter of an hour.'

He smiled faintly, his expression revealing deep scepticism about the proposed time scale. 'I'm ever optimistic.' She threw him a withering glance. It bounced off. He crossed to the door. 'As soon as may be, my dear.'

In fact, he was pleasantly surprised when Sabrina joined him some twenty minutes later. His critical gaze could find no fault with her appearance either. She was, he thought, a rare woman.

While the last of the boxes were carried down they took leave of their host.

'If anyone asks for us, tell them urgent business called me home,' said Falconbridge.

'I will, though it will be hours yet before anyone in this house will be stirring.' Don Pedro held out his hand. 'In the meantime, I pray you may have a safe and uneventful journey.'

'Amen to that.' Falconbridge shook his hand warmly. 'And thank you, sir. For everything.'

'*Vaya con Dios.*'

Sabrina raised her hand in farewell as the carriage

drew away. Then she leaned back in her seat and breathed a sigh of relief.

'We did it.'

Falconbridge shook his head. 'We're not out of the woods yet, my dear. I'll want a lot more distance between us and Aranjuez before I'll dare to hope so.'

'With any luck Machart and company will be sound asleep at this moment. We'll be long gone by the time he wakes.'

'I pray you're right.'

He did not labour the point but she knew him well enough to know that he had doubts on the matter. In consequence, she kept an eye on the countryside through which they passed, half-expecting to encounter a French patrol. However, they met none. By then fatigue was making its presence felt and Sabrina slipped into a doze.

She had no idea how long she slept but when she came to again the sun was much higher. Her companion smiled.

'Feeling better?'

'Yes, I thank you.' She glanced out of the window. 'We're making good progress.'

'So far.'

'You expect pursuit?'

'Not expect, no, but it remains a possibility. Thus, it behoves us not to tarry.'

'At least this time we are going in the right direction, away from the lion's den.'

'The lion's territory is large and his reach is long,' he replied.

Sabrina looked out of the window again but could see nothing to occasion any alarm at present. She leaned back in her seat regarding her companion steadily for a few moments. The handsome face gave nothing away.

'This is all familiar to you, is it not? The risk, I mean, and the adventure.'

'Every soldier encounters risk at some point. It just comes in different guises. We do what the job demands.'

'Do you enjoy it?'

'It has its moments,' he replied. 'All the same, I shall be glad when this task is satisfactorily completed.'

It occurred to her that the end of the mission meant the end of their brief relationship. The knowledge cast a cloud. Somehow, in a matter of days, she had grown so accustomed to his presence that it was hard to imagine life without it. There could be no denying that what she felt for him was more than mere liking for an agreeable companion, but neither was it infatuation. Her feelings were quite different.

This man's absence was going to leave a gap that could not easily be filled, if ever.

He saw the shadow cross her face and mistook the reason for it. 'Don't worry. I am sure that you will see your father soon.'

'God willing.' She paused. 'And you will return to regular duty for a while.'

'Yes, unless Major Forbes has found another task for me to perform.'

Her heart thumped. If he were sent on such another mission she might never see him again. 'Do you think it likely?'

'Where Forbes is concerned, anything could happen.'

'But surely if you are promoted to Lieutenant Colonel you will outrank him.'

Falconbridge laughed. 'What a very pleasing thought.'

'Yes, although I suppose he would still have the ear of General Ward.'

'And of Wellington.'

'A fearful trinity,' she observed.

'It is an apt description.' He paused, eyeing her keenly. 'And you, my dear, what will you do once your father is freed?'

Sabrina shook her head. 'In truth I hadn't thought beyond that moment, but I suppose we will go on as we did before. Perhaps Forbes will find another mission for me, too.'

His expression became more serious. 'Indeed I hope he will not.'

'Why so?'

'I would not see you exploited in this way again.'

She smiled wryly. 'He exploited my feelings, but that is all. I could have refused.'

'No, you could not,' he replied. 'You are too loyal and too brave.'

She felt a start of surprise for there had been nothing in his voice or look to suggest he was anything but sincere. It stirred a strange emotion in her breast.

'Not so brave. It was a calculated risk.'

'All the same, very few young women would have agreed, I think.' He paused. 'Forbes is a scoundrel if he ever subjects you to such a risk again.'

'I shall exercise due care.'

'I pray you will. I would not have you come to harm, my dear.'

Again the sincerity in his tone was unmistakable and her heart beat faster in response. 'Nor I you,' she replied. 'But I'm sure you will not heed my advice and ignore Major Forbes.'

He returned her smile. 'He's a hard man to ignore.'

'He has a certain way with him, does he not?'

'That's putting it tactfully. He's a devious rogue with a smooth tongue and considerable skill in manipulating people.'

'Exploitation of others is part of the job. The intelligence service could scarcely operate without it.'

'Its dealings are usually with those inured to its ways or hardened by long experience,' he replied. 'You are neither.'

'Yet it was my choice to be involved. I just hope it proves to be worth all the effort.'

'I really believe it will.'

They had lapsed into silence after this and did not speak again until the carriage stopped half an hour later. It was a welcome respite and Sabrina was relieved to get down and stretch her legs. She was hungry, too, and readily agreed to the light luncheon that Falconbridge suggested. However, a few words with the *patrón* revealed a limited menu.

'He says that today he has *fabada.*'

Sabrina grinned. 'Well, I suppose that narrows the choice.'

'What choice?'

'Do you want it or not?'

He laughed. 'I happen to like *fabada,* but can you eat it?'

'I have no objection, provided it is well-cooked.'

Indeed it proved to be and they helped themselves to a huge tureen full of the delicious fava bean and pork stew. It was accompanied with bread and a jug of the local wine. Sabrina ate hungrily.

Her companion smiled. 'I never met a woman so easily pleased by such simple fare.'

'Simple does not mean bad,' she replied. 'When one is hungry most food seems delicious.' Then, eyeing him askance, 'Or do you imply that my palate is unrefined?'

He seemed taken aback. 'By no means. I meant it as a compliment.' Then he saw the mischievous sparkle in her eyes. 'As you well knew, you rogue.'

She grinned. The thought occurred to him that he would miss her company when this was over. Somehow it had grown on him, and in lots of unexpected ways. If she had flirted or tried to attach him he would have found it easy to resist, but this innocent charm was harder to overcome. Just then he wasn't even sure he wanted to.

Before either of them could say more they were interrupted by the sudden appearance of Corporal Blakelock.

'Beg pardon, sir, but there's a group of riders heading this way. I spied 'em with the glass from the top of yonder knoll a few minutes ago.'

Falconbridge was on his feet in a moment. 'How far?'

'A couple of miles off, I reckon, sir.'

'How many?'

'Hard to say from the dust they were kicking up, but I'd guess at least fifteen. Could be more.'

'French?'

'Very likely, sir.'

Sabrina looked at Falconbridge. 'Machart?'

'Probably, but we're not going to stay around long enough to be sure.'

'We can't outrun them with the carriage.'

'No. We'll have to ride.' He turned back to Blakelock. 'Get the carriage and chaise out of sight and have the horses saddled at once. We leave as soon as may be.'

'Aye, sir.'

When the other departed on his errand, Falconbridge looked at Sabrina. 'Have you suitable clothes for riding?'

'Of course.'

'Then I suggest you change as fast as you can.' He headed for the door. 'I'll see you outside shortly.'

She needed no second bidding. Calling for Jacinta she issued swift instructions. Within minutes the necessary box was brought indoors and, after withdrawing to a private chamber, the two women stripped off their travelling dresses and pulled on breeches, boots and jackets.

'You will need this.' Jacinta handed Sabrina her

sword and, while her mistress buckled it on, returned for the case that held her pistols. 'Primed and loaded,' she observed.

'Good.' Sabrina thrust one into her waistband and gave her companion the other, before sliding a slim blade into her boot.

Jacinta picked up a wicked-looking dagger and fastened the sheath to her belt. Finally she took out two cloaks. 'It gets cold in the hills at night.'

Hastily shoving their discarded clothing back in the box they took a final glance around. Sabrina glanced at her companion.

'Let's go.'

By the time they rejoined the others, the horses were saddled and ready. Blakelock had returned to the knoll behind the inn to watch the progress of the advancing force, and he returned at a run.

'They're about a mile away, sir, but if they've been pushing their horses hard it gives us an advantage.'

'Then let's make the most of it,' said Falconbridge.

He saw Sabrina and Jacinta mounted and swung himself into the saddle of a rangy chestnut gelding. Then the whole party set off. For a while no one spoke. The pace was too swift anyway to admit of conversation and everyone was anxious to put as much space as possible between themselves and pursuit. At some instinctive level Sabrina knew their pursuer was Machart, and also knew what the consequences of capture would mean. In another part of her was determination not to let that happen, and she settled down to ride.

Having followed the road for another three miles or so they turned off and headed away across country towards the hills. With Ramon as their guide they followed little frequented tracks and sheep paths, using rocks and trees for cover.

'It won't take the Frenchman long to work out what we've done,' said Falconbridge, 'but while he does we'll be moving well ahead of him.'

Sabrina regarded him steadily. 'He strikes me as the sort who does not give up easily.'

'You may well be right. We'll know soon enough.'

They rode until dusk and made camp on a wooded hillside. Even though there was no immediate sign of pursuit, Falconbridge wouldn't allow a fire so they ate cold rations brought from the inn: bread and cheese and a little cured ham. Sabrina ate her portion in thoughtful silence, listening intently. The only sounds were of crickets and the muted murmur of male conversation, occasionally punctuated by the stamp of a horse's hoof on dry earth. It was cooler now and the air sweet with pine and wild herbs. Above her, the first stars shone in the deepening blue. It brought back memories of the times she had camped like this with her father and, unbidden, a lump formed in her throat.

'Are you all right?'

A familiar voice brought her back to the present. 'Oh, yes. Thank you.'

Falconbridge regarded her quizzically for a moment and then seated himself on a convenient rock nearby. 'I regret the basic nature of the accommodation,' he went on. 'It's not what I had planned.'

'I've slept in worse, on some of Father's expeditions.' She grimaced. 'I recall one inn where the beds were so flea-ridden that we had to sleep in our cloaks on the floor.'

'You miss him, don't you?'

'Very much.'

'These last months must have been lonely.'

'Not as lonely as they would have been without Jacinta and Ramon and Luis. They have been very kind to me.'

'It speaks of the regard in which they hold you and your father.'

'I just hope he will rejoin us soon.'

The tone was wistful and in that moment he glimpsed the vulnerability that she tried so hard to conceal. Although she undoubtedly knew how to use them, the sword and pistols were merely part of the disguise designed to keep unwanted attention at bay, like the outwardly confident manner she assumed. At times it slipped a little, as now. The effect was to touch him more deeply than he had ever thought possible. Suddenly he found himself wanting to know more, to understand what drove so lovely a young woman to lead such a demanding and often comfortless life. She would not be out of place in London society; indeed, few of the young women there could hold a candle to her.

Aloud he said, 'I'm sure he will. And he will be very proud when he learns of the part you played in obtaining his freedom.'

'He hasn't got it yet. First we have to shake Machart off the scent.'

'Yes, but I believe it can be done.'

'I hope so. I should not like to fall into his clutches.'

'I'll try by every means to prevent it.'

'I know you will.'

The tone was soft but something about it and the accompanying look caused his heart to beat a little faster. Could a man be mistaken about such a look? He had been mistaken once before. Yet here was no Clarissa. Nothing in Sabrina's manner had ever struck him as underhand or devious—unconventional perhaps, but not treacherous. She was a free spirit but, as he had observed before, loyal and brave and, of course, very lovely. Imagination transported him back to a moonlit terrace and the touch of her lips on his. What had been intended as a mere subterfuge had turned into a moment of heart-stopping delight. The spark that had been kindled had not been extinguished and he knew it, but to repeat the experience would be to take advantage of her youth and inexperience. He was responsible for her welfare. He had made a promise to Albermarle and, he now realised, a promise to himself as well. He smiled and squeezed her shoulder gently.

'Best try to get some rest, Sabrina. We have a long, hard ride ahead of us tomorrow.'

He made his own rude bed close by and, laying his sword beside him, stretched out. Soon she could hear the soft, even tenor of his breathing. Only a few feet separated them. She could still feel the comforting pressure of his hand. He had used her name, too, with an easy familiarity that bore in it not a shade of offence. It sounded so right on his lips. How easy it would be to encourage him, to invite his kiss, to let him lead her aside and lie with him beneath the pines and share his warmth; share his passion. The thought ought to have been displeasing but it was not. She drew her cloak closer and shut her eyes, mentally rebuking herself. She could not afford to think of him in that way. To do so would lead only to heartache.

* * *

The night passed uneventfully and at first light they set out again, keen to use every available hour of daylight to put distance between themselves and pursuit. The pace was slower than Falconbridge would have liked but the trail was narrow and rocky and, in places, steep. Sometimes they had to dismount and walk.

At any other time Sabrina would have admired the scenery more; the peaks of the cordillera, the wooded slopes, the lakes and creeks combined to form a landscape that was spectacular. Once, she glimpsed ibex, and once, an eagle soaring on the warm air currents. Small lizards basked on sunlit rocks and the trees were full of birds. However, she found herself listening not for their songs but for the sound of hoofbeats that would indicate pursuit. She had no fear of their getting lost; Ramon knew this country well and she trusted him to guide them. It was the knowledge of how far they were from help that created the tension she now felt. Rests were few and short and always one of the men was on lookout. Even if they only walked, Falconbridge kept the group moving forwards.

'We'll make better speed when we're through the mountains,' he said, reining his horse alongside. He did not add barring brigands and accidents, but he didn't need to. Sabrina had travelled enough to know the risks. Just then, though, her attention was on the man beside her. The apparently casual ease with which he rode and controlled his mount was the mark of the true horseman. She guessed that he had been taught to ride almost as soon as he could walk.

Becoming aware of her quiet scrutiny, he shot her a sideways glance. 'I'd like to ask if I pass the test,' he said, 'but I'm rather afraid of the answer.'

'Test?'

'Yes. It's not often I am the subject of such close observation.'

'I beg your pardon.' She paused. 'And, yes, you did pass—with flying colours.'

One dark brow lifted a little. 'Now I am intrigued. Dare I enquire as to the nature of the test I have passed?'

'I was just thinking that you ride very well.'

'I'm flattered.'

'Not at all.'

'Of course, I should know that by now,' he replied. 'And, since you are also sparing with your praise, I shall take your remark as a compliment and treasure it. I know I may have to live on it for some time.'

The sober expression that accompanied these words did not deceive her in the least. 'I cannot imagine any words of mine being taken to heart by you.'

'Can you not?'

'No, for you are proof against praise or censure.'

'I dispute that. No man can consider himself beyond praise or censure, and to do so would argue a considerable degree of conceit.' He hesitated. 'Is your opinion of me really so low?'

'No, for I find that it has improved upon better acquaintance.'

He bit back the laughter that threatened. 'I am relieved to hear it, truly. I should not like to think I had sunk lower in your estimation since our first meeting.'

'That would scarcely have been possible, sir.'

This time he could not prevent the laughter from escaping, even as he inwardly acknowledged the hit. 'Wretched girl! I shall take consolation from your praise of my riding skills.'

'It's my belief that you learned from an early age and were taught by someone who knew what he was about.'

'Yes, an old groom by the name of Jackson. I never met a man who knew more about horses, and he was good with us boys, too.'

'You and your brother tried his patience a few times I take it.'

'I think we'd have tried the patience of a saint

when we were young. Lord knows we got into enough scrapes.'

'You were fond of your brother back then?'

'Yes. We were very close as boys. Hugh was the person I looked up to most.'

'That must have made the rift between you much worse.'

'Yes.' It was an understatement, he thought. The discovery that his adored older brother had feet of clay had proved a shattering experience.

'I'm so sorry,' she replied. 'I never had brothers or sisters; at least none who survived past infancy. I always thought it would be pleasant to have a sister—someone to laugh with and to confide in.'

He heard the underlying wistfulness in her tone and glimpsed the loneliness she must have felt at times. Having a caring father was surely a blessing, but a young woman without a mother or older sister to turn to for guidance was at a distinct disadvantage.

'There must have been occasions when you would have welcomed some female company and support.'

'Yes, there were.' For an instant Jack Denton flashed into her mind. 'I am sure I would have made fewer mistakes if I'd had that help.'

'I cannot imagine you making very many mistakes,' he replied. 'You have too much common sense.'

'Yes, now, but I was not always nineteen years old.' She bit her lip. 'Experience is a good teacher but sometimes a painful one, is it not?'

He eyed her curiously, wondering what she was alluding to, but knew better than to force a confidence. If she wanted to tell him she would do it of her own volition.

'Yes, it is,' he agreed, 'but it makes us wiser.'

'And warier.'

'Yes.'

It was true. Experience had certainly made him warier, but what had prompted her to say that? His curiosity mounted. What had happened in the past to make her say that now? And wary of what? Or whom? Was it that earlier experience that had made her so adept at keeping him at a distance? For the first time it occurred to him that there had been another man in her past. Yet why should there not have been other admirers? Other men had eyes, too. From what she had said it did not seem as if the affair had been entirely happy, but it had clearly left its mark. Was she still in love with him? The notion jarred.

Before he could follow it up, Willis' voice broke in and claimed their attention.

'Beg pardon, sir, but my horse is going lame. He's favouring his near foreleg.'

Falconbridge gritted his teeth and signalled a halt. Then he and Willis dismounted and the latter bent to examine the site of the suspected injury.

'There's a lot of heat in the tendon, sir, and some swelling. It's a sprain, I reckon. Probably take a week to mend.'

Falconbridge also ran a hand down the leg and his fingers verified the words. 'Unfortunately, you're quite right. Unsaddle the beast and turn it loose. You'll have to ride double with Blakelock.'

It was far from ideal, but they were left with no choice now. However, it was going to slow their progress and everyone knew it.

Chapter Eight

It was later that same afternoon when they paused to rest the horses that they first caught sight of their pursuers. The wooded defile they had followed earlier had led into a wider valley. Ramon had climbed to the top of a rocky outcrop, scanning the countryside with a keen eye. Suddenly he became very still, all his attention focused on the spyglass. Then he lowered the instrument and hurried down to rejoin the others.

'Riders coming, *señor.*'

Falconbridge swore softly. 'They stick to the trail like leeches.'

'I think they have a tracker with them,' replied Ramon. 'A man named Valdez.'

'How can you be certain?'

'I'm not certain, but Valdez rides a dun-coloured horse and there's a dun leading the way down there.' He handed Falconbridge the glass. 'See for yourself, *señor.*'

He trained the glass on the line of horsemen strung out along the trail. It took only moments to verify what Ramon had said. 'How do you know this Valdez?'

'Anyone who knows this region has heard of the man. He has a reputation for hunting and tracking that is second to none.'

Luis regarded him quizzically. 'Then, if it is he, we are in trouble, I think.'

'Believe it. He will not give up until he has his quarry.'

'But why would he help the French? It is not patriotic.'

'For some men gold outweighs all else.' Ramon looked at Falconbridge. 'I think we should not linger, *señor*.'

The other nodded. Then he snapped the glass shut and stowed it in his saddlebag. 'Mount up everybody. We're leaving.'

They rode fast now, pushing the horses harder. From time to time Sabrina looked over her shoulder half-expecting to see their pursuers, but they were not yet in clear view. Occasionally they were forced to stop to let Willis get up behind Ramon or Luis, and thus relieve Blakelock's mount. She knew they couldn't afford to lose another horse.

When they halted briefly Ramon put an ear to

the ground. 'Nothing yet, but they won't be far behind.'

'Then we ride,' said Falconbridge.

Sabrina urged her horse on, trying not to heed her aching muscles. She wondered what would happen when eventually they were forced to stop. If it came to a confrontation they would be outnumbered. Suddenly, death or capture was more than a vague possibility. For the first time since their mission began she felt the prickling of fear. Resolutely, she pushed the thought aside, unwilling to dwell on it until she had to.

They rode on until the sun was low on the horizon, and made camp beneath a tall ridge. Having tended to the horses' needs they ate cold rations, for again it was not prudent to light a fire. Falconbridge organised guard duties so that there would always be someone on watch. Sabrina looked out from their vantage point over the quiet land, blue in the gathering dusk. She could detect no sign of life or movement. Common sense dictated that even their pursuers had to rest at some point, but gradually they would make up the ground until they caught their quarry. She shivered inwardly.

A shadow fell across her and she looked up quickly to see Falconbridge standing there. Not for anything would she let him see her fear and therefore summoned a smile. He returned it.

'You looked to be deep in thought. Am I intruding?'

'By no means.'

'Then may I join you awhile?'

'Of course.'

He sat down beside her and for a moment or two said nothing. Aware of him to her fingertips, she knew this was to be no casual conversation.

'There is something on your mind.'

He met her gaze and smiled faintly. 'Am I so transparent?'

'No, but under the circumstances it seems likely.'

He nodded. 'I cannot pretend to be unconcerned by our present situation.'

'You think that Machart and company will overtake us.'

'I fear so. If we had not lost a horse we might have outrun them, but as it is…'

'Then it will come to a fight.'

'Quite likely.' He paused. 'Do you remember the conversation we had in the garden the day you accepted Ward's offer?'

'Yes.' How could she forget, when every detail was etched on her memory? 'You think that what we discussed then is about to happen, don't you?'

'It is a possibility only. Anything might happen, but it is as well to be prepared for every eventuality.'

The grey eyes were cool, almost sombre now. For a few seconds more they held hers; then he reached into a small pocket inside the waistband of his breeches and withdrew a small package, about an inch square. It looked like a piece of oilcloth.

'I want you to have this.'

'What is it?'

'A last resort.' He paused. 'I had hoped it would never be necessary to mention it, but as things stand I can do no other.'

Sabrina's brow wrinkled. 'I don't understand.'

'It's poison, swift and deadly. In extremis, it offers a way out.'

For a moment she was quite still, staring at the package in his hand. The implication sent a chill along her spine like the touch of iced velvet. Now, the truth of their earlier conversation was forcibly borne upon her. *If you are captured, death is the best you can hope for. Before that there is always interrogation.*

'I may not always be able to protect you, Sabrina.'

'I see.' Suddenly she did see, and with awful clarity.

'It is a precaution only,' he continued, 'but it would please me to know that you had this with you.'

For a moment, Machart's lupine stare imposed itself on her imagination. It was horribly vivid and her mind recoiled. Wordlessly, she nodded and took the package, slipping it into a small inner pocket of her jacket.

Falconbridge watched it safely stowed. He had wondered what her reaction would be. She was so young and, just then, seemed so very vulnerable. If only he and his men had been involved he might have regarded their situation with greater *sang-froid*. What he felt now was fear, not for himself but for her, and the maid, too. He knew only too well what men like Machart were capable of, and the knowledge filled him with silent fury. The thought of any man doing them hurt was an affront. The idea of any man laying violent hands on Sabrina was past bearing.

'I wish with all my heart that you had not come on this mission,' he said, 'but in truth I have enjoyed your company.'

Rather shyly she said, 'And I yours.'

'In spite of my conspicuous lack of gallantry?'

'I have not found you ungallant. Well, perhaps once,' she amended, 'but I understand the reason for it now.'

He surveyed her closely. 'Does that mean I might entertain the hope of forgiveness?'

Under that penetrating gaze she reddened a little. 'I bear you no grudge.'

'I am glad, for of all people I should least desire your enmity.'

'I feel none.'

The words caused his heart to beat faster. Unable to help himself he leaned closer, glimpsing in her face what he had unconsciously hoped to see and what she could not hide. For a moment they remained thus, before his lips brushed hers. He felt the familiar spark leap between them, igniting desire. Then his arms were round her shoulders drawing her closer.

She knew she should resist and, equally, knew she did not wish to. Every part of her wanted this, wanted to be in his arms, to taste his mouth on hers, to breathe the scent of him. It felt so right. Surely this could be no act on his part. Yet he had not mentioned any emotion stronger than liking. It would be anathema to have him think her an easy conquest, to forfeit all respect. She never wanted to see him look at her as Jack Denton had once looked at her. His good opinion mattered too much. He mattered too much. That knowledge was enough to make her pull gently away from him.

'Forgive me, I…'

'What is it, Sabrina?'

She shook her head, unable to find the words to explain. She had half expected him to be angry, but instead he took her hand in his and squeezed it gently.

'You need not be afraid of me.'

'I know.' That was true, she thought. It was not him she feared.

'Nor will I ever seek more than you wish to give.'

Her stomach lurched and she lowered her gaze from his, lest he should read the dismay his words had caused. He wanted her, but not in the way she had hoped. If she encouraged him it would lead only to a furtive and illicit coupling, a brief affair that would mean nothing to him beyond the pleasure of the moment, but which she knew would break her heart. Better to lose him than to let that happen.

'I cannot give you what you want, Robert.'

Her use of his name thrilled through him even while his mind assimilated the rest of what she had said. Was this hesitation urged by love of another man? His throat tightened.

'Forgive me, I did not mean…'

'The act is unnecessary. Machart is not watching now.'

Suddenly there was tension in every line of his body. The grey eyes burned into hers. 'An act? Is that what you think?'

'What else should I think?'

She tried to disengage her hand but his grip

tightened. 'I'll not deny that I kissed you first as an intended ruse, but it took only seconds to know that it was no ruse, that Machart was merely an excuse.' He paused. 'This time it needed no excuse. I kissed you because I wanted to and because I hoped you felt the same. Was I wrong?'

'I would be lying if I said so.'

'Then you fear I am not to be trusted. Is that it?' When she did not answer his jaw tightened. 'Well, I suppose I cannot blame you.'

'It's not that exactly.'

'Then what?'

'I…it's hard to explain.'

He was almost certain now that it involved another man but he needed to be sure. 'Will you not try?'

She took a deep breath. What would be his reaction if she told him the truth? Would the truth disgust him? There was more than one way to lose a man's regard, such as him finding out that she had once been taken for a slut by a fellow officer.

He saw her hesitation. In the gathering dusk her face looked pale, the expression in her eyes almost fearful. Again he was reminded forcibly of her youth and her vulnerability and he regretted his earlier surge of anger.

'Sabrina?'

The tone was soft and coaxing, the hand on hers

warm and strong. If she succumbed, she was lost. She took another deep breath.

'I'm sorry, but I cannot. Not now.'

'I see.' He gave her hand a last gentle squeeze and then released his hold. 'Perhaps you are right. Some things are better left unsaid, are they not?'

'Yes.'

'I can only apologise for my behaviour and assure you that it will not be repeated.'

He made her a polite bow and withdrew. As she watched him walk away, a cold weight settled in the pit of her stomach. The last vestiges of sunset splintered through the water in her eyes. She had lost him, but at least she had not lost his respect.

Falconbridge took the first watch that night, wanting time apart from his companions. He found a suitable vantage point among the rocks and settled down to wait, his gaze searching the darkening trail. However, the evening was quiet save for the usual chirring of the insect population, and the occasional murmur of conversation from his men. As he watched, he tried not to let his mind dwell on the recent scene with Sabrina, but it kept returning unbidden. He blamed himself for what had happened, for letting what had been a business arrangement get so out of hand. Her private life was none of his business. Once again she had pulled things back from the brink. He grimaced. At his age he ought to know better. It was just that as soon as she was near, all his good intentions vanished like smoke in the wind. The knowledge made him angry. Had they not got enough problems without his complicating things further?

'I shall conquer this,' he muttered, 'for both our sakes.'

The night passed uneventfully and at first light they saddled the horses and moved on. Now they made better progress but, although the open terrain offered that advantage, it also made them more vulnerable, since they could no longer conceal their presence. Falconbridge was keenly aware of that fact. Before they stopped for the night they needed to find a location that was at least defensible. During the ride that morning he made no attempt to single out Sabrina or to engage her in private speech, though his manner towards her was courteous and correct in every way.

She followed his lead in this. It should have been a relief but the feeling it engendered was quite different. This polite stranger was nothing like the man she had come to know, and she felt the loss keenly. However, pride forbade the utterance of those sentiments she felt in her heart.

Jacinta, riding alongside, cast surreptitious glances

her way from time to time, but did not comment. When she spoke it was of general topics only, though the expression in her dark eyes was more knowing.

Only when they had paused for a brief rest at midday and Sabrina only picked at her portion of food did she allude to the subject at all.

'You must eat to keep up your strength.'

'I'm just not hungry.'

'I think it is not the quality of the food which causes this loss of appetite.' She glanced to where Falconbridge sat talking to the men.

Sabrina followed her glance briefly and then looked away. 'No, I guess it's anxiety about our situation.'

Jacinta nodded. 'There is much to be anxious about, but that is not it either.'

Her companion sighed. It was pointless to deny there was anything wrong; Jacinta had known her too long for that. 'You're right, but I can't talk about it.'

'Time to talk may be running out. Perhaps you should speak while you can and,' she continued, ignoring Sabrina's attempt to interrupt, 'I don't mean to me.'

'There's nothing to speak about.'

'No?'

'No.'

'If you say so,' replied Jacinta. 'After all, you best know your own heart, do you not?'

With that she resumed eating. Her companion shot her a sideways look but Jacinta's gaze was fixed on the distant view. Sabrina sighed. Just then she was afraid to acknowledge what was in her own heart. She stared at the portion of stale bread in her hand. The other woman was right about that at least; she did need to eat. With a determined effort she bit off a lump and began to chew.

Soon after this, the party set off again. Sabrina mentally girded herself for the effort. The long hours in the saddle and the swift pace were tiring. Every muscle ached and flesh grew sore. She thought fondly of a hot bath and a soft bed but knew they were a fantasy, many days' ride away. If they could not outrun the men who followed them she might never be afforded such luxuries again. It was a sobering thought and helped focus her mind on the task in hand.

In the mid-afternoon, as they walked to let the animals breathe awhile, Falconbridge called a brief halt so that he might find a vantage point from which to use the spyglass. What he saw did not please him. He made no attempt to disguise the truth from the others. In any case, his expression would have been enough to tell them.

'They're gaining,' he said.

'We cannot outrun them, sir,' said Blakelock. 'Not when we're a horse down and the rest almost spent.'

'No. We need to find somewhere to take cover.' He did not add, and to make a last stand, but it was understood.

For this purpose they selected a knoll which, though set back some way from the road, permitted a clear view and afforded some large rocks which would give cover under fire. It also precluded the possibility of the enemy sneaking up on them un-awares. They made their camp and secured the horses before setting a watch. The men had rifles and ammunition which, Sabrina knew, would at least give them a chance. It all depended on how many pursuers there were.

Falconbridge used the remaining daylight to study the oncoming force. Eventually he was able to give an accurate estimate of their numbers.

'Twenty,' he said, passing the glass to Blakelock.

The other confirmed it with a nod. 'That's the size of it, sir.'

He did not comment on the fact that their own

party numbered only seven, or that two of the number were women.

'We may be able to hold 'em off for a while, sir, but not for too long.'

'No,' replied Falconbridge, 'but perhaps for long enough.'

He returned and summoned the others. Then he told them the situation. They heard him in stony silence.

'I cannot disguise from you the fact that capture is highly likely,' he said then.

'We can give a good account of ourselves first though, eh?' said Luis.

'We can do better than that.'

'How so?'

Falconbridge reached for the inner pocket of his coat and drew out the slim leather wallet that resided there. 'Whatever happens, these must get to Wellington.'

Jacinta looked from them to him. 'And what are they, *señor?*'

'The documents that I went to Aranjuez to collect. They contain sensitive military information that could change the whole course of the war.' He paused. 'There is no possibility that all of us can get away, but one man might be able to. The rest will have to stay and keep the French occupied for as long as we can to cover his escape.' He looked directly at Ramon. 'Only you have the local knowledge that might enable you to succeed.'

Ramon stared back. 'What you say is true, but how do you know I can be trusted with this? We have known each other only a short time.'

'Miss Huntley trusts you. That's good enough for me.'

Hearing these words, Sabrina felt her heart give a peculiar lurch and she threw Falconbridge a swift glance. However, his attention remained on Ramon.

'Will you do it?'

'I have a duty here, *señor,* and that is to protect *Doña* Sabrina.'

'That's right, and that's why she and Jacinta must go with you. The rest of us will hold off pursuit as long as we can to buy you time.'

Sabrina shook her head. 'We cannot ride as fast as Ramon could alone and we would only slow him down. We must remain and take our chances here.'

'I applaud your courage, my dear, but—'

Sabrina shook her head. 'There is no time to argue, Robert. Ramon must go. Those plans must be delivered or this whole mission will have failed.'

Ramon met her eye. 'I promised your father.'

'And I know what my father would say if he were here now.'

Hearing her reply, Falconbridge felt his heart swell with pride and pleasure. She had so much courage and spirit. Most of the women he had ever met would have been weeping wrecks by now. He would have spoken then, but Jacinta was before him.

'*Doña* Sabrina is right. You have to go, Ramon.'

'*Si,*' said Luis. 'Only you have a chance of success.'

Ramon's dark eyes burned. 'A chance to save myself and leave my friends to die, you would say?'

'No, *amigo mio,* it is a chance to help drive the French from Spain. That is something worth dying for.'

'We knew the risks when we came,' said Sabrina. 'Don't let all this count for nothing.'

The silence that followed her words was deep. Ramon looked round but saw in every face the same resolution.

'I will carry the documents to safety, but I will not leave you to die.'

Falconbridge frowned. 'I don't follow.'

'You are right when you say I have local knowledge, *señor,* but it is not confined merely to the geography of this region. I know its people, too.' He glanced back down the trail. 'People like Valdez, for example—and also El Cuchillo.'

They stared at him in slack-jawed astonishment for all present knew the name of the guerrilla leader.

'You know El Cuchillo?' said Luis.

'Our paths have crossed before.'

'You never told me this.'

'You never asked.'

'That is not the point.'

Blakelock frowned. 'What has El Cuchillo got to do with anything?'

'His camp is in these hills, and not so far from here, either,' replied Ramon. 'If I can find it I may be able to bring reinforcements.'

'Why would he help us?'

'He has helped the British before.'

Falconbridge nodded. 'That's true, but even if you found him and he agreed to come, time is not on our side.'

'Then the sooner I leave the better.'

'Agreed. But do nothing to jeopardise the safety of those papers.'

'I give you my word.'

They watched Ramon stow the leather wallet inside his jacket. Jacinta prepared some rations in a small bundle and then they went with him to the horses. He mounted and raised a hand in salute.

'*Hasta luego.*'

Sabrina summoned a smile. She thought that the chances of them meeting again were remote, in this life anyway, but it served no purpose to say so. Instead she watched in silence as he turned the horse's head and rode away.

'I pray he may succeed,' murmured Falconbridge.

The sound of that voice jolted her from her thoughts. For the first time it sounded less than completely confident, and in that moment she glimpsed the strain he must be under, being answerable for their safety and for the success of this mission. He had always seemed so self-assured and so impervious to doubt or fear. It was oddly touching to discover that he was as human as the rest of them underneath that cool exterior.

'If anyone can do it, I think it is he,' she replied.

'You have great faith in him.'

'He has never let me down yet. Whatever happens, he will ensure the plans get to Lord Wellington, somehow.'

'Then this mission will not have been in vain.'

'I know it will not.' Her eyes met his. 'In the meantime, we must do as Luis says and give a good account of ourselves.'

'You have never done anything else.'

The words were quietly spoken but the tone was unmistakably genuine, like the look in his eyes. A look that caused her heart to beat faster. A look that must be resisted at all costs. Besides, she had doubts of her own which she needed to voice.

'If…when…Ramon delivers those papers to Wellington, will my father still be freed? Even if I do not return, I mean?'

'When the papers are delivered, the mission will have succeeded. The agreement will be honoured.'

He saw her smile then, a sad and wistful smile that tore at his heart. Just then he would have given anything to have her safe, to have her a thousand miles from here in some haven where nothing could harm her again.

'I am glad,' she replied, 'and all this will have been worthwhile.'

The words reminded him with force about why she had come on this mission in the first place. Her decision had had nothing to do with him per se, though when they were thrown together, she seemed to find his company agreeable enough. It was he who had overstepped the mark, and she who tried to keep their relationship within professional bounds. He had no right to make things harder than they already were.

He smiled. 'All may yet be well.'

'Yes.' She hoped, rather than believed, it to be true.

Chapter Nine

The French force came into view in the early evening. They were riding slowly, no doubt having pushed their horses before. From her position on the knoll Sabrina could see the blue uniforms and distinctive grey shakos. At their head was a rider on a dun horse.

'The man, Valdez,' said Luis, and spat into the dust.

Blakelock smiled grimly, lining the distant figure in his sights. 'Shall I blow his brains out, sir?'

'No, he is mine,' replied Luis.

'Don't fire yet,' said Falconbridge. 'Let them get closer.'

Sabrina glanced at Jacinta and received a faint answering smile. She wished they, too, had rifles. Pistols were only of real use at closer range. Once they were discharged would there be time to reload before the enemy reached the top of the hill? After that it would be hand-to-hand fighting. Her

stomach knotted. The encounter with brigands she
and her father had once experienced was vivid still
in memory, and there had been far fewer of them.
Brigands were bad enough. Trained soldiers were
another matter entirely. Even if Falconbridge and the
other men could pick off some of the French con-
tingent, they would still be badly outnumbered.

She turned again to Jacinta. 'I'm so sorry to have
got you into this.'

'It was the French who got us into this, not you,
Doña Sabrina.'

'It's true,' said Luis. 'We were involved from the
moment they invaded our country. We will make
them bear the consequences.'

Sabrina looked down the hillside and saw that the
troop had halted. The figure on the dun horse was
riding ahead alone at a slow walk, his attention on
the ground immediately in front of him.

'The bastard's looking for sign,' muttered
Blakelock.

Willis nodded. 'Aye, and it'll not take him long
to work out what's happened.'

Luis bared his teeth in a feral smile. 'Good. It
means I shoot him all the sooner. That will teach
the scum to betray his countrymen.'

A few minutes later the dun horse stopped and
its rider looked directly up at the knoll. Then he
turned back and rejoined his companions. Evidently

words were spoken, and they saw him point towards their place of concealment. The troop dismounted. Leaving their horses they began to fan out, moving slowly forwards towards the slope.

'Here they come,' said Falconbridge. 'Get ready.'

Sabrina's heart hammered in her breast and in spite of the heat she felt cold sweat start along her skin. Just feet away Blakelock's finger squeezed the trigger. There followed a loud report and a French trooper cried out and fell. Almost simultaneously a second shot rang out and the tracker dropped like a stone.

Luis smiled with grim satisfaction. *'Bueno!'*

Blakelock threw him a sideways glance. 'Not bad shooting—for a Spaniard of course.'

'Keep watching, Englishman. I'll show you how it's done.'

Seeing two of their number go down, the rest of the French force dived for cover among the rocks. Moments later they began to return fire. Luis darted a glance at the two women.

'You must stay down.'

'Thank you for that,' replied Jacinta. 'The thought would not otherwise have occurred to us.'

He returned her a pointed look but had no time to reply because, just then, the answering fire intensified. Lead shot whined around them. The higher ground afforded the defenders an advantage and two more French soldiers fell. Then some of their comrades advanced, dodging among the rocks and bushes, while the rest gave covering fire.

Falconbridge looked across at Sabrina. 'Are you all right?'

'Yes.'

'Good girl.'

His smile gave her fresh courage and she returned it. 'I was never in a battle before.'

'When you shoot, aim for the widest part of the man's body. Make each shot count.'

'I will.'

He nodded and then turned his attention back to the task in hand. They needed to lower the odds before the French reached their position and they were reduced to hand-to-hand combat. He tried not to think about what would happen then; tried not to think about Sabrina and Jacinta run through by French sabres, and his men slain. Soldiers accepted the risks of warfare, but women were another matter. He knew he would defend them to the death, but would that be enough? Lining up his target he squeezed off another shot. A man yelled, clutching his arm. Falconbridge smiled grimly and reloaded.

Sabrina crouched behind a rock, pistol drawn. With pounding heart she risked a peek round the edge of the sheltering stone and saw blue-coated figures only fifty yards away. Soon they would be overrun. Her jaw tightened. This was no time for cowardice. If she went down, it would be fighting. Glancing at her companions, she knew there was no company she would rather die in.

A blue-coat rose up from behind a rock. Without thinking she lifted the pistol, aimed and fired. The man cried out and pitched backwards. Hurriedly, she reached for ball and powder to reload. Beside her Jacinta loosed off a shot of her own. Somewhere nearby a man cursed. Around them the air thickened with smoke and the acrid scent of powder. They heard Willis swear and clutch his sleeve. Blood welled through his fingers. Sabrina shoved the pistol in her belt and dropped into a crouching run, reaching him a few moments later.

'How bad is it?'

'Just a crease, ma'am,' he said between gritted teeth.

'Hold still. I'll bind it for you.'

She improvised a bandage from a handkerchief and neckcloth and tied it firmly. He smiled his thanks. Then retrieving his rifle, he reloaded. A blue-coated figure loomed above their crouching figures. Sabrina saw the shadow and looked up in horrified surprise. Her throat dried. She had a fleeting impression of the raised sword before a shot rang out and the man slumped. She spun round to see the smoking rifle in Falconbridge's hands, and swallowed hard, her gaze meeting his for a moment. The expression in his eyes sent a shiver through her; it was utterly uncompromising, the look of a man who would kill to defend his own. She stammered out her thanks and saw him nod.

'My pleasure.'

Out of the corner of her eye she saw a blur of movement and turned in horror to see that the vanguard of the French force had reached the top of the knoll. Falconbridge followed her gaze and his jaw tightened. Letting fall the rifle he drew his sword and launched himself into the attack, fighting now for all he held dear. He felt the blade connect with flesh; heard a cry and saw his opponent slump. Moments later another took his place. Again Falconbridge was on the offensive, keeping up the momentum, not giving his enemy even a moment to pause, using every means at his disposal to win. Finesse had no part in this; it was fierce and dirty with fists and boots supplementing steel.

Just a few feet away Sabrina drew her own blade and prepared to meet the nearest foe. The Frenchman's face registered surprise and then amusement as he took in the nature of his opponent. The hesitation cost him dear as the edge of her sword slashed his arm. Blood bloomed through the torn fabric. For a split second he stared at the wound in outrage and disbelief. Then his expression hardened and he pressed forward his attack. She fought as well as she knew how but determined resistance wasn't enough. Superior skill and strength forced her into retreat, step by step, until her back slammed against stone. Trapped against a boulder with no room to manoeuvre she knew she was lost. The Frenchman smiled. Sickened she watched him raise the blade for the *coup de grâce*.

And then, before her terrified gaze, her opponent checked, his face a mask of astonishment. The sabre dropped from his fingers and his legs buckled. Jacinta tugged her sword point from between his ribs. For a moment her gaze met Sabrina's and the dark eyes glowed with inner fire. Then she smiled.

Sabrina found her voice. 'Thank you.'

'*De nada.*'

Before she could say more, an armed figure rose up behind her. Sabrina yelled a warning. Jacinta spun round, but not quickly enough to avoid the swinging rifle. The butt connected with the side of her head and felled her instantly. The assailant stepped across the prone body towards Sabrina. Too late he saw the mouth of the pistol pointing at him. There was a sharp report and he fell, clutching a hole in his chest. However, Sabrina's attention was no longer on him.

'Jacinta!'

In a moment she was kneeling beside her companion, desperately trying to rouse her. A bloody gash and a lump testified to the site of the injury. Jacinta groaned. Sabrina felt relief flood back. She wasn't dead, only stunned. Her frantic gaze cast about for something to staunch the wound with. Then, without warning, she was seized from behind. Strong hands drew her upright. She fought them, kicking and struggling to free herself but the grip was like steel, pinning her arms behind her back and holding them like a vice. Casting a wild look around, she saw with sinking heart that the knoll was overrun and the fighting all but over. Blakelock and Luis were now held at gunpoint. Only Willis and Falconbridge were still engaged in combat but, hopelessly outnumbered, they were driven to stand at bay against a high rock. Then she heard a voice.

'Throw down your weapons. Further resistance is useless.'

She saw Falconbridge hesitate and for one dreadful moment thought he was going to refuse. Then he glanced around, taking in the whole scene, and nodded to Willis.

'Do as he says.'

The two men let fall their swords. As they did so

the speaker advanced and a French officer strode into her line of vision. With him went the last vestige of hope and her stomach churned as she recognised Machart. For a moment he, too, cast a comprehensive look around. Then his gaze returned to Falconbridge.

'I was hoping we'd meet again, Monsieur le Comte. Though I think that is not the name by which you were known on the occasion of our first meeting.' He paused. 'Arroyo de Molinos, was it not?'

Falconbridge returned the gaze with a cool and insolent stare. 'I have no idea what you're talking about.'

'Come now. I admit my memory was faulty at first but I never forget a face,' the other went on. 'You have put me to a deal of trouble, monsieur, but I feel certain the effort will be repaid in due course.' He turned his attention towards Sabrina, his gaze taking in every detail of her altered appearance. His face registered sardonic amusement, though the smile stopped well short of his eyes. 'It is a pleasure to see you again, madame. I look forward to renewing our acquaintance.'

Her stomach wallowed. She fought it, knowing this man would be very quick to sense fear. With a supreme effort she forced herself to meet his gaze and to remain silent. She would not bandy words with him.

He gestured to his men. 'Bind the prisoners and fetch their horses.'

'You are out of your jurisdiction here,' said Falconbridge, 'and have no authority to detain us.'

Machart appeared untroubled. 'I believe I have the authority to apprehend a group of English spies. Of course, if I am mistaken I shall apologise, but I do not think I am mistaken.'

'Where are you taking us?'

'To Castillo San Angel, where we shall discuss the matter of identities.'

Sabrina darted a glance at Falconbridge but his expression was impassive and he remained still while they bound his wrists. Then her attention was reclaimed by rough hands binding her own. She made a token gesture of resistance but it was useless. When tested the cords yield not a whit. A few minutes later she and the others were manhandled down the slope and forced to mount their horses. It was then that she realised Jacinta wasn't with them. Had they left her for dead? Then she remembered what happened to the wounded after a battle, and fear congealed to a lump in her stomach. Perhaps the French had believed her already dead. If Jacinta had been conscious she would have had enough sense to remain quite still. How bad was her injury? There were predators in the mountains other than the human sort. Could she survive out here alone, at least long enough to make it to the nearest village perhaps? If so, there might be hope for her. She was brave and resourceful. If anyone would survive it would be her. At least she was not a prisoner and there was some comfort in that.

The cavalcade set off and her attention refocused on staying in the saddle. The pace was swift and conversation impossible. Besides, Falconbridge was in front of her. Suddenly her fear was all for him. *Everyone talks by the third day.* She was certain now that Machart would use every means at his disposal to find out what he wanted to know. She had never heard of Castillo San Angel but it bode ill for her and her companions. Where was it exactly?

They had not long to wait and find out, for in the early evening they came to a small castle, perhaps once the seat of a minor nobleman. Sabrina eyed it uneasily. It seemed to be quite old, judging from the state of the perimeter wall, and an attempt had been made to repair the worst areas of crumbling masonry. The stout timbers of the gate were faded and cracked. As they rode through she could see weeds growing among the stones in the courtyard and the buildings had an air of dilapidation. The place must have been commandeered for use as a military base, she decided. Certainly it held an uncomfortably large number of French troops.

Sabrina and her companions were dragged from the saddle and taken through an archway, along a wide inner corridor and down a flight of stone steps. They found themselves in an underground vault lit by torches. Although it now doubled as a prison, it had originally been intended solely for storage. The dim light revealed barrels and sacks and coils of rope. It was distinctly cool down here, the air musty. Several doors led off the main chamber. Their captors unlocked one of these and she and Falconbridge were shoved into the room beyond; the others taken to the adjoining chamber. Machart paused on the threshold. Then he spoke to his men.

'Untie their bonds.'

He watched as the order was obeyed. Then he smiled faintly. 'You see, I am not so unfeeling as to separate a husband and wife. Enjoy each other's company while you can.'

With that, he and his men withdrew and the door slammed shut behind them. A key turned in the lock. At the sound, Sabrina shivered inwardly. From the passage outside she heard men's voices and then the sound of retreating footsteps. Automatically she massaged her bruised wrists. Falconbridge frowned.

'Are you all right, Sabrina? Have they hurt you?'

'No, I'm unharmed.'

'Hardly that,' he replied, looking round. 'I'm so sorry that I have brought you to this.'

She shook her head. 'It isn't your fault.'

'Who else should bear the blame but I?'

'You tried to dissuade me from coming along, but I insisted.'

'I should have moved heaven and earth to prevent it.'

'It would have made no difference.'

He returned a wry smile. 'No, I suppose it wouldn't, at that.'

She glanced around. The room was bare save for a small stool and a rough wooden cot on which lay a sacking mattress filled with straw. It was covered by a dirty blanket. A bucket in one corner served as a privy. A small, barred window set high in the wall was the only source of light. She guessed it corresponded roughly with ground level outside. The only exit was the door, three inches of iron-studded oak.

'They did not bring Jacinta,' she said.

Falconbridge frowned and immediately felt a twinge of guilt. In all the confusion he had not noticed the maid's absence.

'She was hit on the head with a rifle butt,' Sabrina continued. 'I was trying to ascertain the damage when we were overrun.'

'It may be just a concussion. If so, she will be recovered soon enough.'

'I pray she will be able to reach help—a village perhaps—though I don't know how far that might be.'

'By my estimation we were about ten miles from Burgohondo, but it's entirely possible she might find a small farmstead en route.' He paused. 'Jacinta strikes me as being resourceful. If anyone could survive it would be she.'

'She is resourceful, and brave, too.'

'She is not alone in that,' he replied. 'I saw you fight back there.'

'Not too well. Had it not been for you and Jacinta I'd have been run through.' She hesitated. 'I have not thanked you properly for saving my life.'

'I beg you will not mention it.'

'How can I not when I owe you so much?'

'You owe me nothing. Comrades look out for each other.' The words were accompanied by a faint smile. They were also meant to absolve her of obligation and keep their relationship on a professional footing. He was right to do it, she thought, but her dominant emotion was one of sadness.

She nodded. 'Yes, of course.'

For a moment he scrutinised her in silence. 'You must be exhausted, Sabrina. Why don't you try to get some rest?'

'What about you?'

'I'm not tired yet,' he lied. 'Besides, after the time we've spent on horseback it will be good to stand for a while.'

She moved across to the pallet, eyeing it with distaste. The mattress smelt musty and she tried not to think about how old it was or how many other occupants the cot might have had. She stretched out and let her aching muscles relax a little. Beneath veiling lashes she saw Falconbridge move away to the door, glancing out through the narrow metal lattice, apparently deep in thought. Once, she might have found this close confinement intimidating, but now his presence was a comfort. She had not been deceived by his earlier protestations; he, too, must be tired yet he had given up the cot to her use. His manner now could not have been more different from the one she had seen at first. It revealed a gentleness that she would never have suspected then.

Unbidden, Machart's face returned and with it, his words. *Enjoy each other's company while you can.* She shivered, trying not to think of the implication behind that, or what the morrow might bring. Now more than ever she was glad that Jacinta was free, and Ramon, too. At least the plans were safe and well out of Machart's grasp, and at the end of it all her father would be delivered from imprisonment. Not a total failure then, she thought.

Falconbridge remained where he was for some time, trying to order his thoughts. He was under no illusions about what lay ahead for him and his men if Machart discovered the truth. Spies were shot. It was a risk one took and while he might regret that matters had not turned out better, he could not be so philosophical where Sabrina was concerned. He could try to appeal to his captor's sense of honour and ask that she be set free, but suspected that Machart's notion of honour was not the same as his own. He could plead her youth and innocence if it would do any good.

He glanced at the cot. She lay quite still, eyes closed, her breathing soft and regular. She had never once reproached him for their predicament or shown any fear. His admiration and his regard had grown proportionately. She was indeed the rarest of women. He would have liked to know her better; to court her as a young woman should be courted. It was too late for that now, but he would no longer try to deny the depth of feeling she inspired in him; a feeling he had never expected to experience again.

He sighed and crossed quietly to the sleeping figure. Reaching for the blanket, he opened it out and laid it over her. Although it was only a meagre covering, it was better than nothing, for the air was cool down here. Then he sat down on the stool and watched her sleep. Her face looked very peaceful, the expression untroubled as though she had not a care in the world. He knew that face so well now, every line and curve. Its beauty haunted his dreams. Clarissa had been beautiful, but her beauty was of a different kind. Sabrina's owed nothing to artifice of any sort. She would be lovely when she was fifty— if she lived so long. His jaw tightened. If by some miracle they got out of this with a whole skin he would make it his mission to ensure nothing harmed her again.

At some point he must have dozed because he came to with a start. His neck and limbs felt stiff. It was darker now and the only light a faint ruddy glow through the lattice from the torch-lit corridor outside. He got to his feet and straightened slowly, wincing as his muscles protested. A glance at the bed revealed that Sabrina was sleeping still, though more restlessly now, huddled beneath the thin blanket. He reached out and touched her hand lightly. The skin was cold. He saw her shiver, and roll onto her side, drawing the cover closer. As he saw it, he knew there was one useful service he could perform.

He lay down beside her and curled his body protectively around hers, holding her close, sharing his warmth. She stirred a little but did not wake. He dropped a kiss on her hair and closed his eyes, trying not to think that this might be all they would ever have. However, as the shivering stopped and her warmth returned, the thought persisted. He would have liked to seize the moment and explore in intimate detail every curve of the body pressed so close to his; to know her in every sense of the word. There was a spark; it would not take much to fan it to a flame. If he did, would she perhaps surrender in the name of some brief, dubious comfort? He sighed. Even if honour had not forbidden it, he cared too much ever to take such blatant advantage.

He slept soon after, weary after the exertions of the day, and woke in the early dawn. Grey light was filtering through the bars in the high window. He glanced at his companion but she was still dead to the world. He smiled faintly. Unwilling to wake her yet, he drew the coverlet a little higher and remained where he was. In truth he did not want this brief intimacy to end. Despite the primitive surroundings it felt good to lie here quietly thus, to hold her in his arms again.

She began to rouse a little later, surfacing from deep sleep to a comfortable doze, and turned instinctively towards the source of the warmth. He gently kissed her parted lips. She smiled and her mouth yielded to his. The kiss grew deep and lingering. With a supreme and heart-thumping effort of will he drew back. Sabrina opened her eyes and looked into his face.

He smiled. 'Good morning.'

She stretched lazily and returned the greeting.

'I won't ask if you slept well for I know that you did,' he continued.

She was suddenly very still and he saw the green eyes widen as the nature of their situation became truly apparent. 'Robert! What…?'

'Have no fear. I merely wanted to keep you warm.'

'Keep me warm?'

'You were shivering last night so I took the liberty of sharing some body heat.' He paused. 'Besides, I was tired, too, and there is but one bed.'

'You mean that you…that we…you were here all night?'

'That's right.'

She knew then that she had not dreamed his kiss. The realisation sent a deeper warmth to the core of her being. This sudden enforced intimacy should have been shocking and repellent but it wasn't. Instead it felt comforting; somehow it felt right and good. It wasn't only that either: his presence took the edge off her fear, rather than adding to it.

Misinterpreting her silence he added, 'It was about shared bodily warmth, Sabrina, nothing more.'

Hearing the gentleness in his voice she felt a lump form in her throat. If he were dishonourable he could have taken full advantage of the situation. He was bigger and stronger and even if she had fought, he'd have overpowered her without undue trouble, secure in the knowledge that even if she had screamed for help no one would have come to her aid.

'I know,' she replied.

It wasn't what he had been expecting. 'Then you do not suspect a more sinister motive?'

'No.'

She made to sit up but his arm checked her. 'Stay awhile. It's early yet.'

She lay quite still, heart thumping, every fibre of her body aware of him. Feeling the tension in her stillness he regarded her quizzically.

'What are you afraid of?'

'Nothing.'

'Not so. Will you not tell me?'

How to tell him it was not him she feared but her own desires? If he only knew how close to the surface they lay...

'Sabrina?'

Suddenly the handsome face was closer to her own, his gaze searching. His lips were dangerously close now. If he kissed her she would not be able to help herself and he would take it as an invitation. The thought of what would inevitably follow turned her loins to fire. How easy it would be to surrender, to give in and let desire take its course. And if she did, what then? If they ever got out of this alive, how would he regard her after? In his eyes, she would be no better than a whore. She could hear the echo of Denton's voice: *Come…you know you want it. We have all afternoon…make the most of it.* Desire was replaced by flooding shame. There could only be one end to surrender now and she knew full well what it meant. Experience was the best teacher. The thought of Robert Falconbridge regarding her in those terms was unbearable. To hide her confusion she turned her head aside. Mistaking the reason for it, he drew back a little.

'It's all right, my dear. You don't have to say anything.' He stroked the hair off her face. 'Go back to sleep for a while.'

She turned onto her side and felt his body curve round hers once more. Closing her eyes, she let herself relax, pushing aside all thoughts of the future, content just to be in the moment. And so he held her while she drowsed and let his arms provide at least the illusion of security.

Some time later they were roused by the sound of voices and heavy footfalls in the passageway without. Falconbridge was on his feet in an instant, listening intently. Sabrina came to stand beside him, her face pale.

'They have come for us.'

'Come for me,' he replied.

'Oh, Robert, I'm so afraid.'

He squeezed her arm. 'If you are questioned, my dear, you must stick to your story.'

She nodded. 'I will.'

'If Machart finds the slightest discrepancy in what we say he will exploit it. For all our sakes we must continue to sing from the same hymn sheet.'

'I understand.'

The footsteps stopped outside the door and a key turned in the lock. The door swung open to reveal four French soldiers. Two of them seized hold of Falconbridge.

'What do you want?' he demanded.

They made no answer save to bind his wrists.

Sabrina started forwards. 'What are you doing? Where are you taking him?'

The questions still elicited no response. They merely hustled their prisoner from the room and locked the door behind them. Sabrina rushed to the lattice and peered out, craning her neck to watch the retreating figures until they disappeared from view. Then, weak-kneed, she leaned against the wood and prayed quietly.

* * *

Falconbridge had known what to expect, but the pain still took him by surprise. Wrists bound, he crouched on the stone floor, gasping, waiting for the next kick from the booted feet in his line of vision. Every breath brought sharp protest from his bruised ribs. Blood trickled from the cut on his lip. His face throbbed from repeated blows. Rough hands hauled him to his feet so he could see his interrogator.

'I'll ask you again. Who are you?' Machart's voice reached him through the haze.

'I've already told you.' He gasped as a fist connected with his solar plexus.

'And I told you, I never forget a face. You were at Arroyo de Molinos.'

Falconbridge gritted his teeth. 'Someone who looked like me perhaps.'

'You play me for a fool, monsieur, and that is most unwise.' Machart nodded to the guards. Several more blows thudded into the prisoner's midriff, doubling him over. 'Tell me the truth and spare yourself more pain. What were you doing at Aranjuez?'

'You know. You were there.'

'What is your relationship with De la Torre?'

'He is my cousin.'

Machart's lip curled. 'Do you know I don't believe you?'

A heavy fist smashed into Falconbridge's jaw. He felt warm blood trickle from the resulting cut.

'No, I think you are a spy,' the Frenchman continued. 'I think your reason for visiting Aranjuez was something other than a social obligation, and I mean to find out what.'

The reply was an insolent stare. It drew down on the prisoner several more hard blows. He bit back the cry of pain that rose to his lips unbidden. This was just the softening-up process. Machart hadn't really got started yet. When he did, Falconbridge wondered how long he could hold out.

'Perhaps a flogging would help to loosen his tongue,' said a voice from across the room.

Falconbridge registered the rodent face of Jean Laroche. As soon as he had set eyes on the intelligence chief he knew his presence here meant serious trouble. Did they already suspect De la Torre of subterfuge? Had they been keeping an eye on him anyway? Or was this interrogation merely because Machart's memory had returned? He hoped for De la Torre's sake it was the latter.

'Not yet,' replied Machart. 'I have a better idea.'

'What?'

'We'll ask the woman.'

Cold dread congealed in Falconbridge's gut. 'Leave her alone. She's done nothing wrong and she can't tell you any more than I can.'

Machart regarded him speculatively for a moment. 'We shall ascertain that soon enough.' He looked beyond the prisoner to the guards. 'Bring her here.'

Chapter Ten

Sabrina heard boots on stone in the outer passageway and got to her feet, hoping it was Falconbridge returning. Her heart leapt as the key turned in the lock. However, it wasn't her companion who entered the cell. Seeing the two guards she lifted her chin, eyeing them with distaste.

'What do you want?'

'Someone desires a word with you, madam,' replied the first.

Her heart sank but there was no possibility of refusal. They took hold of her arms and escorted her out of the cell and back towards the stairs. She took a deep breath, resisting panic. It was happening, the thing she had subconsciously been dreading. From somewhere she dredged up the remains of courage, praying it would not be she who broke under questioning and so betrayed her companions.

She was taken along another corridor and brought at length to a wooden door. The guards knocked and a familiar voice bade them enter. The hairs on the back of her neck stood up. Then she was drawn across the threshold to be confronted by Machart and Laroche.

'Ah, Condesa, what a pleasure.'

Machart's greeting went unheeded. All her attention was on Falconbridge, her shocked gaze taking in the details of his battered face.

'What have you done to him?'

'Nothing much—yet,' replied Machart.

The pleasant tone sent a shiver through her. Unwilling to let him see her fear she faced him, forcing herself to meet his eye.

'By what right do you hold us here? By what right have you assaulted my husband?' It surprised her how naturally that word had tripped from her tongue.

'By the authority of His Majesty King Joseph. Your husband is an English spy.'

'That is nonsense.'

'Is it? We shall see.'

She darted a swift look at Falconbridge and met his steady gaze. In that instant she understood her own heart. If this was the end of the road she would die with him, and gladly, too. He would have no cause to be ashamed of her at the last.

'I have brought you here to help clarify a few points that have eluded us so far,' Machart continued.

He moved closer, his predatory gaze lingering a moment on her face. One hand stroked her cheek. Sabrina jerked her head aside. Machart bared his teeth in a smile.

Falconbridge glared at him. 'Leave her alone.'

'If you wish us to leave her alone you will tell us what we want to know,' said Laroche. 'It would be a pity to spoil such beauty.'

'You cowardly scum.' The defiant tone gave no hint of the sick dread that gripped him now.

'Oh, I don't think it will be necessary to go to such extremes,' said Machart. 'I believe I know what will work just as well, and will be infinitely more enjoyable.' He turned to the guards. 'Tie him to that chair.'

Falconbridge struggled but it was a token resistance only. Two minutes later he was securely bound. The sick feeling in his gut intensified but his fear was not for himself.

Laroche frowned. 'What do you intend?'

'To discover the truth,' replied Machart. 'If you will permit me some time alone with madam, I believe we shall arrive at it very soon.'

'As you will.' Laroche rose from his seat. 'Just don't take too long.'

'Not long at all, I assure you.' Machart glanced at the guards and jerked his head towards the door. 'Get out.'

When they and Laroche had left, he turned back to Sabrina. 'Now, madam, you are going to help me discover what I wish to know.'

'I will never lift a finger to help you.'

'On the contrary, I think you will be invaluable.' He glanced at the bound figure across the room. 'And you will do everything I demand.'

Falconbridge fought the restraining cords but they held fast. 'If you harm her, you filth, I'll kill you.'

'It seems to me that you are not in a position to make threats,' replied the Frenchman. 'Besides, it is not my intention to harm the lady.'

Sabrina gave him a cold stare, though her heart was thumping in her breast. 'Then what do you intend, Colonel?'

'I've been looking forward to renewing our acquaintance, madam. I intend us to forge a more intimate bond.'

Her jaw tightened as the import of the words became clear. 'Never.'

Machart seized hold of her waist and dragged her up against him, bringing his mouth down hard on hers. Taken by surprise, sickened and half-stifled by fetid breath, she struggled hard. It availed her nothing. He took the kiss at leisure before allowing her to come up for air. Furious she struck out at him, the slap ringing loud in the quiet room.

'Let go of me, you oaf!'

The response was a chilling smile. Without warning a large hand shot out and closed on her throat. She gasped, her hands clawing, trying to break his hold, but he held her easily. Through the drumming blood in her ears she heard Falconbridge's shouted protest; then the Frenchman's face was thrust towards her own.

'Looking forward to renewing the acquaintance and intending to make the most of it,' he continued.

His hold never slackened as he forced her backwards across the room to the desk. With his free arm he swept everything from its surface, scattering documents, sending paperweight, blotter and pens flying. Then he forced Sabrina down, pinning her against the wood with his weight.

'Soon now your husband will tell me everything I wish to know.'

Across the room, Falconbridge fought his bonds, unaware of the blood that trickled over his wrists. 'Let her go, you blackguard.'

'After going to such trouble to find her again? I think not.' Machart released his grip on her throat and reached for the fastenings of her breeches. Gasping for breath Sabrina tried to rise. A slap across the cheek sent her reeling back. Then he resumed, accomplishing the task with little trouble. 'No, I have other plans entirely.'

Sabrina felt her clothing loosen and then coarse hands sliding beneath her shirt to her breasts. She tried to scream but her bruised throat permitted only a faint croak. Frantic hands clawed at the face looming over hers. He slapped her again. Moments later her wrists were imprisoned and clamped to the desk. Then his mouth closed over hers, hot and hard, forcing her jaw open, his tongue thrusting in. She could feel his erection against her thigh. Sick with horror she writhed beneath him.

Machart released her mouth and looked into her face. 'Believe me, madam, when I've finished you will not think of your husband's embraces again, I promise you.'

'No!' Sabrina thrashed. 'Please, no! Let go of me!'

'Let go?' His smile mocked her. 'Later perhaps, but first your husband is going to watch while I take you.'

Falconbridge's grey eyes locked with the Frenchman's for a moment. 'You cur! You filthy little cur!'

'Jealous, monsieur? You should be. Watch and you will learn.' He leaned closer and spoke to Sabrina. 'You are about to discover what it is that you've been missing.' He paused. 'Don't you want me to tell you?' Leaning forwards he murmured words for her ear alone. Their effect was to make her struggle harder. Seeing her desperation increase, he smiled. 'I'm going to give you the time of your life.'

Suddenly four years rolled away. Machart's face blurred and dissolved until all she could see was Jack Denton's leer, hear his mocking tone as he held her down: *Like it rough, do you? Well, by God, Jack's your man.* The memory brought welling fury and disgust that overrode fear. Her current persecutor was strong, too, but she knew she would rather die than submit.

Machart reached for the fastenings of his own clothing. She felt him shove her thighs apart. In desperation she brought her knees up, hand groping along the top of her boot, seeking the blade concealed there. He misinterpreted the movement and smiled.

'Not so reluctant after all then? Be assured, *ma chère,* you'll get what you want.'

Sabrina stifled a sob, her fingers scrabbling against leather. Machart fumbled for the last buttons on his breeches. They held. She heard him curse softly, saw him look away, intent on the task. It was enough. She darted a glance towards her boot and located what she sought. Her fingers closed round the hilt of the knife. The last buttons released their hold and Machart leaned forwards, his weight crushing her against the desk. Sabrina took a deep breath and drew the blade, bringing the point up under his ribs in one swift movement and driving it in as hard as she could. Flesh proved more resistant than she had imagined. For a few seconds he froze an expression of sheer astonishment on his face as he took in the knife.

'You bitch!'

With a sharp indrawn breath he pulled it out and clapped a hand to his side.

Feeling the warm blood on his palm he glanced down and his expression became murderous. Then he lunged for her. She rolled to evade the groping hand and tumbled over the edge of the desk to land sprawling on the floor amid the strewn stationery. Her fingertips brushed something small and solid, a glass paperweight. She grabbed it just before Machart's fist seized her jacket and hauled her upright. Swinging round, Sabrina struck out. The paperweight caught him across the side of the head and sent him staggering backwards. He lost his balance and fell, hitting the floor with a heavy thud, and then lay still. Trembling with revulsion she stared at the silent form, unable to believe what she had done. Then her horrified gaze turned to the other occupant of the room. His eyes spoke of pity and anger and pride.

'Oh, my dear, brave girl.'

The words were softly spoken and they recalled another man in another place, another witness to her humiliation. She had been much younger then but all her former sense of shame and fear returned. For a moment she thought she might be sick. With shaking hands she hurriedly reordered her clothing, appalled to the depths of her soul that he of all men should have observed the scene, and wanting nothing so much as for the earth to open up and swallow her whole.

'Sabrina, can you find the knife?'

She took a deep breath and looked about distractedly. The blade lay just feet away beside the desk. With a grimace of distaste, she bent and retrieved it. Moments later Falconbridge was free.

'Good girl.'

He staggered to his feet, stifling a gasp. Instinctively she reached out to steady him. Then his arms were round her, warm, protective, holding her close. For a while her body shook with reaction. Unable to speak she drew in long sobbing breaths, her face white. Its deathly pallor shocked him to the core.

'My dearest girl. I'm so sorry. So very sorry.'

At last she found her voice. 'I think I've killed him, Robert.' She ought to have been glad but the feeling engendered was one of sick horror.

'If you have, no man deserved it more.' He drew in a sharp breath, dreading to ask the next question. 'Sabrina, did he...?'

'No.'

His throat tightened and he knew a moment of relief more intense than any in his life before. Silently, he thanked God. 'I never saw anything so brave as you this day.'

Tears flowed down her face unbidden. 'I did not feel brave, only frightened.'

'That is scarce to be wondered at.' He held her gently at arm's length. 'Let us not waste the chance you have won for us.'

Suddenly the wider peril impinged upon her thoughts once more. 'What are we going to do, Robert?'

'Get out of here,' he replied.

She looked at his cut and swollen face. 'You're injured. They must have hurt you terribly.'

'I've known worse.'

He released his hold and crossed the room. His bruised ribs protested as he bent to retrieve the Frenchman's sword. Then he hurriedly checked the drawers in the desk. One side proved quite useless, the other revealed a pistol which he lost no time in appropriating.

'Machart dismissed the guards but the chances are they haven't gone far,' he said. 'We need to take care of them first. Then we can set our companions free.'

'Tell me what I must do.'

'Take this.' He handed her the pistol. 'If you need to use it, shoot to kill.'

Her stomach wallowed at the thought, but she nodded. Quietly, he opened the door and glanced out. The corridor was empty of other human presences. Clearly the guards had taken Machart at his word. Sabrina's heart thumped and with every step she expected to hear a shouted challenge. However, none came. Not until they reached the stairs leading to the underground vault did they see any sign of life, one man on duty. Falconbridge ducked back out sight.

'Can you distract his attention while I come up behind him?'

Dumbly, she nodded assent. Shaking her hair loose over her shoulders she opened the front of her shirt to reveal the upper curves of her breasts. Then, assuming what she hoped was a provocative stance she summoned all her courage and strolled forwards. The guard turned, regarding her with astonishment; then he reached for his musket, levelling it at her.

'Who goes there?'

She surveyed him coolly, praying her voice would not shake. 'I am the Condesa de Ordoñez y Casal.'

'The Condesa is Colonel Machart's prisoner.'

'No,' she replied. 'As from now, his mistress.' Seeing him hesitate she forced a smile. 'The

Colonel really knows how to appreciate a woman, doesn't he?'

Seeing her dishevelled appearance the guard returned a knowing grin and opened his mouth to reply. The words were never uttered because the hilt of a sword dealt him a blow to the head and felled him in an instant. Falconbridge surveyed the still form and then looked at his companion.

'Wonderful girl! Get his musket and powder horn. We'll need them.'

While she obeyed, he retrieved the bunch of keys from the man's belt. Then he and Sabrina hurried down the steps to the cells. A minute later the door was unlocked and their companions were free. His men beamed.

'Good to see you, sir.'

'Aye, that it is, sir.'

Falconbridge nodded. 'It's good to see you, too, and you, Luis.'

As they emerged from their prison and got a proper look at Falconbridge, the men frowned.

'The filthy scum gave you a rough time, sir,' said Blakelock.

'I'll live,' he replied.

Luis caught sight of his companion and smiled. '*Doña* Sabrina! Are you all right? We heard them take you away earlier.'

'Quite all right, Luis.'

'I am truly glad to hear it.'

Falconbridge tossed the musket to Willis and gave Blakelock the sword. 'Here. It's a start, but we're going to need more than these if we're to have a hope of getting out of here.'

Sabrina met his eye. 'What are you going to do?'

'Go back along the corridor and check those other rooms. It's a risk but there's no other choice.' He paused. 'In the meantime, we'll take one of those coils of rope.'

Luis hastened to obey, selecting the most suitable and slinging it round his chest like a bandolier. Then they retraced their steps. Leaving Sabrina and Luis at the entrance to the passageway the other three moved quietly forwards. With thumping heart she watched as Willis put his ear against a door, listening. He opened it and glanced in. No shouts or challenges resulted but he shook his head. Further along Blakelock grinned. She heard him hiss to the others. Then all three vanished into the room, to emerge a short time later with swords and muskets.

Luis grinned and moments later he, too, was armed. *'Estupendo!* Now we go over the wall, eh?'

Falconbridge nodded. 'That's the general idea, and preferably before anyone finds Machart or that guard.'

The junction of the passageway revealed the door that led onto the courtyard. Falconbridge looked around the corner and mentally cursed as he counted at least a dozen soldiers there. He ducked back quickly.

'No go. Let's try the other way.'

They fled down the passage towards the archway at the end. From there it was no more than twenty yards to the wall. A crumbling flight of steps led to a small lookout platform on what remained of the rampart. It was currently empty. Falconbridge looked swiftly left and right and, having ascertained the coast was clear, jerked his head towards the steps.

'Up there. It's our only chance.'

They ran for the wall and began to climb. The steps were in a parlous state, some only a few inches wide, the rest having crumbled away. Nor was there any kind of handrail and the fall, though it wasn't high enough to kill, would likely result in a broken limb. Luis went first, testing each step gingerly. Beneath his weight the ancient stonework broke away in places sending down small showers of rubble. However, he reached the platform unscathed. Quickly, he slid the coil of rope off his shoulder and tied one end to a stone merlon. Then he turned and signalled to the others. Willis went next, and then

Blakelock, disappearing over the edge of the drop. Falconbridge turned to Sabrina and smiled.

'Ready?'

She nodded and began to climb, trying not to look down and to concentrate on where she was putting her feet. She reached the platform a short time later, closely followed by Falconbridge. He squeezed her arm.

'Your turn now.'

Before she could reply, they heard shouting in the distance.

'At a guess they've found Machart,' he said. 'Hurry, Sabrina.'

She needed no second bidding. Unheeding of rough stone or the rope burning the palms of her hands, she slid swiftly down to where the others waited. A short time later he joined them, and together they ran for the cover of rock and scrub, trying to put as much distance as possible between themselves and the walls of the castillo. Without horses though, the chances of success were small and everyone knew it.

'It won't take them long to find out how we escaped,' said Falconbridge. 'We can expect mounted pursuit fairly soon, I think.'

Sabrina shivered inwardly. If they were recaptured, they would die this time, but perhaps not quickly. The French would want revenge for their slain. She thought of the pills Falconbridge had given her and was glad. Better a swift end thus, than a protracted one at the hands of their enemies.

They ran hard until at length they were forced to slow down to catch their breath. Even then the Castillo was still only about a mile away. Not far enough. Sabrina pressed a hand to her aching side, forcing herself on. Falconbridge kept pace beside her, his smile lending her strength. She knew he must be in pain himself from the beating at the hands of Machart's guards, but he made no mention of it. To judge from the bruising on his face it must have been hard for him even to smile. If he could keep going, so could she.

Eventually they paused, taking shelter behind a group of scattered rocks. Luis flung himself down, ear to the ground, listening intently. Then he frowned.

'Many horses coming, though some way off yet.'

Falconbridge gritted his teeth against the pain in his ribs. 'We can't outrun them. Take cover. We'll have to make a stand here.'

They knew it wasn't going to be much of a stand, given the limited weapons and ammunition available. Their defiance would be counted by minutes, not hours. Nevertheless, it was the only option now. Surrender would likely not delay the inevitable outcome by very much. They took cover and waited for the appearance of the enemy. Sabrina crouched behind a large rock, resting her cheek against the rough surface. There could be no doubt now that she would not see her father again. She had gambled and lost. The long-dreamed-of reunion would never happen. He would be grieved by her loss but at least he would be free to continue his work for the war effort. She glanced at the man beside her and smiled faintly. If they had only met under other circumstances things might have been different. There might have been time to get to know each other better, time for talking and laughing, time in which to relax and to be herself. Unfortunately, time was the one thing they didn't have.

'I'm truly sorry things have turned out like this,' he said. 'I'd planned it all rather differently.'

'What was it the poet said about the best-laid plans?'

'Best-laid? Under other circumstances I'd want to laugh.'

She hesitated, and then took courage in both hands. 'I wish we had met under other circumstances.'

His gaze held hers. 'Yes, so do I, and yet I would not have missed knowing you. In truth, I have never met a braver woman.'

His words brought an inner glow of pleasure. At least she had not lost his regard. Since they had little

time left, and since there might never be another opportunity, she needed to say what was on her mind.
'I would not have missed knowing you, either.'

'I thank you. It is a compliment I have done little
to deserve.'

'Not so. You saved my life.'

'Only to fail you when it mattered most.' His lips
curled in self-disgust. 'When I think of you in the
clutches of that lecherous brute, it sickens me to my
stomach. Yet I could do nothing. Nothing.'

'It was not your fault, Robert.'

'Yes, it was. I should have insisted you ride on
with Ramon. Instead, I as good as delivered you to
Machart.'

'Machart was a sadistic beast, but he is unlikely
to trouble us any more.'

'And I thank God for it. To be tortured is one
thing, but to be forced to watch while he… No civilised man could countenance it. I was not afraid until
that moment.' He reached out and took her hand in
a warm clasp before raising it to his lips. 'I honour
your spirit and your courage.'

The words, so sincerely spoken, brought a deeper
glow of pleasure. She made no attempt to disengage
herself from his hold. It did not repel her. Rather,
its warmth and strength were comforting, like his
nearness now. 'There are men who consider them-

selves civilised in every way who do not baulk at it.'

He regarded her intently. 'You say that with some authority.'

'With authority enough.'

Curiosity mounted. There was so much he wanted to know and so little time left them. However, before he could speak, Blakelock's voice interjected.

'Here they come, sir.'

Falconbridge followed his gaze into the middle distance and saw the oncoming soldiers. His heart sank. Even from here it was possible to make out their blue uniform jackets and grey shakos. He relinquished his hold on Sabrina's hand and lifted the musket, aware of bruised muscles protesting.

'Let them come then. We'll account for as many as we can.'

She threw a sideways glance his way and nodded. 'Yes, we will.' Then, hoping her hand would not shake, she drew the pistol from her belt.

Chapter Eleven

Falconbridge grimaced, mentally counting the number of the oncoming force. With sinking heart he reached twenty. This was going to be a fight to the death. Knowing what to expect at the hands of the enemy there was no point in contemplating surrender. Better a quick ending here. He glanced at the faces around him and saw the same resolution in each one. A man could feel proud to die in such company. His gaze rested a moment on Sabrina. As though she sensed his regard she turned her head and met his gaze with a smile. He returned it, albeit crookedly, and his admiration increased. Truly, she was the rarest of women: the woman he would defend to the death. Setting his jaw he lined the first oncoming soldier in his sights. Alongside him his companions did the same.

As the shots rang out and three of the French vanguard fell, the others drew rein, and for a few moments there was shouting and confusion. Then a command rang out and the rest of the force drew their sabres. Falconbridge heard the order to charge and cursed softly. Men on the ground were no match for cavalry. This was going to be a slaughter pure and simple.

Another volley of shots brought down three more of the French, but it did not slow their advance. The thunder of hooves grew louder. Sunlight glinted on naked blades. With no time to reload, Falconbridge thrust Sabrina behind him.

'Behind that rock. Stay down.'

'If I am to die then I'll go down fighting with you.'

His throat tightened. A man could not be mistaken about such a look as hers. Suddenly there were so many things he wanted to say, but had time for none of them. Instead, he nodded. 'So be it.'

Heart thumping, she watched him draw the sword at his side, knowing they had no chance now. Soon the sabres would cut them down. If not... Her fingers felt for the small package inside her jacket and felt its reassuring presence. She would never be a prisoner of the French again.

More shots rang out and on the warm air she heard the sound of galloping hoofs. It could only mean reinforcements. She swallowed hard. There came more shots and then shouts and cries of pain. At any moment the vanguard would be upon them.

For the space of several heartbeats she waited. Then, slowly, she became aware that the impetus of the French charge was lost, and those riders remaining had veered off, turning their attention another way. Her bewildered gaze took in the large host of roughly-dressed horsemen that was bearing down on them. She was not alone in her astonishment.

Luis looked round at his companions. *'Que pasa?'*

'Your guess is as good as mine,' replied Willis.

Sabrina stared at the newcomers. 'Wait, aren't those redcoats among them?'

Willis narrowed his eyes, looking intently in the direction she had indicated. 'By heaven, you're right, ma'am.'

'But what are redcoats doing among those others?'

Falconbridge grinned, ignoring the pain in his cut lip. 'I think Ramon found help after all.'

For a moment or two the implication was lost and she could only stare in disbelief at the oncoming horde. Then she experienced a sudden surge of hope so intense it was almost painful. Turning she met his eye. What she read there caused her heart to leap.

'You mean we're not going to die after all?'

'We're certainly going to die,' he replied, 'but not today I think.'

Tearing her gaze away, she watched with bated breath as the opposing forces met amid shouts and the clash of arms. There followed a short spell of fierce hand-to-hand fighting as the desperate French tried to stave off the unexpected assault, but, hopelessly outnumbered, they were cut down one by one. Soon the area was littered with the fallen, the scene confused by riderless horses. Then, as the last of the enemy fell, the battlefield grew quiet.

Sabrina heard voices in Spanish and saw a few figures dismount, moving among the fallen. Those French still living were swiftly dispatched. She drew a deep breath, fighting the churning sensation in her stomach. Then she became aware of mounted figures moving towards them. The first was a British officer. For a moment he and Falconbridge surveyed each other in silence.

Falconbridge smiled wryly. 'I'm glad to see you, Tony.'

'And I to see you,' the other replied.

'Your arrival was most timely.'

'So I see.' The officer paused, looking at Sabrina. 'Will you not introduce me to this lady?'

'Forgive me. I have the honour to present Miss Huntley, my companion on this mission. Miss Huntley, Major Lord Anthony Brudenell.'

'We are much obliged to you, Major,' she replied.

Brudenell's blue gaze swept her from head to foot and then he smiled. 'I wish I could take the credit, ma'am, but that rightly belongs to El Cuchillo and his men.'

Sabrina's gaze went to the horseman who had reined in alongside. Like most people she had heard of the guerrilla leader, for his reputation preceded him. Her imagination had supplied a figure from high romance, something very different from the person before her now. He was perhaps in his early forties, and she guessed of average height. Like most Spaniards he was dark. The swarthy, bearded face was not handsome, but it was arresting, the left side being marred by deep scars across the cheek and brow. Piercing black eyes took in every detail of her appearance but gave nothing away. He favoured her with a slight inclination of the head, then turned to the man beside her.

'I am glad we arrived in time, Major.'

'You are not alone in that, *señor*,' replied Falconbridge. 'In truth, I thought it was all up with us.'

The conversation continued but Sabrina's attention was arrested by a familiar figure that had appeared from the group, ranged behind the guerrilla leader. Then her heart leapt.

'Jacinta?'

'*Doña* Sabrina!'

The two women embraced. Sabrina's voice caught on a sob. 'How glad I am to see you.'

'And I you.'

'I prayed you would live.'

'I received a concussion only,' replied Jacinta. 'It gave me a headache for a while, that is all.'

'Thank God.'

'Amen to that.'

'But how came you to be with El Cuchillo and Major Brudenell?'

'By good fortune only. It seems that when Ramon located the guerilla hideout, Major Brudenell was already there on business of his own. When he heard the name of Falconbridge he brought assistance as fast as he could. They found me near the place where we fought with Machart's men. I heard the French mention Castillo San Angel before they took you away. That is how our friends knew where to come.'

'Where is Ramon now?'

'Taking those papers to Lord Wellington. As soon as he knew aid was on its way to you, he set off.'

As the pieces of the story fell into place they brought about a feeling of relief so intense that Sabrina found herself trembling. Never in a thousand years could she have hoped that matters might have so happy a conclusion.

'I am sorry to interrupt,' said a voice behind them,

'but it would be as well not to linger here.' They turned to see Major Brudenell. 'I will have my men bring you a horse, ma'am.'

'I'm much obliged, sir.'

'At least that won't be hard to arrange,' replied Jacinta as he walked away. 'There are enough loose ones hereabouts.'

'True enough.'

'I will go and see that he provides something suitable.'

As Jacinta set off in Brudenell's wake, Sabrina experienced a moment of surprise. Then she saw Falconbridge approaching and understood the reason for the sudden departure.

'Can you bear the thought of another long ride?' he asked.

Sabrina smiled. 'If it takes us away from here I find I can bear the thought very well.' She surveyed him critically. 'But I think it is you who will find it hard going. Those cuts and bruises need attention.'

'Presently,' he replied.

'Do you fear my ministrations?'

'By no means, but Brudenell is right. We shouldn't linger here.' He grinned. 'When we make camp I'll submit willingly to your attentions.'

'I intend to hold you to that.'

'Indeed I hope so, ma'am.'

It was hard to know what to make of that and Sabrina decided it was safer not to pursue the matter. There was no time, in any case, for Brudenell's men returned with mounts. She swung into the saddle of a cavalry horse and watched her companions mount, too. Then the entire cavalcade set off.

They made camp that night in the hills. Sabrina took the opportunity to fetch clean water and cloths, and asked Luis to find out if any of the company had any medicinal salves or embrocation. The enquiry proved positive, for some time later he returned with a small pot which he presented to her triumphantly.

'Salve,' he said, 'and most efficacious for bruising.'

She sniffed the contents and wrinkled her nose. 'How do you know it's efficacious?'

'Does it not smell terrible?'

'Yes.'

'That proves it. The worse the smell, the better is the ointment, eh?' Seeing her dubious expression he added, 'Trust me in this.'

'Of course.'

He threw her a beaming smile and took himself off. Sabrina watched him go and shook her head.

'Trust him in what?' asked a familiar voice.

She turned to see Falconbridge and grinned. 'In

matters medical.' Putting down the cloths and bowl of water on a nearby rock, she bade him be seated. He obeyed without argument.

'I would trust Luis at my back in a fight any day of the week,' he observed, 'but I had no idea he was an expert in medicine, too.'

'I think it self-styled expertise.'

'Ah.'

She dipped a cloth and began very gently to bathe the cuts and bruises on his face. They looked painful, but so far as she could tell the damage was superficial. That anyone should have hurt him in that way brought a surge of anger. For men to fight each other in combat was one thing, to torture and maim quite another. Her hand moved to the cut on his lip and she saw him wince.

'I'm sorry. I didn't mean to hurt you.'

'No matter. Besides, if it hadn't been for you, things would have been much worse.' He paused. 'When you dealt with Machart you saved both our lives.'

She shuddered visibly. 'He is…was…an evil man.'

'Yes. I could almost wish the brute here again just so that I could have the pleasure of killing him for certain.'

'If he is dead then I hope he's in the hottest part of hell.'

Her quiet vehemence took him by surprise and he eyed her speculatively. 'I imagine that is his likely destination, and no man could deserve it more.'

Sabrina said nothing, merely dipped the cloth again and continued her ministrations. In spite of his injuries her touch was causing unexpectedly pleasurable sensations along his skin. Now that she was so close to him he could smell the scent of leather and horses on her clothing, but beneath it the scent of the woman. It was subtle and arousing. The last time he had been this close was when he had shared the cot with her in the cell back at Castillo San Angel. It had been a brief enough interlude but one he knew he would remember all his days. If she had given him any encouragement he would have taken it further, but she had not. Neither would she now, in all likelihood, for what woman could respect a man who had let her down so badly? He had gathered from previous conversations that something had happened in the past to make her exceedingly wary of giving her affections. His failure to protect her in her time of greatest need would only have reinforced that tendency.

Becoming aware of his regard, Sabrina kept her attention on her work. Having bathed his face, she laid down the cloth and reached for the pot of salve. Then, very lightly, she applied a little to the bruised areas of skin, taking care to avoid the open cuts. Falconbridge wrinkled his nose.

'What on earth is that stuff?'

'Goodness knows. Luis assures me it's good for bruises.'

'Good for embalming, too, from the smell of it.'

Sabrina grinned. 'Perhaps it has a two-fold purpose. I must ask him.'

'It might be better not to know.'

She completed her task and then paused. 'Take off your jacket.'

'Why?'

'I want to check the bruising on your ribs.'

His initial reaction was to say it wasn't necessary but just as quickly he decided against it. He didn't want to lose her company or to end this unforced intimacy.

'Would you mind helping me with this?'

'Of course.'

She stepped in closer and gently eased the coat off his shoulders. Falconbridge winced again, and with perfect sincerity. The blows he had received earlier were now very painful. The other events of the day hadn't helped either. Sabrina eyed him closely, wondering at the extent of the hidden damage.

'Pull up your shirt.'

Gingerly he obeyed and heard her gasp. Glancing

down he saw that his ribs were a mass of ugly red-and-black bruises.

'Dear God, Robert, you should have said something sooner! These must be agony.'

He smiled wryly. 'I've felt better.'

'Let me put some of this on for you.'

'I suppose it can't do any harm.'

'Luis says that a strong smell means an effective treatment.'

'In that case I should be as right as rain by tomorrow, unless the French sniff me out first.'

She returned the smile and then set to work again, gently smoothing the salve onto the bruised areas of his back. She was careful, trying by all means not to hurt him, but once or twice she heard a sharp intake of breath. It occurred to her to wonder then just what he had endured before she had been brought onto the scene. Looking at the damage caused by that beating, she was even less sorry for the injuries she had inflicted on Machart.

Gradually, she worked round to the front again, kneeling beside him now to ensure that no bruises were left untreated, applying the salve with light, deft touches along the muscles of his stomach and waist. Once, not so long ago, it would have been unthinkable to touch him or any man so intimately. Yet now it seemed quite natural and right. She could feel his leg warm against her side but the closeness did not repel her. On the contrary, what she felt now was melting warmth in the region of her pelvis. She drew in a deep breath of her own and finished the task.

He let the shirt fall. 'Thank you.'

'You're welcome.'

He tucked the fabric carefully into his breeches and then reached for his coat.

'May I importune you this one last time?' he asked.

'One last time?' She tilted her head to one side, regarding him thoughtfully. 'Really? Or was that just a figure of speech?'

He smiled. 'It probably was.'

She took the coat from him, gently easing the garment onto his arms and then drew it up over his shoulders. He got to his feet and turned to face her. For the space of several heartbeats neither one of them spoke. He wanted so much to kiss her but after what had happened he feared that such attentions must be unwelcome. Instead, he reached for her hand and raised it to his lips.

'Thank you.'

'You have no need to thank me.'

'I think I do.' His expression grew serious. 'That is twice you've come to my aid today. I should hate it to become a habit.'

'Should you?'

'This reversal of roles is deucedly uncomfortable, I find.'

She nodded sympathetically but there was a familiar gleam in her eyes. 'It must be, especially with so much bruised flesh.'

'Wretch! I was serious.'

'I know, but it is no use repining over what cannot be altered, Robert.'

'True, but I hope one day to make it up to you somehow.'

'It really doesn't matter.'

'Yes, it does. It matters a great deal.'

'Ah, bruised pride.' She saw him stiffen slightly and went on, 'I recognise it, you see, since my own has taken a heavy battering, too.'

'Of course, forgive me. What happened today has hurt both of us, in different ways.'

'Some hurts go deep, do they not?' She sighed. 'As deep as years.'

He regarded her intently now. 'What hurts, Sabrina?'

She bit her lip, hesitating, wanting to tell him but fearing to, as well, dreading his reaction.

'It seems to me that we have been here before,' he said. 'Will you not tell me what it is that so troubles you?'

She made no immediate reply and for a moment

he thought she would refuse. Then she drew in a shuddering breath and nodded.

'What happened with Machart…it happened to me once before.'

He stared at her, appalled. Whatever else, he had not expected that. 'Oh, my dear girl.'

'Today brought it all back, every last sordid detail.'

'I'm so sorry. You don't have to tell me, Sabrina.'

'Yes, I do. I wanted to before but the time wasn't right.' She turned to face him. 'Will you hear me?'

'You know I will.'

'You may think ill of me afterwards.'

He smiled gently. 'May not I be the judge of that?'

Resuming his seat on the rock he gestured for her to join him. So they sat together and she told him about Jack Denton, of the way they had met, of their stolen moments together and her growing infatuation with him.

'…and then one afternoon we went out riding to see some cave paintings that he said he'd found by chance, while out on patrol.' She paused. 'I was a little apprehensive; we were alone and the place remote, but he was…persuasive. Of course, when we reached the cave there were no paintings.'

Falconbridge was very still. 'And then?'

'I discovered how badly mistaken I had been in his character. He…he tried to kiss me…' The memory had lost none of its power to chill. The kiss he took then was unlike those first chaste salutes. Hot, searing, demanding, it shocked her, like the tongue thrusting into her mouth and the crude hand exploring her breasts. When she tried to pull away his hold only tightened. 'I tried to get away but he threw me down on the floor of the cave…tore my clothing.'

An expression of disgust crossed Falconbridge's face. She quailed before it, but knew she had come too far to go back now.

'I tried to fight him but he was too strong. I begged him to stop.' In her mind she could still hear his reply.

'Come now, you little tease. You've led me on for weeks. You know you want it as much as I.'

Furious and frightened, she fought Denton in earnest, biting, yelling, kicking. If anything it seemed to inflame him further.

'You can't get away, my sweet, so don't think it. Besides, when I'm done, you'll be begging for more.' He smiled. 'We have the whole afternoon before us and I mean to make the most of it.'

Panicking, she struggled harder, feeling his greedy mouth fasten on her breasts. She twisted

in revulsion, got a hand free, clawed at his face.
He caught her wrists and pinned them. His smile
chilled her.

'Like it rough, do you? Well, by God, Jack's your
man.'

His free hand shoved her skirts round her thighs
and then unfastened his breeches. Terrified now,
she screamed. His knee thrust her thighs apart...

Sabrina took another deep breath to steady herself.
'Just when I was certain that…that all was lost, a
hand reached out and dragged him away. It was
Captain Harcourt.'

'Harcourt?' The name registered at once and
Falconbridge was aware of other pieces of the puzzle
dropping into place.

'Yes, it seems he had noticed Denton's attentions
to me and, knowing the man's reputation, had kept
an eye on him. When he saw us ride off together,
he followed.'

Her companion's gaze hardened. 'A fortunate
circumstance.'

She nodded miserably. 'He hit Denton several
times before pushing him up against the rear wall
of the cave with a sword at his throat. I don't recall
everything he said, but I heard him utter the promise of death if Denton ever came near me again or
disclosed a word of what had passed. Denton swore
to keep silence so the Captain let him go.'

'Did he?' The tone was icy. 'And what of you?'

'He carried me back to his horse and took me home. He was very kind and uttered no word of reproach or blame, but all his gentleness could not dispel the searing sense of shame and humiliation that I felt.' She drew in a ragged breath. 'He took a back route to town, riding by little-frequented streets to minimise the chances of meeting anyone we knew. When we reached his lodgings he gave me into the care of his wife. She tended me and mended my garments as best she could. When I was calmer and reasonably presentable, they took me home.'

'Your father's reaction I can well imagine.'

'He never knew.'

'What!'

'Mercifully, he was elsewhere when we returned and I never told him what had happened. Nor did the Harcourts, at my insistence. Had we done so, he would certainly have called Denton out. Lord Wellington had expressly forbidden duelling among his officers, so even if he were not killed or injured, the affair would have put paid to my father's career. I could not bear to think that such ill fortune might befall him on account of my folly.'

'I see.'

'At first, I thought the whole sordid affair was over but it seems that, one evening, when Captain Denton was in his cups, he revealed something of it to two of his fellow officers. It was enough to lead to speculation and rumour. Captain Harcourt learned of it in the officers' mess and nipped the conversation in the bud. However, enough damage had been done by then to have an impact.' She swallowed hard. 'Nothing was ever said directly but there were covert looks and sly smiles from some of Denton's acquaintance. Ladies who had been friendly before now grew cool or, in one or two cases, shunned me completely, and invitations to their houses ceased. Had it not been for the kindness of the Harcourts, I would have been lost. Being of excellent social standing and also generally popular, their continued friendship and public refusal to give credence to rumour did much to aid my cause.'

'You seem to have been fortunate in your friends.'

'I did not know how fortunate until then,' she replied. 'After that, my relationship with the Harcourts became much closer. They took on the role of guardians, particularly in my father's absence, and saw to it that I came to no more harm.'

'And Captain Denton?'

'He was killed by the French in an ambush a few months later.'

Falconbridge's face was expressionless, save for the cold anger that burned in his eyes. 'How old were you when all this happened?'

'Fifteen.'

'Good God!'

'It is not a pretty story, is it?'

'Hardly.'

Her heart sank as she looked at his expression. He was sickened all right. Perhaps it had been a mistake to tell him, to be so totally frank. Perhaps she had lost his regard by doing so.

'The blackguard should have been whipped at the cart tail,' he went on. 'What man worthy of the name takes such advantage of a young girl?'

'I was very foolish.'

'Weren't we all when we were fifteen? In any case, foolishness is not a crime. Cold-blooded seduction of a minor most certainly is.'

'Then you do not blame me for what happened?'

'Good heavens, no. Why would I?'

'I was afraid you would think me light.'

His jaw tightened. 'I have never thought such a thing of you. Nor would I ever think it.' He paused. 'Is that what you believed when I kissed you before?' Seeing she remained silent, his brow creased. 'It was, wasn't it?'

'I couldn't be sure. I'm sorry. I see now that it was foolish.'

'I hope you do.'

'I was so afraid of what you would think.'

'Does my opinion matter so much then?'

'Yes, it does.'

'Then be assured that I hold you in the highest regard and always will.'

Part of her was glad, another part saddened. High regard was valuable but it was not the same as love; nor was it enough. Yet what man would want to marry a woman with such a history, even if it was not all her fault?

Before either of them could say more, a redcoated figure appeared in their line of vision. He stopped a few feet away and saluted.

'Beg pardon, sir, but Major Brudenell asks if you would be good enough to attend him.'

Falconbridge cursed mentally. Aloud he said, 'Very well. Tell him I'll come presently.'

'Yes, sir.'

The soldier departed. Falconbridge looked at Sabrina. 'Forgive me. I must find out what Brudenell wants.'

'Of course.'

'We will speak again later.'

She watched him walk away and thought sadly that there could be little more to say on the subject. He had assured her of his regard and she had believed him, but he had not spoken of anything deeper than regard. For her to admit to her own feelings, while being unsure of his, was impossible.

It did not pay to wear one's heart on one's sleeve. To make a fool of herself again after her previous experience would be foolish beyond permission. Better they remain as friends instead.

Falconbridge listened with close attention as Brudenell outlined his plans for their collective return to Ciudad Rodrigo.

'For it will be safer if we return as a group. El Cuchillo's men will guarantee us safe passage out of the Gredos, of course, but there is still some way to go before we can consider ourselves in friendly territory.'

Falconbridge nodded. 'You're right, and I accept the offer.'

'Good.'

'Miss Huntley has been exposed to enough danger already. I would spare her any further risk, in so far as I may.'

'She is a courageous young woman.'

'The bravest I ever met.'

Brudenell did not miss the tone in which it was said, or the accompanying expression on his friend's face.

'She is also very attractive.'

'Yes, she is.'

'Some fellows have all the luck when it comes to assignments.'

Falconbridge met his gaze. 'My brief association with Miss Huntley has been a privilege.'

'I should say so. If I'd known beforehand, I'd have asked Ward to swap our roles. Then I could have spent three weeks in close proximity to a pretty girl.'

'Damn it, Tony.' The grey eyes turned steely. 'What exactly are you implying?'

'Nothing at all.' With a sense of shock Brudenell saw the glacial expression. 'My dear fellow, I was joking.'

'I don't much care for the joke. Nor will I suffer Miss Huntley's name to be used in such a way.'

'Good God, Robert. You cannot seriously think I meant anything by it? If so, then I apologise.'

For a moment Falconbridge remained quite still, his gaze locked on the other man. Then, suddenly, the tension left him.

'Apology accepted.' He made a vague gesture with his hand. 'I beg you will forgive my ill humour. It has been a trying day.'

'Forget it.'

'It's just that Miss Huntley is a most esteemed… colleague.'

'Of course she is, my dear chap.'

Falconbridge managed a wry smile. 'Well then, I'll relieve you of my tiresome company. A good night's sleep will no doubt cure my foul temper.'

Having bidden his companion farewell, Brudenell followed the departing figure with his eyes. Then he whistled softly.

'I think it's going to take more than sleep to cure what's wrong with you, my friend.'

Having left Brudenell, Falconbridge walked apart a little way, needing time to think. Finally he found a tall pine and eased himself down onto the dry grass beneath. Annoyed with himself for what had taken place just now, he admitted that his response had been an overreaction. Of course his friend had never meant to slight Sabrina. It was just that following so close on the heels of her confidence to him, he had been instinctively protective. She was vulnerable in so many ways, and so strong in others. It was part of her considerable charm. She had told him that she valued his good opinion, an admission that caused both surprise and delight. Then he told himself not to attach undue significance to that remark. It meant only that she had come to value him as a colleague. He smiled in self-deprecation. A colleague? When he'd seen her in Machart's clutches he'd realised she meant a lot more than that, but he'd been powerless to help her. So far from acting the hero, it had been he who had needed rescuing. It was hardly the stuff of romance. Yet it seemed to him that their adventures together had forged a friendship between them at least, for she had trusted him with her confidence. Her tale made a lot of things much clearer and he could only look on his earlier behaviour with regret. Though well intentioned, he realised it had not done him any favours.

Chapter Twelve

Sabrina ate with Jacinta that evening and then retired early. Sleeping under the stars was not a new
experience and she made the best of it, using the
cavalry saddle as a pillow and the attached blanket roll for warmth. Although she was tired, sleep
proved elusive, for her thoughts kept crowding in.
Soon now their mission would be over and, God
willing, her father restored to her. That day could not
come too soon. But what of Robert Falconbridge?
Would she see him again afterwards, or were their
lives destined only to touch briefly?

No answer to this presented itself and eventually
she fell into a fitful doze, only to wake in the early
hours feeling chilled and stiff. Once when she had
been cold, a man had warmed her, but that had been
in a special set of circumstances that would never
be repeated. A lump formed in her throat. How
much she would have given just then to feel his
arms around her. Mentally she gave herself a shake.

It wasn't going to happen. To her horror she felt a tear slide down her cheek and hurriedly dashed it away. Then, pulling the blanket higher, she turned over.

It was dawn when Jacinta woke her with a cup of coffee. Gratefully she accepted the offering, feeling the warmth carve a path to her stomach. Jacinta joined her, eyeing her critically.

'Did you sleep well, *Doña* Sabrina?'

'Yes, very well, thank you.'

'Neither did I.'

Sabrina threw her a swift sideways glance, and then smiled ruefully. 'Is it that obvious?'

'Dark shadows under the eyes give away the game, no?'

'The ground is very hard when one has become used to a bed.'

'So it is.'

'To say nothing of hours spent in the saddle.'

'That, too, is guaranteed to make the muscles stiff.' Jacinta took another sip of her coffee. 'Or a beating like the one Major Falconbridge received.'

Sabrina lowered her gaze. 'Yes. The bruising was very bad.'

'Machart?'

'He.'

'*Puerco!*'

'That is an insult to pigs.'

'Luis said it was you who killed the swine.'

'I do not know if he is dead, only that I injured him.'

'A good thing if he were dead. The world would be well rid of such a one.' Jacinta paused. 'May I ask how you hurt the brute?'

'With a sharp knife between the ribs.'

'*Así?* You make me proud.'

'It was not about pride; it was about survival.'

Briefly she summarised what had occurred. As she spoke, her companion's face paled.

'If I had not stabbed him he would have raped me and killed us both afterwards,' said Sabrina. 'I had no choice. Even so, it is no easy thing to live with the knowledge that one may have killed a man.'

'Yet you shot men before.'

'I know, but it's different somehow. A gun lends distance to the act; a knife brings one horribly close.' She shook her head. 'I'm not explaining it very well.'

'You need feel no guilt over this matter. Be thankful you had the chance to be avenged.' Jacinta's dark eyes glittered. 'I was not so happy.'

Sabrina frowned. 'When your village was destroyed, you mean?'

'The French soldiers looted it first. They killed all the men, even the very old and the sick. After that they rounded up the women, my mother and sisters among them. They were taken to a barn where the soldiers took it in turns to rape them.'

'Oh, Jacinta, no.'

'Oh, yes. When they had finished, they closed up the doors after them so that none could escape. Then they set the barn alight and burned it to the ground, along with every house in the village.' Her companion paused. 'The only reason I didn't die with the rest was because my mother had sent me out earlier on an errand. I was on my way back, but when I saw the soldiers I hid in a ditch until they went away. By then, all my family were dead and our home gone. I didn't know what to do or where to go, but I knew I could not stay, so I set off for the hills. A week later your father found me. I was half-dead from lack of food. If it had not been for his intervention, I would have perished.'

'Dear Lord.'

Sabrina's throat tightened as she struggled with the enormity of it. Never until now had she known the full story of Jacinta's past. Having being told she could only stare at her in horror. Jacinta met her gaze and held it.

'The soldiers who did those things were led by a man just like Machart,' she went on. 'You need feel no guilt for his death. Only remember what he would have done if you had not thrust that blade between his ribs.'

Sabrina shivered inwardly. 'When I agreed to come on this mission I knew the risks, but they seemed unreal somehow, as though they could never happen to me. I cannot believe I could have been so naive.'

'And yet, these things will make you stronger.'

'I hope so. As I hope all this will achieve my father's freedom.'

'I pray for it, too. He is among the best of men.'

'Yes, he is.'

'And Major Falconbridge?'

'I did not think so when first we met. Now…yes, I believe he is.'

'Good. Then he is worthy of you.'

'You mistake—our relationship is not of that kind. We are merely friends.'

Jacinta lifted one dark brow. 'If you say so.'

'I do say so.'

'If you repeat it often enough, you may come to believe it, but it won't alter the truth.'

'And what is that?'

'Do you need me to tell you?'

Sabrina sighed. It was impossible to feign anything with Jacinta. 'No, but I cannot reveal my feelings until I know his.'

'They are written all over him.'

'Are they?'

'Ha! The man is transparent.'

Before the remark could be explored further, Luis hove into view. He greeted both women and then informed them that the column was due to move out.

'El Cuchillo's men like to make use of the cooler hours,' he explained.

'Do they come with us then?' asked Jacinta.

'Until the far edge of the sierra. There is safety in numbers, eh?'

'I expect there is, even though the numbers be comprised of bandits.'

'Never look a gift horse in the eye.'

'Mouth,' amended Jacinta. 'Never look a gift horse in the mouth.'

Luis frowned. 'That is nonsense. How can one look a horse in the mouth? It cannot be done.'

Jacinta muttered something under her breath. Sabrina grinned and got to her feet.

'Frankly, I'm not looking forward to seeing any part of a horse today, but needs must.' She glanced at Jacinta. 'Come on, let's pack our things and saddle up.'

Luis nodded and took his leave. They watched him walk away and then set to. It didn't take long to roll up the blankets and stow the mugs in the saddlebag. Then, hefting saddles and bridles, they walked to the picket line where the horses were tethered. It took a relatively short time to tack up and mount. Sabrina stifled a groan as her aching muscles protested. Jacinta read her expression correctly.

'Are you ready for another delightful ride through the mountains, *Doña* Sabrina?'

'I can hardly wait.'

In fact, the pace was slow and easy, for which she was grateful. Moreover, now that she was in the centre of so large a company, the fear of a surprise attack receded. She estimated that El Cuchillo's force numbered at least fifty. They were rough, silent men who rarely spoke and whose expressions gave nothing away. Occasionally she intercepted the odd glance towards Jacinta and herself, but that was all. Never by word or deed were they shown the least discourtesy. Every man there was armed to the teeth and all looked as though they could kill without a qualm. It was reassuring to know that they were allies, and she was glad of their protection. No French patrol was going to take them on, assuming any such were in the vicinity. It left her at leisure to admire the mountain scenery and to think.

She saw little of Falconbridge that morning, for he was riding at the head of the column with El Cuchillo and Major Brudenell. She missed his company and their lively conversations and thought that it was impossible to be bored in his presence. It also occurred to her that life was going to seem very dull without it when all this was over. Perhaps they might meet sometimes, until the army moved on. At a guess, Wellington would try to take Salamanca; the city was of great strategic importance. That implied another battle to drive the French back. She bit her lip, unwilling to think of the implications. Captain Harcourt had once told her that a man's luck could only hold so long. The idea of anything happening to Falconbridge was deeply unsettling. She thought she could bear his absence as long as he was alive and well somewhere in the world.

The column halted at midday by the edge of a wide creek. After the horses were watered and tethered, the men broke out provisions. While they were thus occupied, Sabrina made a necessary trip into the undergrowth and then strolled down to the water's edge to bathe her hands and face. The sun was hot now, and the water wonderfully refreshing. Had she been alone she'd have been strongly tempted to strip off and bathe. Unfortunately, that wasn't an option just then.

She was so engrossed in thought that she failed to hear the quiet footsteps approaching until a man's shadow fell across her. She turned with a start and then felt her heart give a little leap as she recognised him.

'Forgive me. I didn't mean to startle you.'

'Not your fault. I was miles away.'

'So I gather.'

She eyed him critically. The cuts on his face and lip had scabbed over but the bruises were livid, particularly the one around his right eye. He noted the scrutiny and sighed.

'I look like a pirate, don't I?'

'Not quite so bad. You must still be very sore.'

'Somewhat,' he admitted, 'though I have to say that salve you applied did help considerably.'

'I'm glad to hear it. I would hate to think you had undergone the treatment for nothing.'

'Far from it.' He held up a small cloth bundle. 'Are you hungry? I've got some provisions here. We could share them if you wish.'

Feigning a calm she was far from feeling, she smiled acceptance, so they sat together by the water and she watched as he unfastened the cloth and examined the contents.

'Hmm. Half a loaf, at least two days old; a chunk of chorizo, possibly rancid; an onion and a wedge of dry cheese.'

'A veritable feast,' she replied.

He smiled ruefully. 'I regret that I cannot offer you something better.'

'It doesn't matter.'

'What shall we essay first?'

'Some bread and cheese?'

He took out a pocket knife and sawed into the loaf. Several minutes later he was still only halfway through it. 'Maybe I should use a sabre instead.'

Sabrina smiled. 'Better not. It might dull the edge.'

He persevered and finally succeeded in dividing the bread, handing her a portion before setting to work on the cheese. This proved marginally easier. He sniffed the chorizo.

'It seems all right. Will you chance it and have some?'

'Why not?'

'We won't go into that.'

She laughed and suddenly he found himself staring. Yet she seemed quite unaware of the effect she was having. Making a conscious effort to get a grip on himself he turned his attention to the food.

Of necessity they ate in silence for a while, the loaf demanding serious effort. Eventually Sabrina dunked her portion in the creek to soften it a little. He watched her quizzically.

'Better?'

'It doesn't do a great deal for the texture,' she admitted, 'but it tastes all right.'

'That's good enough for me,' he replied, and immediately followed suit. Having done so, he tried the bread again and rolled his eyes in mock appreciation. 'Absolutely divine.'

'And to think you once told me I was easily pleased.'

For answer he held up the onion. 'Can I tempt you?'

Sabrina shook her head. 'I draw the line there.'

'I think you may be right.' He discarded it and regarded her with another rueful smile. 'This must rank as the worst meal I have ever offered you.'

'By far the worst,' she agreed.

'Will you allow me to make amends and treat you to a better one when we return?'

Her heart gave another peculiar little lurch. 'I'd like that.'

'Then I promise that you shall be wined and dined in style.'

'With a fresh loaf?'

His grey eyes glinted with amusement. 'Loaf and cheese. I guarantee it.'

'I look forward to it, sir.'

'And I,' he replied. 'Besides, after all the dire culinary experiences you have been forced to endure, it is the least I can do.'

'Only one dire culinary experience to date.'

'You are generous.'

He reflected that it was true. Never once had she complained about the fare or indeed any of the trying conditions on this trip. She was truly a gem among women.

Keenly aware of that penetrating gaze, she wondered at the thoughts behind. If he had meant the invitation, then she would see him again after they got back. The thought made her happy and anxious together. Was it a token gesture, an acknowledgement of services rendered on their mission? Or was it because he genuinely wanted her company? How much she hoped it was the latter, that they might truly remain good friends. Then another, more pressing, thought occurred to her.

'You have invited me to dine but I shall have nothing to wear.'

'Really? What a delicious prospect.'

She gave him an accusing look. 'My dresses are in the trunk that we left back at that inn.'

'The landlord has instructions to send them on with the carriage when an appropriate driver can be found. The man will be well paid for his trouble.'

'You seem to think of everything.'

'I do my best. Of course, this being Spain, it may take a little time for the carriage to arrive, but you will get your things eventually.'

'That is a relief.'

'In truth I feel slightly disappointed, given the alternative.'

Sabrina grabbed the food cloth and flung it at him.

It landed against his chest in a shower of crumbs. Much to her chagrin she heard him laugh.

'You are not to feel disappointed,' she admonished.

'Oh, good. Does that mean my hopes will be met?'

She glared at him. 'It does not, you dreadful man!'

The expression of contrition which followed was belied by the expression in his eyes. For a moment or two Sabrina regarded him with outrage. Then her sense of humour got the better of her and she began to laugh, albeit ruefully.

'I should be proof against this by now.'

'But I'm so glad that you are not.'

'Does it amuse you to tease me then?'

'What do you think?' he replied.

'I fear it does.'

'Only because I know I can expect the like in return. I have not been disappointed yet.'

Sabrina eyed him askance. 'How am I to take that?'

'As a compliment, my dear.' He paused, his expression suddenly serious. 'Very much so.'

Under the intensity of that look the blood mounted to her neck and face. Before she could think of a suitable reply the men around them began to stir. Noting it, Falconbridge sighed.

'I think that is a hint.'

'I'm afraid so.'

'It would be so much more pleasant to stay here for the rest of the afternoon.'

'Yes, but I fear that is not an option.'

'Come then.' He got to his feet with a stifled groan, and then held out a hand. 'Allow me.'

She took the offered hand and felt his fingers close round hers, drawing her easily to her feet. The touch sent a familiar charge along her skin. He retained his hold a little longer, relinquishing it with apparent reluctance. Then they made their way back to the horses.

He untied her horse's reins and held the bridle while she mounted. Then he retrieved his own horse. She expected him then to return to his place at the head of the line but he did not, reining his mount alongside hers.

'How do you find your cavalry charger?' he asked.

'A very willing beast, though quite a change from my usual mounts.'

'I imagine it is a change for him, too, since he has to carry only half the usual weight.'

'I had not thought of it like that.'

'No, but I'm sure he has.'

She laughed and patted the bay's neck. 'He will

be back in service soon enough I have no doubt. The army always needs good horses.'

'True—and when those horses have been taken from the French they are the more highly prized.'

They lapsed into silence after this, but it was companionable, rather than awkward and she knew there was no company she would rather have. It felt so right to be with him. Once she had thought never to feel that about any man again and yet, in a short space of time, her feelings had changed so completely that she hardly recognised herself.

From time to time as they rode he pointed things out: a pair of eagles in flight above a distant peak; a small snake basking on a stone or brown trout finning lazily in the shallows of the stream.

'You have an eye for detail,' she said.

'It's useful in this line of work.'

'Have you always had it?'

'I grew up in the country. Perhaps that affects the way one sees things.'

'I am sure it does.'

'My brother and I always seemed to have a gun in one hand and a fishing rod in the other.'

'You had similar tastes.'

'Very similar tastes.'

Realising the implication she reddened. 'I beg your pardon. I didn't mean…'

'I know you didn't. Pray, do not be concerned.'

He paused. 'Yes, Hugh and I were alike in many ways.'

'You were close?'

'Very close—then.'

Though the tone was perfectly even she sensed the hurt beneath. It was dangerous ground and, having no wish to alienate him, she sought to change the subject.

'It's all right,' he replied. 'You need not fear to offend my sensibilities. I am equal to hearing my brother's name spoken.' Even as he said the words he knew them for truth, and that a shift had occurred somehow without his even being aware of it. 'I think I have you to thank for that.'

'I'm not sure I understand.'

'It was you who first made me face the things I had kept hidden for so long.'

'It was unintentionally done. I had no wish to pry.'

'I know. That is why I spoke of it.' He paused. 'Perhaps it was overdue.'

Sabrina remained silent, not wanting to interrupt him now, knowing just how hard it was to reveal the secrets of the past.

'You once asked me if I had forgiven my brother for what he did,' he continued. 'The thought has stayed with me ever since. The answer is the same:

I still cannot forgive or forget, but I think it is time to draw a line under the affair.'

'I'm glad. The past should not be allowed to blight the future.'

He shot her a penetrating look. 'No, it should not, though I fear that too often it does.'

She nodded, accepting the veracity of that remark. Was she not a prime example? 'My father once said that it is not misfortune that shapes us, but how we respond to misfortune.'

'He was right. Either we go under or we become stronger.'

Recalling her recent conversation with Jacinta, Sabrina felt the words resonate strongly. 'I cannot imagine the circumstances that would drive you under.'

'Everyone has their breaking point. I am no different in that respect.'

'Everyone talks by the third day?'

'Exactly.' He smiled faintly. 'In any case, there are many kinds of hurt and even the strongest of us are not immune.'

'I think that time helps us put things in perspective.'

'Time helps,' he agreed. 'But it is thanks to you that I have been able to put things in perspective.'

'To me?'

'You made me face up to the past, to voice the

feelings I had buried for so long. Once they were out I had no choice but to confront them. I cannot pretend it was comfortable, but it was necessary.'

'It is not easy to face down our demons.'

'No, it isn't, but past demons shrink before present evils.' He paused. 'When I was forced to watch while Machart assaulted you…it was the worst hour of my entire life. Nothing could compare to the horror of that.' The grey eyes met and held her own. 'I could not bear to see you hurt or demeaned in that way…in any way. I'd give my life to prevent it.'

She stared at him in complete astonishment, trying to gather her scattered wits. Never in a thousand years would she have expected to hear such words from him. Somehow she found her voice. 'I think that is the nicest compliment I have ever been paid.'

'You deserve only the highest of compliments.' He smiled wryly. 'And a decent dinner, of course.'

Chapter Thirteen

The conversation remained with her long afterwards and its effect was to leave a warm glow inside. Though she would not allow herself to refine too much upon it, nothing could diminish the pleasure of knowing she had his esteem.

As their journey progressed there were fewer opportunities for private speech, and though she was often in his company it was invariably in the presence of others. One of them was Major Brudenell for whom she had formed a real liking. Quite apart from the fact that he had been instrumental in saving her and her companions from the French, he had easy, unaffected manners and was invariably pleasant company. It was not hard to see why he and Falconbridge were friends as well as colleagues.

'We've been through a fair few campaigns together,' he confided one evening as they sat around the fire. 'He's a good fellow to have at your back in a fight.'

'Yes, he is,' she agreed.

He regarded her in momentary surprise. 'Of course, you would know that.'

'He has demonstrated as much on several occasions.'

'I own I did not think he would ever permit a woman to accompany him on a mission,' he said. 'No offence meant, of course.'

'None taken,' she replied. 'Major Falconbridge did not wish me to come, but he was given no choice.'

'I see.'

'In fact he did everything he could to dissuade me.'

He smiled. 'Quite unsuccessfully it seems.'

'He did his best.'

'He is known to be most assertive on occasion.'

'Oh, he was. All the same it did no good.'

'Marvellous. I wish I'd seen it. It's not often anyone bests him thus.'

They both laughed. Neither of them noticed Falconbridge, who had just returned from inspecting the picket line. He paused on the edge of the ring of firelight, surveying the scene. The two were sitting close, as old friends might, clearly enjoying each other's company. As he looked on he experienced a stab of emotion uncommonly like jealousy. It took him aback and almost at once he felt ashamed. His friend had never shown anything other than gentlemanly courtesy towards Sabrina. Nor was he a womaniser. He had a wife back in England to boot. There was not the least occasion to be jealous. Taking a deep breath he stepped forward into the ring of firelight and joined the group who were gathered there.

Brudenell glanced up and, seeing who it was, smiled. 'Ah, Robert. Miss Huntley and I were just talking about you.'

Falconbridge helped himself to a mug of coffee. 'Indeed?'

'Nothing damning, of course.'

'I'm relieved to hear it.'

'It seems the lady holds you in high regard.'

Falconbridge felt his heart skip a beat. Schooling his expression he surveyed the two of them calmly. 'I am honoured.'

'Yes, you are. Miss Huntley tells me you have demonstrated your worth many times.'

His face reddened and he was glad of the flickering shadows around them. 'The lady is generous.'

'Not so,' she replied. 'I spoke only the truth.'

For a moment she met his gaze across the fire. Was that a depth of warmth he glimpsed there, or was it merely the reflected glow of the flames? Before he could respond, Brudenell leapt in.

'There you are, straight from the lady's own lips.' He turned to Sabrina. 'I am in total agreement, ma'am. He's a good fellow to have with you in a tight spot.'

Falconbridge's hand clenched round the coffee mug. 'Brudenell, you talk too much. It's a bad habit.'

Far from being disturbed by the intelligence, his friend only laughed. Falconbridge glowered quietly, privately wondering if there wasn't a badger sett nearby that he could stuff him into. After that he'd very much have liked to take Sabrina aside for private discussion. No, he amended, not discussion. What he would have liked to do was take her in his arms, to repeat the heart-stopping delight he had experienced once before. Unfortunately, the circumstances were not conducive to it. The best he could do was to change the subject as soon as possible.

The conversation moved seamlessly on to other topics, interspersed at intervals with good-humoured jesting. It passed the evening agreeably until it was time to turn in. For a long time afterwards Falconbridge lay awake, looking at the stars, and feeling strangely happy. His mind returned to what Brudenell had told him earlier. *The lady holds you in high regard.* The words had been spoken in a bantering tone but their import meant far more than that. His friend could not know how cheering their effect had been, or how they gave him hope.

* * *

Their party remained with El Cuchillo's men until they came at last to the western edge of the Sierra de Gredos. There the guerrilla leader reined in and gestured towards the plain below.

'This is where we part, my friends. Follow the path yonder and it will bring you safely down. From there it should be but a few days' ride to Ciudad Rodrigo.'

Falconbridge nodded. 'And you?'

'We have other fish to fry.'

'Then I wish you God speed.' He held out his hand and the other man took it in a firm clasp. 'And I thank you again for your most timely assistance. It will not be forgotten, I assure you.'

A ghost of a smile played around El Cuchillo's lips. 'Allies must help each other. Besides, it is no hardship for us to harry the French, believe me.'

'Wellington shall hear of your part in the matter.'

'And we shall make good use of the guns he has supplied.'

'I imagine you will.'

El Cuchillo nodded. Then he touched his hat. *'Vaya con Dios.'*

With that the Spanish force rode away, heading back along the trail that led into the hills. For a little while Falconbridge watched them go. Then he turned his horse and led the descent to the plain. They reached it without incident. The pace was swifter then and they made good progress, though keeping a sharp look-out for any sign of French troops. However, they encountered none.

'With any luck we really shall be back in Ciudad Rodrigo in a few days,' he said, bringing his horse alongside Sabrina's mount.

'I pray we will meet Ramon there.'

'And I.'

She shot him a sideways glance. 'You do not doubt him?'

'Not in the least, but, in spite of his local knowledge and survival skill, he has had to make a perilous journey alone.'

'A calculated risk, surely? If you had any serious doubts on the matter you would not have given him the plans.'

He smiled. 'Quite right. All the same I try never to count chickens before the eggs are hatched.'

'I can see the sense in that. Nevertheless, you must have had faith.'

'I did. For that matter I still do.'

'But you take the precaution of keeping your fingers crossed as well.'

'Right now, my dear, everything is crossed.' He threw her a penetrating look. 'You must be looking forward to the end of this journey.'

'I confess I am. Even so, I shall never forget it.'

'Nor I.'

'It has had its moments.'

'Moments that I think neither of us will forget,' he replied.

Something in his tone caused her pulse to beat a little quicker, though when she looked at him his expression was impossible to read. She could only hope he, too, had taken some positive things from their time together.

'Some I would rather forget,' she admitted, 'but by no means all.'

There followed a small hesitation. Then he said, 'What will you choose to remember?'

'The night of the ball.' It was out before she had time to think of all its implications and what construction he might place on the remark. As these things belatedly occurred to her she felt suddenly much warmer. Striving for casualness, she added, 'And you?'

'There are many things I will remember,' he said. 'The ball not least.'

In an instant she was back in a moonlit garden with his arms around her and his lips on hers. Of course, that had been a ruse to deceive Machart, but the moment would stay with her always. Was her companion thinking of that, too? Had it meant anything to him? He made no direct reference to it so she must assume that it had not. In any case, it was dangerous ground. She managed a smile.

'I think there will be little opportunity for dancing for a while.'

'Opportunities can be created,' he replied.

'Yes.'

'We must seize those that come our way.'

She drew another deep breath, knowing full well that if there was ever another opportunity to dance with him she would seize it. The force of the re-alisation shocked her. Did he feel the same, or was he speaking in general, rather than specific terms? Again there was no way of knowing.

'I shall make every effort to do so.'

He smiled. 'I shall remind you of that, in the event that such an opportunity arises.'

Just then another horse drew alongside and he looked round to see Blakelock.

'Beg pardon, sir, but Major Brudenell asks if he might have a word.'

Falconbridge quashed a desire to tell Blakelock and Brudenell to go to blazes, and nodded instead. 'Certainly.' Then he turned back to Sabrina. 'Will you excuse me, ma'am?'

'Of course.'

With real regret she watched him trot on ahead, and presently he and his colleague were engaged in private conversation.

* * *

Afterwards she found herself thinking of the future with mixed feelings: on the one hand, it would be wonderful to bathe and change into feminine garments and sleep in a bed again; on the other, she would see less of Falconbridge. He had intimated that he would like to see her again, but she knew it could not be often. His duties would command his attention and he would have little time to think of anything else. Gradually, the immediacy of their adventure would fade, though perhaps he might remember it from time to time and recall her with affection. In the meantime there was every chance that her father would be freed. Her spirits lifted at the prospect. He was the reason she had come on this mission and his safety mattered more than foolish dreams of romance.

When they stopped to rest the horses a little later she was joined by Major Brudenell. It seemed that his thoughts had been turning on similar lines to her own.

'No doubt you will be glad to get back to civilisation, ma'am.'

'Yes, indeed.'

'This rough living gets wearisome after a while, even for soldiers. It must be doubly so for a lady.'

'I am not unused to rough living, sir, for I have accompanied my father on numerous expeditions into the back of beyond. All the same, some creature comforts will be most welcome.'

'I'm sure. As I am sure that you must be longing to see your father again.' He paused. 'Major Falconbridge outlined the circumstances to me.'

'Ramon is the key to my father's release now.'

'Ah, yes, Ramon. A most persuasive gentleman as I recall.'

'He can be.'

'He rode into El Cuchillo's lair as if he owned the place. There must have been at least twenty muskets pointing his way, and he didn't turn a hair.'

'I wish I had been there to see it.'

He shook his head. 'I felt trepidation enough riding in there, and I'd been invited.'

'Well, I'm glad El Cuchillo didn't have him shot or I wouldn't be here either.' She paused. 'I understand that is due as much to your good offices as Ramon's intervention. All the same, I'm surprised the guerilla agreed to help us. We must have seemed expendable in his eyes.'

'I got the impression that he didn't have much choice—something about him returning a favour.'

Sabrina grew thoughtful, recalling an earlier conversation in which Ramon had admitted to knowing the guerrilla leader. He had not explained the connection and neither she nor her companions would have dreamed of prying. Now it appeared that the connection was more than one of casual acquaintance.

'I don't know the details,' Brudenell continued, 'but it appeared to be about a matter of honour.'

'Indeed?'

'Yes. Then, when Ramon told me the name of the officer leading the mission, I added my voice.'

'I'm glad you did.'

'To be honest I don't think it made any difference. I'm sure El Cuchillo had already decided by then.'

It was intriguing, though it brought her no nearer to an answer. Only Ramon could clarify matters there. Perhaps when she returned he would tell her.

'The strange thing was that once El Cuchillo had said he would help, your friend got on his horse and rode off in the opposite direction. Said he had urgent business elsewhere. Didn't even wait to see if the chap would keep his word.'

'Ramon must have known he would.'

'Evidently. I thought then that he must have had a very good reason for leaving.'

'He did.'

'Major Falconbridge has since apprised me of the facts.'

'Had it not been of the gravest importance, Ramon

would not have left. I can only pray he has reached his destination unscathed.'

'I have every confidence he has, ma'am. Who would dare to try and stop such a man?'

Sabrina could only hope he was right.

She was still thinking about it when Falconbridge joined her later.

'Most interesting,' he said after she had summarised what Brudenell had told her. 'Your friend Ramon is a dark horse.'

'Maybe so, but I'd trust him with my life.'

'You already have, and he has proved himself worthy of your regard.'

She nodded. 'Do you think he has got those plans to Lord Wellington by now?'

'I sincerely hope so.'

'I little thought events would turn out this way. I had visions of a triumphant return in which you handed over the papers to the great man himself, while Ward and Forbes looked on in open-mouthed admiration.'

He laughed out loud. 'I must say I like the sound of that. Unfortunately, things rarely do turn out exactly as we imagine. The important thing is that Wellington does get those papers.'

She hesitated. 'How soon do you think it might be before my father is released?'

Looking into her face just then Falconbridge was touched by its earnest expression. 'If Ward has any notion of honour it will be very soon.' He squeezed her shoulder gently. 'I will do all in my power to ensure that it is so.'

His touch and his kindly expression warmed her. 'Thank you.' She paused. 'Will there be a ceremony for your promotion to Lieutenant Colonel?'

He choked off a laugh. 'About as much ceremony as it takes to hand over the paperwork and tell me to clear off and get on with it.'

'Oh. I thought it would be more elaborate than that.'

'A forlorn hope, my dear. Of course, on the day I'm given a Field Marshal's baton they may well organise a parade.'

'You'd be able to command one then.'

'So I should.' He grinned. 'I'm very flattered that you think I might attain such high rank.'

'I think you would make an excellent Field Marshal.'

'Have a care, lest you turn my head.'

'You would not let your head be turned by me or anyone else.'

'Oh, you turn heads, my dear, I assure you.'

She flushed faintly. 'Hardly—not dressed like this at any rate.'

'It would make no difference if you wore

sackcloth. Not that I advocate any such thing, you understand.'

'I'm relieved to hear it. Mine is not a penitential nature.'

His eyes gleamed. 'So I've noticed.'

'Sackcloth is not part of my plans, even if I do not get my trunks back.'

'What would you do then?'

'Then I should be forced to wear breeches and boots henceforth.'

'What a dreadful notion. I shall spare no effort to see that your gowns are returned to you with all haste.'

'I would be most grateful.'

He raised one eyebrow. 'How grateful exactly?'

'It is most improper of you to ask, you horrid man.'

Falconbridge laughed softly. Was there ever such a girl?

It was a thought that stayed with him when the journey resumed a short time later. Their earlier conversations had led him to hope that his company would not be unwelcome to her in future. It gladdened his heart. Once he had thought never to experience that feeling again. If he had ever considered the notion of a more settled life it had always been in the dim and distant future when the war was over.

It had involved the pursuits of a country gentleman and was far removed from any thought of romance. Now, in a few short weeks, all those notions had been turned on their heads. The thought of losing Sabrina's company was unpalatable because he knew how devilishly dull life would be without it. For all its perils he had enjoyed their shared adventures. A sage in ancient times once said that journeys cause men to reveal their true characters. The saying held good for women, too. Despite the short duration of their acquaintance he realised he knew Sabrina better than he had ever known Clarissa. Guile and duplicity were as far from her nature as the earth was from the stars. Events had tested her severely and she had not been found wanting. Falconbridge smiled in self-mockery. He had once proclaimed that he was married to his career; now he realised that his career wasn't enough.

'Penny for 'em,' said Brudenell, coming alongside.

Falconbridge started. 'Oh, er, I was just thinking about our return to Ciudad Rodrigo.'

'I'm looking forward to it myself,' admitted the other. 'This saddle is making life damned tedious.'

'Getting sore, eh?'

'Let's just say I'd give a great deal for a hot tub.' Brudenell lifted his sleeve and sniffed at it, wrinkling his nose in distaste. 'I'm starting to smell like a dead ferret.'

Falconbridge glanced ruefully at his own travel-stained garments. He couldn't recall the last time he'd bathed. 'Make that two dead ferrets.'

'These adventures are all very well, but I'm beginning to think a spell of routine duties would suit me nicely.'

'I suppose there's something to be said for routine.'

'Aye,' replied Brudenell, 'hot water, clean linen and a soft bed to start with.'

'The hallmarks of civilised living.'

'Not forgetting feminine company, of course.'

His friend smiled faintly. 'At least I have not lacked for that.'

'No, you lucky dog. It was a cruel fate that rewarded you with the company of the delightful Miss Huntley, and me with El Cuchillo.'

'Cruel indeed.'

'It's worse than that. For reasons that I cannot fathom, the lady likes you.'

Falconbridge felt his face redden. 'I fear I have done little enough to deserve it.'

'Not what she says, old boy. Of course, I tried to put her on her guard and tell her what an undeserving brute you are, but she was having none of it.'

It drew a deprecating grin. 'Unkind, Tony. You might have put in a good word for me.'

'What, and seen myself quite cut out?' Brudenell sighed. 'Not that it did me any good. She is oddly impervious to my charm.'

'So she should be. You're a married man.'

'That isn't the point.'

'Isn't it? I rather thought it was significant.'

His companion returned the grin. 'You're a hard man, Robert.'

'Hard? I have it on good authority that I'm quite odious.'

'Good Lord. Who dared to say that to your face?'

'Miss Huntley.'

Brudenell chuckled softly. 'Did she, by God?'

'Oh, yes, and a lot more besides.'

'Really? What more?'

'If you think I'm going to tell you that, Tony, you're delusional.'

Far from dismaying his friend, it served only to fuel his enjoyment. 'How I should have loved to be a fly on the wall.'

Falconbridge regarded him with a jaundiced eye. 'I have no doubt you would.'

'Offensive, was it?'

'Deeply.'

'Wounding?'

'Most hurtful.'

'Bruised your pride?'

'It may never recover.'

'Splendid.' Brudenell beamed. 'I take it you'll be seeing her again when we get back then?'

'I wouldn't miss it for the world.'

Chapter Fourteen

Three days later they surmounted a hill and saw the Agueda River below. Beside it lay Ciudad Rodrigo. Sabrina smiled, letting her eye travel from the big gun batteries on the Great Teson opposite the town, to the familiar details of its fortress and churches and ancient stone bridge. Somewhere down there was her godfather and, she hoped, Ramon. Perhaps soon her father, too.

'There were times when I thought we would not live to see this place again,' said Jacinta.

Sabrina nodded. 'And I. It seems strangely like coming home.' She paused. 'I don't know why I should feel that when my acquaintance with the place is so slight.'

'Home is where we happen to be, no?'

'True—in our case anyway.'

'Besides, it is people who make places significant.'

'Yes, you're right.'

For the first time it occurred to Sabrina that it might be pleasant to put down roots and have a permanent home. Involuntarily her gaze flicked towards Falconbridge. Then she pulled herself up sharply. She could have no expectations there; he was married to his career and would go wherever the army decided to send him. Today, Ciudad Rodrigo, next week, Salamanca perhaps. She thought that anywhere would seem like home if he were there, and everywhere empty without him.

As they rode slowly towards the town she could not help comparing it with the first occasion. Then she had been trying to forget Robert Falconbridge. Now she knew she never would.

'Damned glad to see the old place again,' said Brudenell.

'Yes. There were moments when I thought we might not,' replied Falconbridge.

It was so precisely an echo of what Jacinta had said that Sabrina looked up quickly. He met her gaze and smiled. 'At least now I can look your godfather in the face—and keep my liver intact.'

'What has your liver got to do with it?' she asked.

'A private matter, between gentlemen.'

'Oh.' She had an idea he was teasing her again, though his expression did not suggest it. 'Well, I'm glad to learn your vital organs are safe.'

He bit back a laugh. 'It's a relief to me, too.'

The cavalcade clattered over the bridge and through the gates, following the road to the Castillo. They dismounted in the courtyard and Brudenell sent a runner to announce their arrival. Then he looked at his companions.

'Well, I suppose we'd better go and give an account of ourselves to Ward.'

'I suppose we had.' Falconbridge turned to Sabrina. 'Are you equal to it, my dear?'

'Certainly.'

'Good girl.'

Before there was a chance for further speech they heard the sound of footsteps behind them. They turned to see Colonel Albermarle. Sabrina's face lit in a smile. Then she was enveloped in a hearty hug.

'My dear girl, how glad I am to see you.'

'And I to see you, sir.'

'I have thought of you constantly since the day you left.' He held her at arm's length. 'Are you well?'

'Quite well.'

'I was expecting your return by coach, not on horseback. Was there some mishap?'

'Circumstances forced us to leave the coach behind,' she explained.

'Indeed. Well, you can tell me the details later over dinner.'

'Of course.'

Albermarle's gaze went from her to the rest of the group and came to rest on Falconbridge. 'You got her back safe, Major. I'm obliged.'

'Precious few thanks are due to me, sir. The credit rightly belongs to Miss Huntley herself.'

Albermarle saw the glance that passed between the two of them and knew there was more to the matter than he was being told. However, he decided that this was not the right time to probe.

'Am I to take it that your mission was successful?'

Sabrina bit her lip. 'Yes and no.'

'I'm not sure I follow you, my dear.'

'Godfather, have you not spoken to Ramon?'

Albermarle frowned. 'Ramon? No, how should I? He is with you.'

The others exchanged looks of consternation. Sabrina heard Falconbridge swear under his breath.

'Am I to understand that Ramon has not returned, sir?' he asked.

'No, he has not, or not to my knowledge.'

Suddenly all the elation of the past few minutes leached away. It was replaced by sudden deep unease as the implications began to dawn.

'Nothing would have kept Ramon from coming

here, save for some misfortune,' said Sabrina. 'Perhaps his horse went lame.'

Falconbridge frowned. 'Perhaps. I just pray it is only that.'

Thinking of the possible dangers their companion might have encountered, she felt her stomach knot. Was Ramon lying dead or injured as a result of an encounter with a French patrol? A glance at Luis and Jacinta revealed that the possibility had occurred to them as well. Willis and Blakelock frowned.

'If his horse went lame it may have taken some time to find another, depending on where it happened,' said Albermarle. 'In which case he'll turn up in the next few days, I expect. He is an able man. I'm sure you need not fear for his safety.'

'It isn't just a matter of his safety, sir,' replied Falconbridge.

'What do you mean?'

'Ramon has the plans we brought back from Aranjuez.'

'You mean you entrusted the documents to this man?'

'That is correct, sir. I would not have done it, save under the most extreme of circumstances.'

Albermarle shook his head. 'This is unfortunate indeed. No doubt you acted for the best but—'

'He could not have done anything else, sir,' said Sabrina.

For a moment her gaze met Falconbridge's and she saw him smile faintly. Then he turned back to Albermarle.

'I take full responsibility for the decision,' he replied. 'It seemed the only choice at the time. I had hoped that Ramon would have returned by now. Unfortunately nothing can be done until he does, or we find out what happened to him.'

'You realise that General Ward will have to be apprised of the circumstances.'

'Of course.'

His expression gave nothing away, but Blakelock's and Willis's did, and Sabrina began to feel deeply uneasy in her turn. Surely they did not think that Ward would somehow blame Falconbridge for this mishap? Then she realised that that was exactly what they did think.

'Well, we'd better go in.' Albermarle shot a glance at his goddaughter. 'No doubt you will want to retire to your lodgings and rest after your journey, my dear.'

'I'll rest later,' she replied. 'Right now I have to go along to this debriefing.'

Luis nodded. 'Maybe we should all go, *Doña* Sabrina. It may be that Major Falconbridge will require corroboration of his report to General Ward.'

The others murmured their agreement. Albermarle looked round in surprise.

'Surely there is no need for all of you to attend?'

'I think there is every need, sir,' replied Sabrina.

He saw the resolution on every face and then shrugged. 'If you insist.'

'We do insist.'

Thus they set off together across the courtyard. As they did so, Falconbridge fell into step with her.

'Thank you,' he murmured.

'For nothing.'

'Not nothing, I think.'

'They cannot blame you for this, Robert.'

'I let vital papers pass out of my hands.'

'You had no choice.'

He vouchsafed no reply, forbearing to say that this was the army and that his superiors tended to see things their way.

They arrived outside Ward's office a short time later. Albermarle spoke to the adjutant on duty and they were shown straight in. Looking round, Sabrina could not but remember the last time she had been here, a reluctant participant in a military scheme. It was no more than three weeks ago, yet how very different her feelings were now.

Ward looked up in surprise as the group walked in. However, he made no remark on the matter and merely rose from his chair.

'Ah, Major Falconbridge and Miss Huntley. Returned safe and sound.' He paused. 'Well, man? Did you obtain the papers?'

'Yes, sir.'

'Where are they?'

'I no longer have them, sir.'

Ward's brows drew together. 'I think you'd better explain.'

Falconbridge summarised events, omitting nothing and exaggerating nothing.

Ward heard him out without interruption but his expression was wintry. 'So the documents are now in the possession of this man, Ramon?'

'That is correct, sir.'

'A partisan, I believe.'

'Yes, sir.'

'What do we know about him?'

'I believe him to be honest and reliable.'

'I didn't ask what you believe, Major. I asked what is known,' replied Ward. 'The documents in his possession are worth a great deal of money in more than one quarter.'

Sabrina, who had been following the conversation closely, stared at him in disbelief. It was followed immediately by a surge of anger. Beside her

Jacinta and Luis stiffened visibly. Suddenly events were taking a turn she could never have envisaged. Even so, she couldn't let the imputation pass unchallenged. Striving to control her voice, she spoke up.

'Ramon is both honest and loyal, sir. He would never do such a thing."

Ward glanced at her. 'Men will do all manner of things for money, Miss Huntley.'

'If he is not here now it is because something happened to prevent it,' she replied.

'Let us hope you are right, ma'am.'

Her face paled but Ward had turned his attention back to Falconbridge.

'The decision to let the documents out of your keeping amounts to a dereliction of duty, Major.'

Falconbridge's jaw tightened. 'Had I not done so, the French would have found them when we were captured. I gave them to the one person who had a realistic chance of getting away and delivering them safely.'

'What Major Falconbridge says it true,' said Sabrina. 'And every member of our party here will attest to it, General.'

Ward surveyed her coolly. 'Be that as it may, the documents are still missing. Of course, your friend Ramon may yet deliver them.'

'If he can, he will,' she replied.

'Again, let us hope you are right, ma'am,' he replied. 'So much hangs on it, does it not?'

The implication of the words was not lost on her and she was suddenly sickened. If Ramon did not come, all their efforts would have been for nothing. Her father would not be freed. Beside her she heard a faint hiss of indrawn breath and glanced at Jacinta. The woman's face was a mask of cold fury, an outward expression of Sabrina's own sentiments.

'Major Falconbridge, you will return to your quarters and stay there. I shall want to talk to you again later. Lord Wellington will require a full report of course.'

'Yes, sir.'

Ward favoured Sabrina with another chilly smile. 'Your servant, Miss Huntley.'

It was dismissal and there was nothing they could do about it. They trooped out of the office and into the corridor. Sabrina turned to face Falconbridge.

'I'm so sorry, Robert.'

'Thank you for what you said back there.'

'It was the least I could do. I wanted to hit the old buzzard for implying those things.'

He gave her a wry smile. 'It is perhaps as well that you did not.'

'Yes, I suppose it is, though it would have served him right.'

Albermarle shook his head. 'Damnable situation

all round, but I cannot blame you for what happened, Major.'

'Thank you, sir.'

The Colonel turned to his goddaughter. 'Will you walk back to your lodgings, my dear?'

'Presently, sir.'

'Then I'll leave you for the time.' He nodded to Falconbridge. 'Let's just hope your man, Ramon, turns up.'

With that Albermarle walked away. For a little space they watched him go. Then Falconbridge looked at Sabrina. 'I had hoped to call on you after you had rested, but I fear that may not be possible for a while.'

Her heart skipped a beat. He did want to see her after all. 'Then I shall have to be patient.'

'I fear you will.' He sighed. 'It's a devil of a mess.'

'But not of your making.'

'You are generous. The consequences for you may be harsh indeed.'

'You must not think that way. Ramon will come. I know he will.'

'I pray he will. The thought of all your efforts being for nothing appals me.'

'I am not the only one who stands to lose something. Your promotion—'

'Is unimportant, compared with your father's freedom.'

The words brought a lump to her throat. 'It may yet be well.'

He hoped with all his heart that she was right.

After they parted Sabrina rejoined Jacinta and Luis and walked back to her lodgings. How different it all was from the way she had imagined it. Her vision of their triumphant return had been a fantasy indeed. When they reached the door, Luis paused.

'I must leave you here, *Doña* Sabrina. Jacinta will look after you for the time being.'

'Where are you going?'

'To find out what has happened to Ramon.'

'He could be anywhere, Luis.'

'Then I must discover where that is.'

'Will you not eat first and rest a little?'

He smiled, revealing strong, white teeth. 'The sooner I leave, the sooner I shall find him.'

Jacinta frowned. 'How do you know you will succeed?'

'I will find him. Everyone must be somewhere, you see.' He paused. 'Besides, Ramon is my friend and I did not much care for the slurs of General Ward.'

'None of us cared for them,' said Sabrina. 'When

Ramon returns he can shove them back down the General's throat.'

'Exactly so.'

'He may also wish to consider where he'd like to shove General Ward's secret papers when next they meet,' replied Jacinta.

Sabrina choked back indecorous laughter.

Luis grinned. 'I will suggest it to him. In the meantime, I must find a fresh horse.'

'When you get one, come back. I will have some provisions ready for you,' said Jacinta.

'*Muchas gracias. Hasta entonces.*'

With that he bowed and left them.

Some time later, in the privacy of her room, Sabrina stripped off her travel-stained garments and climbed into a hot tub. She sank into the water with a sigh of real pleasure. It seemed so long since she had bathed properly or worn clean clothes. She scrubbed herself vigorously and washed her hair before leaning back to relax and let the heat unknot her aching muscles. The water was cooling before she felt ready to climb out. Having dried herself off she donned one of her older gowns, a rose-pink muslin that had remained behind in the wardrobe. When her hair was dry she brushed it out and tied it back with a ribbon.

A close scrutiny in the mirror revealed that her

appearance was at least acceptable, although her face and neck were lightly tanned from the time spent in the open air. The effect was not entirely displeasing though, for the colour enhanced her hair and eyes. Some hand cream would help restore the softness lost through outdoor living. As she began to massage the cream in she realised she was still wearing the wedding ring that Falconbridge had given her when they set out for Aranjuez. She had grown so accustomed to its presence it had almost become part of her hand. It cost her a real pang to remove it, but to do anything else was totally inappropriate. She laid it carefully in the small jewel box on the dresser and closed the lid. That part of the adventure was really over.

Satisfied that she was presentable again, she went downstairs in search of something to eat. She was met by Jacinta, also bathed now and dressed in clean garments.

'I will make you a tortilla,' she said. 'It will keep the wolf from the door until dinner.'

'Make enough for yourself, as well,' replied Sabrina. 'You must also be hungry by now.'

Jacinta nodded. 'It will be good to have some fresh food again, no?'

'Yes, it will.'

'And bread that is not the consistency of brick.'

Sabrina smiled sadly, recalling the meal she had

shared with Falconbridge when they had sat by the creek together. The rations had been scanty and poor but his conversation had not. Just being in his company was sufficient compensation for stale bread and cheese. Would they ever have the dinner together that he had promised her? Circumstances seemed to be ranged against it. General Ward had made no secret of his displeasure. If Ramon did not return… She didn't want to think about the consequences of that, for Falconbridge or for her father.

Almost as if she knew her thoughts, Jacinta met her gaze. 'If anyone can find Ramon now, it is Luis.'

'I hope you are right.'

'One does not suffer a friend to be insulted. You spoke up for Ramon before General Ward. Now Luis will do his part.'

'Ramon is my friend, too,' replied Sabrina. 'My father also holds him in the highest regard. He would have been deeply angered had he been there today.'

'Yes, I believe he would. For his sake, too, Luis will find Ramon.'

Later, when they had eaten, Sabrina went out into the garden, wanting some fresh air and some space in which to think. Without making any conscious choice she followed the path to the stone bench she had sat on with Robert Falconbridge the last time she had been out here. He had tried every means to dissuade her from accompanying him on the mission. Every detail was etched on her memory. Even then she had been aware of him, his sheer physical presence, his look, his touch. She could never have thought then that one glorious moonlit evening he would take her in his arms and steal her heart.

She was so rapt in thought that she failed to hear the footsteps on the path until the visitor was close. She caught sight of a red uniform jacket and her heart leapt. Then she realised with a stab of disappointment that the newcomer was a total stranger. He bowed and smiled.

'I have been charged to deliver this letter, ma'am. Compliments of Major Falconbridge.'

Her heart gave another lurch. 'Thank you for your trouble, sir.'

'No trouble at all, ma'am.'

When he had gone she sank back onto the stone seat and broke open the wafer with a trembling hand. The missive contained one sentence only: *Since a Field Marshal's baton appears to be out of reach for the present, I comfort myself with the slender hope that you might consent to dine with a humble Major, as soon as he can arrange it. F.* Sabrina read it and felt laughter bubble up in her throat. He had meant it then. Suddenly all her earlier gloom lifted. All might yet be well. Having re-read the note half a dozen times, she carefully refolded it and tucked it safely inside the bodice of her gown. Then she went indoors to find pen and paper.

Some time later an orderly arrived at the officers' quarters. 'A note for Major Falconbridge,' he announced. 'Arrived just now, sir.'

Brudenell gestured across the room. 'The Major is yonder.'

Falconbridge took the letter and dismissed the man. Then he studied the direction. The handwriting was unfamiliar but it was unquestionably feminine in nature. Hope leapt. Taking a deep breath he opened it, eagerly scanning the contents. It contained just one sentence: *Whilst the loss of a baton is deeply regrettable, the notion of dining with a lower-ranking officer is, on balance, to be preferred.* There was no signature but it needed none, and his face lit with a grin.

'Good news?' inquired Brudenell.

'Very good news.'

'It's about time.'

'Yes, it is.'

Refolding the paper, Falconbridge stowed it carefully inside his breast pocket. It was about time, he thought; time to draw a line under the past and get on with his life. At least now he knew what he wanted the future to be.

His thoughts were interrupted by the arrival of an adjutant summoning him to Lord Wellington's headquarters in the Palacio de los Castro. He exchanged glances with Brudenell and then nodded.

'I shall come directly.'

When the adjutant had departed, his friend frowned. 'What does the old man want now?'

'To hear my report, I imagine. Unless of course he wishes to tell me himself that Ramon has returned with the papers.'

'That would solve a few problems, would it not?'

'Aye, it would.'

'You did the best you could, Robert. Damned bad luck his getting delayed like that.'

'It's a pity Ward doesn't see it in the same light.'

'No, well, he wasn't surrounded by hostile French troops wanting to carve him into slivers, was he?'

'Even so...' Falconbridge moved to the door '...I made an error of judgement. The trouble is that others besides myself will be made to pay for it.'

When he arrived at Wellington's door a short time later it was to see Ward and Forbes there as well. His heart sank. Schooling his face to a neutral expression he halted in front of the desk.

'You wished to see me, sir?'

Wellington looked up from the letter he had been writing and leaned back in his chair, surveying his visitor coolly. The stern lines of his face gave nothing away but the piercing eyes missed nothing. Under their fixed scrutiny his visitor felt the knot in his gut tighten.

'Damned bad business, Falconbridge.'

'Yes, sir.'

Ward nodded and interjected, 'You should not have let those papers out of your hands.'

'I believed I had no choice, sir, with capture imminent.'

'You should have brought the documents yourself.'

'That would have meant leaving my companions to die, sir.'

'All soldiers know the risks of war.'

'Miss Huntley is not a soldier.'

'No, but she also knew the risks.'

Falconbridge's eyes became steel grey. 'Not a good enough reason, in my opinion, for leaving her to the mercy of the French.'

Ward glared and made to reply but Wellington was before him. 'The situation was an unenviable one and I have no doubt you did what you thought right, Major. Nevertheless, the fact remains that a third party now has in his possession the most sensitive of information.'

'Information that our man in Madrid went to great lengths to obtain,' said Forbes.

'I believe that Ramon will deliver it if he can,' replied Falconbridge.

Ward snorted. The sound drew a swift quelling glance from Wellington but just as quickly his attention returned to Falconbridge.

'You appear to have great faith in this man.'

'I do, sir, and so does Miss Huntley. Ramon was a good friend of her father's.'

'Well, we'll see soon enough whether your faith is justified.'

'Touching the matter of John Huntley, sir...'

'Well?'

'His freedom was the condition that caused Miss Huntley to agree to go on the mission in the first place. She has performed her part in exemplary fashion, sir, and kept her side of the bargain.'

'But you did not return with the papers you went for,' said Ward.

'That is not her fault. It is mine, and she should not be punished for it.'

Wellington lifted one eyebrow a little. 'I should have thought there was no question of her being penalised in any way. Major Forbes, have not negotiations already begun for the release of prisoners?'

'They have, sir.'

'John Huntley among them?'

'Yes, sir.'

'Good. You will keep me informed of how things progress.'

Falconbridge breathed a silent sigh of relief. At least that much might be salvaged from the affair. Before he could pursue the thought any further he became aware that Wellington was addressing him again.

'For the rest we can only wait and hope. In the meantime, in the absence of information, I must try and outguess the French. You may return to your duties, Major Falconbridge.'

Being thus dismissed he walked back to his quarters with the words ringing in his ears. Waiting and hoping were indeed the only options available to him just then, on the career front anyway. On a personal level, he felt a different kind of hope. Sabrina's face drifted into his mind and he recalled a promise he had made. That at least was a matter he could do something about.

Chapter Fifteen

The following morning Sabrina received a courteous letter from Major Falconbridge inviting her to dine with him and Brudenell that evening. Her face lit with a smile as she read the invitation. He had kept his promise, and done it with tact and sensitivity. The occasion coincided with ladies' night in the officers' mess. Moreover, as Colonel Albermarle was also invited to join the party, she would have a highly respectable escort. For all sorts of reasons it promised to be an enjoyable occasion and she lost no time in returning a note of acceptance.

However, it threw up another difficulty. Her boxes still had not been returned to her and the choice of gowns remaining in her wardrobe was slim. In the end she selected one of her newer muslin frocks. The gown was fashioned in a simple but becoming style and, when combined with a silken shawl, a fetching hairstyle, a necklace and earrings and a pair of long gloves, the effect was of simple understated elegance.

Heads turned as she and Colonel Albermarle made their entrance, and Falconbridge felt the first stirrings of pride that she was to be his guest that evening. Beside him, Brudenell was following her progress, too.

'My word, Robert, but she's a beauty.'

'That she is.'

'What on earth does she see in you?'

'Lord knows.'

They moved forward to meet their guests. For a moment Falconbridge took her hand, letting his gaze travel the length of her. Then he smiled.

'You look wonderful.'

'Thank you.'

He felt another surge of pride, fully aware of the covert looks coming their way, and knowing every man there would like to be in his shoes. In consequence, he forgot that he had retained her hand far longer than was necessary or correct.

Beside him Albermarle coughed. 'Well, then, shall we sit down?'

Sabrina smiled and took her place beside their host. The meal was excellent, a real treat after the Spartan rations they had endured in the latter days of their journey. A tasty vegetable soup was removed with trout, cooked *à la plancha,* and then a sirloin of beef, chicken in a lemon sauce and a game pie. Dessert was a light and frothy syllabub, with fruit and sweetmeats.

The conversation flowed easily throughout. As ever, Falconbridge and Brudenell were excellent company, being well informed on a variety of topics, and often witty. Many times Sabrina found herself laughing at the tales of their past exploits. These, she had no doubt, had been carefully censored and were thus totally unexceptionable, but always hilarious. Albermarle, too, relaxed and became expansive, keeping up his part in the conversation. Aware of having the company and undivided attention of three distinguished men, Sabrina found herself positively enjoying the covert and envious looks that came her way from some of the other ladies present. It occurred to her then that both Brudenell and Robert were very handsome in their different ways. Even so, she had eyes for only one.

Becoming aware of her attention Falconbridge smiled and, seeing that the other two were temporarily engaged in discussion, seized his chance. 'You look thoughtful, ma'am.'

'I was thinking,' she admitted.

He lowered his voice a little. 'About what?'

'I shall not tell you for fear you should grow conceited.'

He grinned. 'Now I am intrigued.'

'Good.'

'Vixen.'

Sabrina laughed. It might have been the candle-light or the wine or the sparkle in her eyes, or all three, but again he found himself staring and felt a sudden rush of heat to his groin.

'If we were alone, my girl, I should compel you to speak.'

'Do you think so?'

'Do you think I would not?'

The tone and the accompanying look sent a delicious shiver the length of her body. Suddenly she wished very much that they were alone together, somewhere out in the back of beyond; that she was in his arms again and yielding to that tender compulsion. Startled by the tenor of her thoughts she lowered her gaze, afraid that he might read too accurately what lay behind.

Fortunately their attention was recalled by Albermarle who had directed a question to Falconbridge. Gathering his wits he made some reply but it wasn't easy while his thoughts were all on the woman beside him.

For the remainder of the evening there was no further opportunity for private speech until the time came for her and Albermarle to leave.

'Thank you,' she said. 'It has been a wonderful evening. And it was a truly delicious meal.'

He raised her hand to his lips. 'I keep my promises.'

'So you do.' She smiled. 'And most handsomely, too.'

Resisting the urge to take her in his arms, he contented himself with a bow. 'It was my pleasure.'

'Capital evening, Major,' said Albermarle. 'First rate.'

'I'm glad you enjoyed it, sir.'

'Hope to return the favour one day soon.'

'I'll look forward to it, sir.'

With real regret he watched his guests depart, following their progress until they were out of sight.

For a while Sabrina and her godfather walked in companionable silence. Then he cast a shrewd glance her way.

'I'd say that young man has taken quite a fancy to you, my dear.'

Her cheeks reddened and she was glad of the concealing darkness. 'Would you?'

'Couldn't keep his eyes off you all evening. Not that it's to be wondered at. You're a devilish pretty girl.'

'Thank you, sir.'

He hesitated and then said casually, 'I think you're not indifferent to him either.'

She bit her lip. 'I like him very well.'

'Thought so. I confess it surprised me at first. I'd a notion you didn't care for him at one time.'

'No, I didn't, but my knowing him better has improved my opinion of him.'

'I see.' He paused. 'Good sort of fellow, Falconbridge.'

'Yes, he is.'

Albermarle made no reply but merely smiled to himself.

Sabrina did not see or hear from Falconbridge for several days after that and guessed that his duties kept him fully occupied. Then one morning he came to call.

'I regret that Wellington has assigned me to another mission. I shall be going out of town for a while.'

Sabrina's heart sank. This was the very thing she had been dreading. Although she had known it must come at some point she had not thought it would be so soon. Somehow she summoned a smile, trying not to let her disappointment show.

'Will you be gone long?'

'A week or so, I believe.'

'I see.'

'I deeply regret the necessity, but my orders are

to leave at once.' He looked down into her face. 'However, I wanted to see you first.'

'I am so glad that you did.' She hesitated, hating to ask but needing to know the answer. 'Is it going to be dangerous, this mission of yours?'

'Would that matter to you?'

'You know it would.'

'On this occasion I think there is likely to be little danger.'

'May I ask where you are going?'

'I am not at liberty to say what it is at present.'

'Forgive me, it was a tactless question.'

He shook his head. 'No, just a natural one. When I return, everything will be made clear.'

'A mystery then.' She laid a hand on his sleeve. 'I beg you will be careful. You have trouble enough at present without adding injury to the list.'

'I promise to heed the advice.'

'I wish I were going with you. I hate the thought of sitting here and doing nothing.'

'You have already done far more than could ever have been expected of you. Besides, you will want to wait for news of Ramon.'

'Yes,' she replied. 'We have heard nothing from Luis since he left.'

'I fear the task will be like looking for a needle in a haystack.'

'He felt he had to do it anyway,' she replied. 'General Ward's comments went deep.'

'Yes, they did.'

She met his gaze and held it. 'If Ramon does not return, will things go ill for you, Robert?'

'I cannot deny that matters are a touch awkward at present, but all may yet be well.'

'If it had not been for me and Jacinta you would have brought those documents back yourself. Your men would have provided a diversion to cover your escape, and they would all have done it as a matter of duty. But you would not leave two women behind to be captured while you left the scene.'

'Nor would any man worthy of the name.' He took her shoulders in a gentle clasp. 'You should not feel guilty on that account.'

'I cannot help it.'

'I took the decision and I stand by it. Do you really think I could have left you there?'

The warmth of his hands and the gentleness of his tone brought a lump to her throat. 'You should have, but I am glad you did not. In consequence, all of Lord Wellington's plans are thrown awry.'

He smiled. 'I think you overstate the case a little. This is a setback, no more.'

'Now you will not get your promotion.'

'It doesn't matter. There will be other opportunities. What matters to me is your safety and well-being.'

'And yours to me.'

His heart beat a little quicker but before he could reply they heard booted feet in the hall. Then Corporal Blakelock appeared at the door. 'Beg pardon, Major, but it's time.'

'Very well. I'm coming.' Falconbridge smiled ruefully at Sabrina. 'There is so much I want to say to you and no time now to do it in, but I'll be back, I promise you.'

She managed to return his smile. 'I'll hold you to that.'

He pressed his lips to her hand, and then left her to join the waiting men. Sabrina watched until they were out of sight and only the warm imprint of his kiss remained.

The days following his departure seemed long and dull. Nor could she settle to anything. Reading, sewing and sketch pad were abandoned in succession. Every time she heard a horse in the street or a footstep in the hall her heart leapt. She knew it could not be him, but lived in the hope that it might be Luis or Ramon or both, and each time the hope was dashed. Then her thoughts would turn back to Falconbridge, wondering where he was and what he was doing at that moment. She had known she was going to miss him, but now his absence left a void that nothing could fill. Moreover, she missed action, the sense of having something important to do.

Needing to make herself useful, she accompanied Jacinta to the market each day and explored the local shops to see what they might have to offer in the way of dress fabric. Her trunks had not yet arrived and there was no absolute certainty of their doing so. In consequence, her wardrobe was drastically reduced, and she needed to furnish herself with some new gowns. The choice proved to be limited but she found two lengths of figured muslin cloth and some thread, with matching ribbon for trim. At least sewing new gowns would provide a worthwhile occupation.

'Perhaps you will have them ready by the time Major Falconbridge returns,' said Jacinta.

'Yes, perhaps,' she replied.

Seeing her downcast expression the other woman continued, 'You need not worry for him. He will come back. That one is like a cat; he has nine lives.'

Sabrina made no reply. This parting, though not wholly unexpected, had come sooner than she had anticipated. Being separated from him was like losing a part of her. It caused a lowering of the spirits quite unlike her usual buoyant self. Her abstracted air had not passed unnoticed in other quarters. Colonel Albermarle, with whom she was dining that evening, was sufficiently concerned to enquire.

'Is something wrong, my dear?'

Unable to open her heart just then, she sought refuge in a partial truth. 'It's only that so many days have passed without news of Ramon or Luis. I really thought they might have returned by now.'

It had been his thought also but he did not say so. 'If they have not there will be a good reason for it.' He regarded her shrewdly. 'It is an anticlimax, isn't it, coming back to routine after such an adventure?'

'I confess it is.'

'Look, I have to ride out to the Great Teson tomorrow morning. Why don't you come with me?'

Sabrina brightened a little. 'I'd like that.'

They went out early, and once on horseback again Sabrina felt her spirits revive. The morning air was sweet and cool and the company congenial. As they rode towards the hilltop batteries, Albermarle pointed out the repairs and improvements underway. Even at this hour the place was a hive of activity. Seeing so many redcoats she began automatically to seek for one in particular, even though her mind told her he couldn't possibly be there. Then she told herself sternly not to be such an idiot.

They returned to the house just before ten to see two horses outside, one a particularly poor specimen. Since she didn't recognise either, Sabrina assumed it must be someone seeking Albermarle.

'Possibly, my dear,' he said. 'I left word where I would be if needed, though I don't know anyone who owns such a nag as that chestnut. Never saw such an ancient, sway-backed, spavined, cow-hocked bag of bones in my life.'

The comment was not unjustified. The horse looked as though it might have walked straight out of the pages of a Cervantes novel.

'Perhaps it belongs to one of the traders hereabouts,' she suggested. 'I'll ask Jacinta.'

The two of them dismounted and went in together. They had no sooner entered the hallway than they saw the maid speaking animatedly to two men in dirty and travel-stained clothes. Seeing the newcomers she looked up, smiling. Then the men turned around. Sabrina's heart leapt.

'Ramon! Luis! How glad I am to see you.'

'Did I not tell you I would find him?' said Luis.

'I knew if anyone could, it would be you.' Sabrina turned to Ramon, examining him critically. 'Are you injured? Have you been unwell? We have been so concerned.'

He smiled ruefully. 'I am well, *Doña* Sabrina, I thank you.'

'Glad to hear it,' said Albermarle, 'but where the devil have you been, man?'

'I regret the tardiness of my return, Colonel, but it could not be avoided.' He looked at Sabrina. 'The day after I left you, my horse put its foot in a hole and broke its leg. I had to shoot it. Then I walked for three days more before I came to a farmstead where I could obtain another beast. Unfortunately, I had no money and it took all my powers of persuasion to make the man part with it. Even then I had to swear a sacred oath to return with payment.'

'It must be some horse.'

'Oh, it is.'

Light dawned. 'Not that ghastly old crock I saw outside?'

'The very same.'

Albermarle snorted. 'The rogue should rather have paid you for taking it off his hands. It's a miracle you got here at all.'

'At times I did wonder if it would not have been quicker to walk.'

Luis grinned. 'When I met him he was not twenty miles from town, carrying the horse.' Then, seeing their expressions of incredulity, he added, 'All right,

I admit I exaggerate a little bit. He was not carrying it just then.'

Jacinta threw him a quelling glance and Albermarle turned back to Ramon.

'Have you got the papers, man?' he demanded.

'I have them safe, Colonel.'

The collective sigh of relief was audible.

'Luis told me that my delay has meant trouble for Major Falconbridge,' Ramon went on, 'and for that I am truly sorry.'

'The matter must be rectified at once,' said Albermarle.

Luis nodded. 'By taking the papers to General Ward, no?'

'Ward be damned. Take 'em straight to Wellington.'

Afterwards, it was as though a load had been lifted from Sabrina's shoulders. The only cloud over her pleasure was that she couldn't let Falconbridge know straight away. A pleasant diversion arrived some three days later in the form of the previously abandoned coach, and with it her missing boxes. Having given the driver a handsome tip, she lost no time in having these carried upstairs. Then she and Jacinta spent an hour unpacking. Initially Sabrina had wondered what condition her things might be in, but, apart from a little creasing, the garments seemed to be untouched by the recent adventure. It came as a relief. Although she did not want for funds, they would not have stretched to the replacement of almost her entire wardrobe.

Jacinta gathered an armful of dresses. 'I will take these for pressing. They will soon be as good as…'

The words were drowned by loud knocking on the door. Then they heard Luis's voice.

'*Doña* Sabrina, you must come!'

Her stomach lurched. Immediately her thoughts went to Robert. Had something happened to him? Was he injured? Captured? Dead? Dear God, not dead. She hurried to the door and threw it open.

'What is it? What's happened, Luis?'

'He is back!'

She let out a long breath. 'Thank heaven. Is he all right?'

'A little tired perhaps, and thinner of course, but otherwise all right.'

She stared at him. 'Thinner?'

'*Si,* but it is to be expected. Probably he has had a little fever. It is not unknown.'

Sabrina paled. 'A fever?'

Jacinta stepped forwards and glared at Luis. 'Who has a fever, you fool?'

He looked affronted. 'I did not say that anyone

had a fever. I only said he might have had one, being thin as he is.'

'Why should Major Falconbridge be thin?'

'Not Major Falconbridge, woman.'

'*Idiota!* Who then?'

'Why, Señor Huntley of course. Who else?'

Sabrina went pale and red by turns. 'My father? My father is back?'

Luis nodded. 'That is what I have been telling you.'

He had no time for more because Sabrina was out of the room and running along the passage to the head of the stairs. She paused there a moment, her gaze searching the hallway below. Several men were waiting there. Among them was a man of middle years with greying brown hair. His face was pale and gaunt, the blue eyes tired. Though of upright carriage he was dusty and travel-stained and indisputably thinner, but she would have known him anywhere.

'Father.'

At the sound of her voice the blue eyes brightened and a tremulous smile formed on his lips. Sabrina raced down the stairs and across the hall. Moments later his arms were round her.

'Oh, my dearest child, how I have dreamed of this moment.'

'And I also.' Her breath caught on a sob. 'I thought

I might never see you again. I feared you would never be freed.'

'I might not have been but for you. Major Falconbridge has told me what you did to obtain my release.'

She looked round and saw him just a few feet away and suddenly a lump formed in her throat. 'This was your mission. This is why you went out of town.'

'Yes,' he replied. 'It was General Ward who charged me with the office, but he had his orders from the very top.'

'Lord Wellington?'

'Apparently so. When he received word that the return of the English prisoners was imminent, he sent me to oversee the handover and to ensure your father's safe return. I did not tell you because I wanted it to be a surprise.'

'The very best of surprises. Thank you. Thank you from the bottom of my heart.'

'No thanks are necessary. It was my privilege.'

Sabrina didn't know whether to laugh or cry and ended by doing both. He smiled gently.

'You and your father must have a great deal to say to one another, so I'll leave you for the time being.'

Unable to speak, she nodded, dashing tears from her eyes with a shaking hand. Her father put an arm about her shoulders and then looked at his deliverer.

'Thank you, Major, for all that you have done. I am most grateful.'

'An honour and a pleasure, sir.' He bowed. 'Your servant, Miss Huntley.'

With that he turned and left them. Sabrina stared at the empty doorway, her heart full.

Falconbridge's mind was also agreeably preoccupied: Sabrina's joy on being reunited with her father had given him a very real glow of pleasure. That he had been able to contribute to her happiness in some small way, gladdened him immeasurably.

On leaving them he had delivered his report to Wellington, informing him that the exchange of prisoners had taken place without a hitch. It was then that he learned of Ramon's return and the safe delivery of the military plans. For a moment or two he wasn't sure he'd heard correctly. When his brain did assimilate the information, his overriding feeling was one of enormous relief. His lordship had no difficulty reading the expression.

'You did well, Major Falconbridge. The information was every bit as valuable as I'd hoped.'

'I am glad of it, sir.'

'It would appear that your faith in that fellow Ramon was quite justified.'

'I never doubted him, sir.'

'The feeling would seem to be mutual.'

'Sir?'

'May I say that you have inspired an extraordinary degree of loyalty among your confederates on the Aranjuez mission. Quite apart from a detailed explanation about why he was delayed so long, the chap was also quite tediously emphatic that what occurred was none of your fault.'

'Was he, sir?'

'Damn it, man, with a dozen like him we needn't have besieged Badajoz at all; we could have talked our way in.'

Falconbridge's lips twitched. 'I'm grateful for his support, sir.'

The hawk-like gaze held his. 'Then perhaps you should go and tell him that yourself.'

'I mean to, sir.'

'Good. Do it soon, would you? Then perhaps I might be left alone to get on with the organisation of this campaign.'

Falconbridge left the room, aware that he was grinning quite inanely but unable to help it. He would have gone directly to speak with Sabrina but tact forbade it. She and her father needed time together.

Thus it was another two days before he presented himself at her door. It was opened by Jacinta who informed him that her mistress was in the garden.

'It's all right,' he said as she made to accompany him, 'I know the way.'

He walked through the salon and let himself out through the open French window, pausing a moment on the pathway among the brightly coloured beds. He saw her sitting on a stone bench by the fountain, apparently absorbed in a book. The sound of the water covered his footsteps until he was close. He paused, drinking in the details, realising that imagination had fallen well short of reality. The dusty and dishevelled companion of his travels was far removed from the feminine vision before him now. She was wearing a pretty pink gown that he had never seen before. It showed off to advantage the curve of a figure whose perfection he had glimpsed more intimately on other occasions. The golden curls were arranged in a knot on the crown of her head, and trailed artlessly over her neck and shoulders.

As if sensing that quiet scrutiny she looked up and saw him. Her cheeks paled, then flooded with warm colour. The book slid unheeded from her lap.

'Robert.' She rose to greet him, holding out her hands. 'How glad I am that you have returned.'

He lost no time in possessing himself of the offering, holding her fingers in a familiar warm clasp as he returned her smile. Then he enquired after her father.

'I hope he is in better health.'

'He is much improved having had good food and plenty of rest. Of course, there is still some way to go yet, but I am sure that it will not be long before he is fully restored.'

'Indeed I am happy to hear it.'

'I cannot thank you enough for bringing him back to me.'

'It was but a trifling service to escort him the last few miles home.'

'Not trifling to me,' she replied. 'You cannot know what it meant.'

'And I must thank Ramon. Lord Wellington told me of his return.'

'Is it not wonderful? I cannot tell you how it felt to see him come back safe, and with the documents intact.'

He smiled. 'I think I can imagine it.'

'He went straight to see Lord Wellington and put the matter right. He felt it was the least he could do in view of his tardy arrival.'

'His lordship informed me that Ramon spoke most eloquently on my behalf.'

'I am quite sure he did.' She was suddenly aware that he was still holding her hands. She really ought to free herself.

He drew her to the bench and sat down beside her. 'I have wanted so much to speak with you,' he went on. 'I have missed your company these last two days.'

Her heart began to beat much faster. 'Have you?'

'More than I can say.' He hesitated. 'If I dared to, I would hope that you have also missed me, just a little.'

She smiled, regarding him askance. 'Are you fishing for compliments?'

'Absolutely. Is there any chance I might get one?'

'No chance at all. Though I did miss you—a little.'

His eyes gleamed. 'Only that?'

'In truth, rather more than that.'

For the space of several heartbeats his gaze searched her face. Then he did release her hands, but only in order to take her in his arms. The precipice yawned at her feet but now it induced no desire to draw back. Sabrina closed her eyes and leapt, relaxing against him, surrendering to the embrace, wanting this. Her entire being delighted in his nearness and in the familiar scents of leather and cedar, and the warmth of his lips on hers. Their touch engendered more erotic thoughts and blood became fire. Her mouth opened beneath his, soft and yielding inviting total possession. He tightened his hold and the kiss became deliciously intimate, but now there was no fear or revulsion, only a deep-seated feeling of belonging.

Eventually he released her and drew back a little, looking down into her face.

'How many times I have wanted to do that.'

'Have you?'

'Ever since the night of the ball.'

A small pulse leapt in her throat. 'Then it wasn't just a ruse?'

'A ruse?' His brows drew together for a moment. 'It may have begun that way, until I actually held you in my arms and kissed you. Then I realised that my feelings had grown deeper than even I had suspected.' He sighed. 'I had no expectation of their being returned, of course. You had made it clear that our relationship was to remain on solely professional lines.'

'I was afraid that if I did not you would think...'

'What?' he prompted gently.

'That you would think of me as Jack Denton once did. I could not bear to see you look at me like that.'

'My dearest girl, I would never look at you that way. You are most precious to me.' He drew her to his breast, pressing his lips to her hair. 'I think I did not know how precious until I saw you in Machart's clutches. The thought of any man doing you harm is intolerable. If I had my way you would never be harmed again.'

'Nor would I see harm come to you,' she replied.

'I imagine that was not always the case.'

'True. The first time I met you I confess I could cheerfully have wrung your neck.'

'Ah.' He pulled back enough to look into her eyes. 'And now?'

'I have no wish to, even though this behaviour can hardly be described as professional.'

'I'm afraid it's about to become even less so.'

Without warning Sabrina was tipped back into the crook of his arm and for a while after that speech was impossible. When next he looked into her face all suggestion of laughter was gone.

'In case I'm not making this plain enough, I love you to distraction and can think of nothing else.'

The green eyes danced. 'That is shockingly un-professional, sir, but I must tell you that the feeling is mutual.'

His heart performed a dangerously original exer-cise. 'It's clearly hopeless so there's only one thing to be done.'

'What do you suggest?'

'Marry me.'

The words brought a sudden surge of joy so in-tense that for a moment it eradicated all else. Sabrina reached up and brought his face down towards hers for a long, lingering kiss. Then she drew back a little in her turn. 'In case I'm not making this plain enough, the answer is yes.'

He grinned. 'Would you do that again, please, for the sake of clarity?'

The matter was clarified several times more before they came up for air.

'I would like us to be married as soon as possible,' he said then, 'but I know that there are other considerations.' He paused, choosing his next words with care. 'Perhaps you want time to get used to the idea of marriage. We have known each other only a short while.'

'How long does it take to know your own heart?' she replied.

'I think I did not know mine until I met you.'

'We have learned more about each other in those weeks than most people discover in years.'

'Then you would not object to our marrying sooner rather than later?'

'I want to be your wife, Robert. It cannot come soon enough for me.'

'Nor for me, either.' He gave her a wry smile. 'I gave you a wedding ring once before, and with precious little ceremony as I recall.'

'I still have it.'

'I'll give you a much finer one, set with diamonds perhaps.'

'If you don't mind, I'd like it to be the original. It has more significance to me than any diamonds ever could.'

'Are you sure, Sabrina?'

'Quite sure.'

'So be it.' He rose, bringing her gently with him. 'May I speak to your father?'

She nodded. 'It will doubtless come as a shock to him.'

'Then we will allow him some time to get used to the idea.' He grinned. 'A little time, that is.'

Chapter Sixteen

The wedding was to be a simple ceremony performed by the chaplain before a small number of witnesses. Falconbridge arrived early with Brudenell, but found it impossible to sit still and wait. Instead, he paced slowly the length of the hallway outside the chapel to try to dissipate the knot of tension in his gut. He heard the clock strike the hour but there was still no sign of his bride. The knot in his gut tightened. Was it all going to happen again? He shut his eyes and took a deep breath, telling himself not to be a fool. Brudenell eyed him shrewdly.

'She'll be here, Robert.'

He forced a smile. 'Yes, of course.'

'It's a bride's privilege to be late on her wedding day.'

'I know.'

'Then stop wearing out those stones and let us go in.'

He nodded and they walked up the aisle to take

their places. Around them the assembled guests smiled, but he saw only a blur of faces. His throat was dry. With an assumption of calm he was far from feeling he took his place with his friend. As he stood there he found himself praying silently.

It seemed an age that he remained there thus, but in reality only a minute or two, before they heard a noise behind them, gasps and murmuring voices. Both men glanced round and then remained thus, staring.

'By heaven and all the saints,' murmured Brudenell. 'You lucky...'

Falconbridge hardly heard him and could not have replied anyway, for he had no breath to do it. For a moment he was quite still, his gaze taking in every detail of the woman who walked towards him, leaning lightly on her father's arm. She was exquisite, every detail perfect from the long-sleeved gown of white satin and lace, to the pearls adorning her ears and throat and the silk flowers nestling among her gold curls, to the small bouquet of red roses that she was carrying. His heart swelled with love and pride. Then, gathering his wits again, he stepped forwards to meet her.

From among the assembled guests Wellington surveyed the proceedings with a keen eye. 'Damned handsome couple, what?'

Beside him Albermarle nodded. 'Indeed they are, my lord.'

'Good man, Falconbridge.'

'Oh, unquestionably, my lord. I've always thought so.'

The ceremony was simple and short, a brief exchange of vows and the placing of the gold ring to bind them together as man and wife. Sabrina stole a look at the man who was now her husband and received an answering smile.

The chaplain smiled, too. 'You may kiss the bride.'

Robert Falconbridge drew his wife close and for a moment looked down into her face. His heartbeat accelerated as he read the answer in her eyes. Then he bent his head and brought his mouth down on hers in a tender and lingering embrace.

Sabrina closed her eyes. For a moment she felt light-headed, dislocated from reality. Yet the warmth of his hands was real enough, like the scent of leather and cedar wood from his uniform and the pressure of his lips on hers. Her blood tingled and, deep within, a flame kindled in her body's core. Its glow remained even after he had drawn back. In shy confusion she became aware of voices raised in congratulation and good wishes. Then his hand closed around hers and squeezed it gently.

'Come, Mrs Falconbridge.'

* * *

Colonel Albermarle had arranged for the wedding breakfast to be held in a private room adjoining the officers' mess where they were joined by a larger group of friends and colleagues. Carried along on a wave of happiness Sabrina was yet keenly aware of the goodwill emanating from those gathered around them. Many were Falconbridge's colleagues who had managed to arrange a few hours off duty and who thronged around to wish him well. Over his bride they were positively foolish, and she found herself the recipient of numerous compliments and gallantries.

Her husband smiled and, seeing he had no chance of claiming her for a while, turned his attention to Ramon who, with Luis and Jacinta, had been watching the proceedings with approbation. All three offered their congratulations. Luis blinked away a tear.

'You must forgive me. I always cry at weddings.'

'It is true,' said Jacinta. 'He does.'

Falconbridge grinned. 'It is a tradition, I believe.' Then, seeing his chance, he turned to Ramon. 'There is something I would like to ask, if I may.'

The other man nodded. 'You can ask.'

'How did you persuade El Cuchillo to help us?'

For a moment Ramon was silent. Then he smiled faintly. 'I called in a favour.'

'I see. You've known him some time, I collect.'

'We go back a long way, he and I. We grew up in the same village.'

'Ah, you were old friends then.'

'We were never friends. I might even say we detested each other. Certainly we had numerous fights when we were boys. By the time we were young men we each had a healthy respect for the other.' Ramon paused. 'Then, one day, his family's house caught fire, trapping his mother and sister within. I had been working nearby and saw the smoke. When I went to investigate I heard the screams, so I broke in and managed to help them to safety.'

'And so you and he became friends in the end, eh?' said Luis.

Ramon smiled ruefully. 'No, we were never that exactly. All the same, he saw the rescue as divine intervention and believed himself obligated to me as a result. He went to the church and swore a sacred oath before the altar that one day he would repay the debt.'

Luis frowned. 'How long ago was that?'

'Twenty years.'

'His memory is long.'

'So is mine.'

'How could you be sure that he would keep his word?' asked Luis.

Jacinta met his eye with a level stare. 'Time does not affect a sacred promise. To break it would dishonour himself and his family, and imperil his immortal soul.'

'That is so,' replied Ramon. 'But, more than all of that, El Cuchillo hates the French as much as he loves a fight. He would never pass up such an opportunity.'

Falconbridge laughed. 'Whatever his motivation, I am glad of it, believe me.'

Watching the little group from across the room, Sabrina smiled. In that moment it truly felt as if all her family were gathered again at last. It seemed, too, that happiness was infectious. All around her, laughter and banter flowed like wine. Even her father was smiling and doing his best to look cheerful, though she knew that inwardly he felt sad, too.

'You need not worry for me,' she said. 'Truly I have married the best of men.'

He squeezed her hand. 'I could not have parted with you had I not thought so, my dear.'

As soon as Sabrina had expressed her wish to marry, he had lost no time in speaking with Albermarle to find out all he could about his prospective son-in-law. The conversation had proved to be reassuring, rather than otherwise, and he had taken comfort from it. Sabrina's obvious happiness and her new husband's evident love and pride did much now to alleviate any lingering doubts.

For his part Falconbridge had taken as much time as he could to get to know his wife's father and, when they did speak, to be as open and honest as possible. It had done him no disservice. Nor did he find John Huntley's company in any way irksome. Both men were well travelled and well read and thus had enough common ground to be able to converse with ease. Though he yet detected some faint reserve in Huntley's manner, he had every hope of their becoming the best of friends.

Colonel Albermarle waited for his moment and, seeing it, lost no time in taking Falconbridge aside to wish him happiness. The two shook hands heartily.

'I thank you for your good wishes.'

'Look after her, my boy.'

'I intend to, sir.'

'And be sure to make her happy.'

'I promise to do my best.'

Albermarle's eyes glinted. 'You'd better.'

'I know.' Falconbridge smiled wryly. 'I am also much attached to my liver and shall not give you any reason to try to remove it, sir.'

The older man beamed. 'I think we understand each other very well.'

'I believe we do.'

The meal progressed in an atmosphere of conviviality. Later there were speeches and numerous toasts were drunk to the bride and groom. Then, somewhat unexpectedly, Lord Wellington got to his feet. As the conversation faded he turned to the newly-weds.

'I shall not repeat what others have said before, although I share their sentiments unreservedly. It merely remains for me to give you this.' He drew a heavy, sealed pack of official papers from the pocket of his coat and handed it to the groom. Then, as the latter stared at it and him in silent bemusement, he added, 'Congratulations, Lieutenant Colonel Falconbridge.'

For a moment there was silence before the import dawned and the room erupted with cheers. Gathering his wits, the recipient got to his feet and shook the proffered hand. 'I really don't know what to say, my lord, except to thank you.'

Wellington raised an eyebrow. 'You may wish you hadn't when we make our push for Salamanca.' For a moment the hawk-like gaze rested on the other man. 'In the interim, you will want to be with your lovely wife. Take three days' leave. That's an order.'

'Yes, my lord.'

Sabrina who had been following every word felt only swelling joy. Three days! Never would she have foreseen anything like this. It was a gesture as generous as it was unexpected. Before she had time to do more than add her thanks, her husband gathered her in his arms and bestowed on her a resounding kiss. She smiled up at him, eyes shining.

'Congratulations, Robert. I'm so proud of you.'

'I could not have done it without you.'

'I keep thinking I shall wake in a moment, and find all this a dream.'

'No dream, my love, but the start of our life together.'

'A wonderful start,' she replied. 'I little thought to be as happy as I am now.'

'I want you to be happy, Sabrina. I will try by every means to make you so.'

She stood on tiptoe and kissed him softly on the lips. Suddenly he found himself longing for the time when they would be alone. The touch of her hand in his, the scent of her perfume, the warmth of her smile went to his head like wine.

Sabrina saw the intent expression and regarded him quizzically. 'You seem rather pensive.'

He grinned. 'You're right. Indeed, I could get locked up for the thoughts in my mind at this moment.'

Her eyes danced. 'Not more unprofessional thoughts?'

'Shockingly so.'

The implications set every sense alight and the knowledge that she would share his bed this night added spice to what had been the happiest of days.

In fact it was not until much later that they returned to the house. Her father had retired long since and the place was quiet. At last they reached the sanctuary of her room and locked the door behind them. Then he took her in his arms for a long and lingering kiss.

'I've wanted to do that all day,' he said then. 'Amongst other things.'

The green eyes expressed apparently innocent interest. 'Oh? What other things?'

Never taking his eyes from her face, he shrugged off his jacket and tossed it over a chair. It was followed by his neckcloth and shirt. At the sight of the hard-muscled torso beneath, her breathing quickened. He moved towards her. Then, turning her gently, he reached for the buttons of her gown and unfastened them. With slow care he slid the fabric over her shoulders and drew off her gown, laying it aside before returning to her petticoat. He unfastened that, too, sending it the way of the gown. With the same unhurried care he removed the pins that held her hair and let it fall, shaking it loose and sliding his fingers through its silken length.

She saw him bend his head and felt his lips on the hollow of her shoulder, travelling thence to her neck and throat and then the lobe of her ear, nibbling gently and sending a delicious shiver the length of her body. He drew her closer for another kiss, his free hand brushing her breast, gently teasing the nipple. She shivered again but not with fear, drawing him close, her hands exploring the muscles of his back, breathing his scent, tasting his mouth on hers.

She could feel his arousal but now there was no fear or disgust, only desire and an answering heat in her loins. She felt him lift the hem of her chemise and then the warmth of his fingers on her thighs and buttocks, stroking, caressing, raising sensations of delight that she had not known existed. He moved to the place between her thighs, drawing a finger slowly through the slippery wetness it encountered there. He heard her gasp, continued stroking, teasing, feeling the shudder through her body and his own hardening response.

An arm slid around her waist and another under her knees, lifting her with consummate ease and carrying her to the bed. He removed the rest of his clothing and came to join her, resuming what he had begun, restraining his passion to increase hers. Very gently he drew the chemise upwards, letting his gaze drink in the details.

'You are so beautiful.'

A rosy flush bloomed along her skin. He pulled the garment higher and she moved to accommodate him, so that he could remove it altogether. The immediacy of her nakedness against his both thrilled and shocked her as the length of his body pressed against hers. His hands resumed their caresses, gentle, sure and infinitely disturbing. With thumping heart she felt him part her thighs, and slowly he entered her. It hurt and she experienced a moment of panic, fighting him. With infinite patience he brought her back, stroking her gently, whispering reassurance. Then the moment was past and he pushed deeper until she had the length of him. She felt him move then, slowly at first but gradually with stronger and more powerful strokes. The movement sent a series of shivers through her body's core. Instinctively she raised her knees, closing her legs around him, moving with him, surrendering completely to the mounting fire in her blood.

He felt her shudder but held back, controlling the urge that would give rein to lust, knowing he must do nothing that would frighten or disgust; tonight she would know only pleasure at his hands, and the desire for more. For a moment or two he was still, holding her there, making her wait. He felt her writhe beneath him, panting, her fingers clutching his arms, her eyes darkened to emerald now as she yielded to her own passion. Slowly he resumed, rocking gently against her, stroking internally, hearing her sharp intake of breath. He continued until another, deeper shudder shook her body; then another and another. He bit back a groan, thrusting into her, letting the rhythm build. He heard her cry out, felt her nails rake his back as she arched against him. And then restraint was gone and power surged in the sudden hot rush of release. He cried out, experiencing a sensation of delight so fierce he thought it might stop his heart. For a little while he remained inside her, not wanting to let this go. Then, breathing hard, he lowered himself onto his forearms, brushing sweat from his forehead, and slowly withdrew to collapse beside her.

Sabrina lay still, her mind oblivious to everything except joy. She had wanted this but had never imagined how marvellous it might be, for nothing in this experience had borne any resemblance to what had gone before. Deliciously sated, she closed her eyes and smiled.

'That was wonderful.'

'Yes, it was,' he replied. 'And it will become more wonderful still.'

It was the truth. Having wanted her from the first he had expected to enjoy this, but had never anticipated the intensity of the joy he would feel.

She turned her head and smiled. 'More unprofessional thoughts?'

'Quite disgracefully so.'

Far from alarming her, the words gave rise only to a sense of pleasurable anticipation. This lovemaking was so different from anything she could have dreamed. Sated and drowsy she snuggled closer and closed her eyes, letting herself drift. She was vaguely aware of a light kiss on her shoulder and smiled faintly, slipping into a blissful doze.

For some time he lay awake, watching her sleep, his gaze taking in each loved detail of her face and the soft rise and fall of her breathing. As he did so the last shadows of the past dissolved and vanished. What took their place was a soft, warm radiance that filled his heart and soul with hope. Life had given back far more than had ever been lost. He smiled; what he had won was treasure beyond counting and he would guard it with his life, for without it his own meant nothing. Taking care not to waken her, he curled his body around Sabrina and held her close. Thus embracing his future, he, too, slept.

* * * * *

HISTORICAL

Large Print

MISS IN A MAN'S WORLD
Anne Ashley

Georgiana Grey disguised herself as a boy, and became handsome Viscount Fincham's page. Having come home love-struck, she must return to London for the Season. When she comes face-to-face with him again, her deception is unmasked…

CAPTAIN CORCORAN'S HOYDEN BRIDE
Annie Burrows

Aimée Peters possesses an innocence which charms even the piratical Captain Corcoran. Then he discovers the coins stitched into her bodice—what secrets does Aimée hide behind her naive façade?

HIS COUNTERFEIT CONDESA
Joanna Fulford

Major Falconbridge can see that Sabrina Huntley is no ordinary miss! With their posing as the Conde and Condesa de Ordoñez, he doesn't know which is worse—the menace of their perilous mission, or the desires awakened by this tantalising beauty…

REBELLIOUS RAKE, INNOCENT GOVERNESS
Elizabeth Beacon

Despite hiding behind shapeless dresses, governess Charlotte Wells has caught the eye of notorious Benedict Shaw. Charlotte declines his invitation to dance—but this scandalous libertine isn't used to taking no for an answer!

 MILLS & BOON®

HISTORICAL

Large Print

MORE THAN A MISTRESS
Ann Lethbridge

Miss Honor Meredith Draycott knows she doesn't need a man—but society takes a different view. Meeting Charles Mountford, Marquis of Tonbridge, she discovers he's more than happy to make her respectable…but only if she acts privayely as his mistress!

THE RETURN OF LORD CONISTONE
Lucy Ashford

Lord Conistone vowed to look after Verena Sheldon. Now, her beloved home up for sale, she needs his help even more. But his dreams of holding her are shattered every time he imagines her reaction should she learn what he has done…

SIR ASHLEY'S METTLESOME MATCH
Mary Nichols

Determined to overthrow a smuggling operation, Sir Ashley Saunders will let nothing stand in his way—until he runs up against Pippa Kingslake! She's careful to protect her own interests…but could her independence end Ash's case—and his rakish ways?

THE CONQUEROR'S LADY
Terri Brisbin

To save her people and lands, Lady Fayth must marry Giles Fitzhenry, the commanding Breton knight. The marriage is as unwelcome as the deep desire which stirs each time she looks at her husband's powerful, battle-ready body…

MILLS & BOON

HISTORICAL

Large Print

SECRET LIFE OF A SCANDALOUS DEBUTANTE

Bronwyn Scott

Beldon Stratten is the perfect English gentleman, and he's looking for a respectable wife. He's intrigued by polite Lilya Stefanov—little does he know that beneath her polished etiquette lies a dangerous secret, and a scandalous sensuality…

ONE ILLICIT NIGHT

Sophia James

Returning to London, Lord Cristo Wellingham is as dangerously magnetic as Eleanor Bracewell-Lowen remembers from their brief liaison in Paris. But why does she still feel such longing for a man who could destroy her reputation with just one glance?

THE GOVERNESS AND THE SHEIKH

Marguerite Kaye

Sheikh Prince Jamil al-Nazarri hires Lady Cassandra Armstrong as governess for his difficult young daughter. Famous for his unshakeable honour, the Sheikh's resolve is about to be tested, as his feelings for Cassie are anything *but* honourable!

PIRATE'S DAUGHTER, REBEL WIFE

June Francis

Fearing for her life aboard a slave ship, Bridget McDonald flings herself into the ocean. Her rescuer, Captain Henry Mariner, knows Bridget's vulnerable—but the only way to protect her is to marry her!